THE MEMORY BELL

KAT FLANNERY

Black Rose Writing | Texas

ISBN: 978-1-68433-708-8
PUBLISHED BY BLACK ROSE WRITING
www.blackrosewriting.com

Printed in the United States of America
Suggested Retail Price (SRP) $19.95

The Memory Bell is printed in Jensen

*As a planet-friendly publisher, Black Rose Writing does its best to eliminate
unnecessary waste to reduce paper usage and energy costs, while never
compromising the reading experience. As a result, the final word count vs. page count
may not meet common expectations.

Edited by Rhonda Skinner and Jonas Saul

Dedicated to
The Garage Gang

There comes a time in our lives when we realize that family doesn't always mean the blood pumping in our veins. It can mean so much more. It is the people who sit next to you through thick and thin, hold your hand and lift you up. It's the ones who will laugh at your dumb jokes, know your heart and love you unconditionally.

Thank you to my fr-amily for always being there, for the ideas and concepts we shared when I was plotting this book, even though some of them were quite outlandish, and we all knew would never make the cut, your enthusiasm was appreciated and I love you all for it.

I am grateful for the excitement you've shown with all of my books and your willingness to throw out ideas for any new story I am working on. I do consider them all and you will see a few of them in this book.

Thank you to my husband, without your encouragement and love I'd never make it some days, my boys who are all men now, I am so proud to say I'm your mom. I love you all to the moon and back. Thank you to Rhonda and Jonas for the exceptional edits and kick in the ass when I needed it.

I cherish every single one of you, and I am so thankful to have you all in my life.

I would not be where I am today if it wasn't for God, because with Him all things are possible.

Love
Kat

THE
MEMORY
BELL

CHAPTER ONE

Detective Bennet James stood over the remains of a hand dug grave. The morning air was brisk for July, and a foggy cloud permeated the air as he exhaled. He'd woken as the first rays of dawn crept through his hotel window, casting sundogs along the planked floor.

Bones were found by the grain elevators at the mill in Oakville. The sleepy town was an hour's drive from Chicago and where he'd been stationed for the last two weeks. It was hell, but anything was better than sitting at home waiting to hear his fate. He flexed his shoulders. The muscles ached from the mounting pressure.

He took a sip of the coffee he'd bought at the local gas station. The bitter blend was cold and old. Probably made the night before and just waiting for some poor soul to drain the last of the dregs from the decanter.

With no details other than the presence of human remains to work with, Ben made quick work of taping off the area and closing all access in and out of the mill. The trains were halted and all productivity near the tracks was at a standstill. He surveyed the grounds. Three metal silos stood in a row to his left with tracks laid in front of them. Directly behind were wooden buildings with peaked roofs, and a single track led to a dead end.

He gathered the mill to be over fifty years old by the way the boards heaved and sagged. Out of commission for some time, he wondered why no one had torn the dilapidated buildings down. Being that the place was pretty much deserted, it'd make things difficult in the investigation. He snorted. It wasn't his investigation, and if things didn't work out for him with the state, he'd never see another one again.

He rubbed his hand across his face. His heart quickened with the familiar feeling of piecing together a puzzle. It was the same feeling he got every time he was dealt a fresh case. Except this one was different. It wasn't his, and even though the thought of having something to occupy his mind was appealing, he doubted Sheriff Rhoads would let him take the lead on it, much less be a part of it.

Ben glanced down at the body. Nothing left but bones and a few fragments of hair which signified the death happened years before. The grave was not shallow, but not deep either. Ben guessed it was four feet into the ground. A blue blanket caught his eye. He fingered the soft cotton with a gloved hand, a crocheted throw pulled apart from the knots someone delicately placed there. Whoever had wrapped the victim in it did so with pristine care.

"Where is the witness?" he asked the young deputy standing to his left. He couldn't remember the boy's name, or was it he didn't care? It didn't really matter. He'd stopped caring about those around him a long time ago.

The deputy looked a bit flushed, and Ben figured the kid living in the small town had seen nothing like this before. Regret settled in his stomach at making the boy stay with him while he looked over the body and its surroundings. Ben remembered seeing his first body, a young girl, only six. Her image still haunted him on nights when sleep wouldn't come.

He blinked, collected his thoughts, and faced the young man.

"You're no longer needed here," he said.

"The men who found the body are over there," the kid stammered. His hand shook as he pointed to the two silhouettes standing twenty yards away.

"Thanks." Ben dismissed him and walked toward the two men sipping coffee from their mugs. A part of him wanted to turn back to his car and leave now that Rhoads had shown up, but his pride and his duty wouldn't allow it. He pulled out the small notepad and pen he kept in his pocket.

"Morning. I need to ask you a few questions."

"Ain't you the new fella?" one of the men asked.

"Yeah."

"You're that swanky detective from the city."

Ben didn't answer.

"Why in hell would you want to come out here?"

He remained silent. It was none of the old man's business why he'd been placed in this shithole town.

"Talk is you got into hot water up there."

"I need to ask you some questions," Ben repeated, an edge creeping into his voice. He wasn't about to discuss his shit with these guys. He shifted from one foot to the other, took a deep calming breath, cleared his throat, and waited.

"Not much to tell," the man said. His thick white moustache spanned the whole of his upper lip and the bottoms of his cheeks.

"Your name?" he asked.

"Walter Smythe." The man leaned in to read what Ben wrote and tapped his index finger onto the paper. "That's Smythe with a Y, not an I."

Ben nodded.

"Can you tell me how you came upon the body?"

"Ol' Russ found it."

He turned to the other man.

"I ain't Russ," the farmer said.

"Who is—"

"That's my dog." Walter whistled. A large St. Bernard came loping up from the field behind the buildings.

"The dog found the body?"

"That's right."

"What were you doing out here?"

"I come out from time to time."

"Why, if the place is closed down?"

The man shrugged.

"Have you brought Russ out here before?" Ben asked, still trying to piece together how the remains were found.

"Sure. I bring him everywhere."

"Why was he in the elevators?"

Walter's wide shoulders lifted underneath the plaid jacket.

"Did the dog take anything from the grave, or disturb it in any way?"

"Once I saw him diggin', I called him over." Walter guffawed. "But the damn mutt just kept on going back. So, I ran over to see what the hell he was after."

"At what point did you figure out it was a body?"

"Right away when I saw the bones."

"Russ dug up most of the grave?"

"Nah, maybe a foot of it." Walter nudged the farmer beside him. "I called Bill, and we determined it was best to call the sheriff."

"Why didn't you call the sheriff first?"

Walter didn't answer.

"Did you remove or touch anything?" Ben asked.

"Nope."

As much as the farmer was rough around the edges, he could tell Walter Smythe spoke the truth.

"One more question. Has anyone gone missing in the last ten years?"

"Not around these parts. Most people who go missing leave for the city."

"Why is that?"

"Small towns ain't for everybody." Walter's eyes narrowed. "Stuff like this don't happen around here."

Ben nodded before he walked away and headed back to his car. He opened the door but didn't get in. Tall silos, train cars, and a field surrounded tracks. Waist-high stalks of yellow waved in the breeze, and from what he knew of farming, it looked to be canola. Why wasn't the body buried in the field? There must be over a hundred acres of land. Until he received the coroner's report, he couldn't guess at anything yet. Before he left, he'd need to talk to Sheriff Rhoads and see about any missing persons reports in the area.

"Well, that is odd." Rhoads sauntered toward him, brows furrowed.

"What is?" Ben asked.

"A body, here, at the elevators, in Oakville." His forehead wrinkled, and a perplexed look crossed his face. "Nobody has been here in years."

"These things can happen anywhere. There are no rules for death."

Rhoads focused on him, but remained quiet for some time before he said, "Not here."

"I'd like to take the lead on this," Ben said. The words surprised him, but he couldn't take them back now. Besides, he needed something to keep him busy. The minor misdemeanors at the old folk's home, break-ins, and an occasional kid in trouble wasn't enough to keep him from going crazy with boredom.

"Not sure that's wise, with your probation and all."

Ben nodded, figuring that would be the answer.

"But I don't see it as more than an unfortunate accident, so go ahead."

Ben wasn't so sure.

CHAPTER TWO

Grace Penner leaned against the small island in her mother's kitchen. She squeezed her hands together until her fingers ached. Anticipation of what would happen, what he'd left her kept her from sleep. She'd risen early, took Zeke for a long walk, and headed over to the house she'd grown up in.

"Gracie, relax," her mother said. "I'm sure Grandpa left you something special."

Her mother took out a fresh batch of muffins from the oven.

"I don't know, Mom. Grandpa was close to all of us grandkids." She was twenty-three-years old and knew the memories of years spent with him should be good enough, but Grace wanted the bell.

She chewed on her bottom lip.

"Yes, he was, and so there will be something there for all of you."

Her mother's hair was pulled into a loose bun at the back of her head, a style she'd worn since Grace was a little girl. Vera Penner didn't care for change, and the house Grace grew up in proved it. The ornaments, pictures, and furniture were still in the same place they were twenty years before.

Careful not to burn herself, Grace plucked a muffin out of the hot tray.

"Those are for the family," her mother admonished, but she didn't make her put it back, so Grace sunk her teeth into the warm, spongy mass.

Her brother, Andy, sauntered into the kitchen, hair a mess and wearing an over-sized white shirt with orange stains all over the front.

"Nice of you to dress up, bro." She took another bite.

"Thanks, Gigi." Andy opened the fridge and pulled out a carton of milk. Instead of pouring a glass, he guzzled the contents directly from the jug.

"Remind me not to drink that later," Grace said to her mom.

"I saw Josh yesterday." He wiped the milk moustache on his forearm.

"Good for you." The mention of Grace's ex had her chewing faster.

"I've been running into him a lot lately." He gulped down more milk.

Josh broke up with Grace a few months before and her heart still ached from it.

"Did you hear about the body found out by the mill?" Andy asked, sensing her reluctance to discuss Josh.

Grace didn't like it and hadn't slept well the last few days because of the news. The town had been buzzing with speculation as they gossiped about who it could be. Grace hoped it was some animal or an ancient grave from years before.

"I think it's kind of cool." Andy stole a muffin from the pan.

"I think it's freaky. What if it was a murder?" she asked, and her voice shook. Grace had installed extra locks and a surveillance camera outside last year after her neighbor's place was robbed. It'd taken weeks for her to sleep through the night. Hearing about the body being found only intensified Grace's fears, and she hadn't slept much since.

"Doubt it," Andy said.

"Until they figure it out, maybe you should stay here, Gracie."

"I'll be fine, Mom." She grimaced when her voice cracked again.

"I can come stay with ya," Andy said.

"Thanks, bro, but I'll be okay." She loved her brother, but he was a bit of a mooch. They were the best of friends, but if Andy moved in, their relationship would deteriorate, and she didn't want that.

Andy shrugged, took another muffin, and left the kitchen.

"Mom, did you by chance get a look at the will?" she asked, going back to the reason they were all here.

"I did not."

"Do you think if I text Dad, he'd tell me?"

Her mom opened the freezer and pulled out a bag of peas.

Grace tapped her fingers on the counter. It was selfish for wanting the heirloom, but the ornament held so many memories.

"Mom." She raised her voice, desperate for an answer.

"I don't know. All of you played with the bell."

"We didn't play with it, Mom." She sighed. "We rang it."

Her mom slid the plate of muffins toward Grace. "Go put what's left of these on the table."

"Fine." She took the platter and walked into the dining room.

The afternoon sun shone through the big bay window where the table sat, and she couldn't help but linger, letting the warmth heat her back. The house was quiet. Soon the family would arrive. She loved when they were all together. Sundays were for families and the Penners spent every one together.

She plopped down onto a chair, took another muffin from the plate, and stared at it for a second before shoving half of it in her mouth. Grace loved sweets and Sunday dinners were full of them.

The front door opened, and the sound of a baby crying carried through the house. Grace smiled. Her sister and nephew had arrived. Soon the house would bustle with laughter and fun as the Penners came together to hand out Grandpa's belongings.

***

Grace's shoulder brushed against Andy's as they squished together on the big chair in the living room. She squirmed, trying to get comfortable. She'd eaten way too much at dinner and wondered what her mother would think if she undid the top button of her jeans. Vera might not say something in front of everyone, but Grace would hear about it later, so instead of appeasing her bulging belly, she groaned.

Andy elbowed her. "You okay?"

"I ate too much," she whined.

"Yeah, you sure packed it away."

Grace pressed her shoulder into his and laughed. "Shut up."

Her dad entered the room, a white piece of paper in his left hand, followed by her uncle Jules carrying a large box.

Grace's stomach tightened.

"Better get comfortable, Gigi," Andy whispered, as he leaned back and yawned. "This could take a while."

Her dad's eyes darkened as he glared at Andy. Her brother pushed himself deeper into the chair.

"Can someone help with handing out the items?" Grace's dad asked.

"I will, Uncle Dave." Ally raised her hand.

Grace smiled at her cousin's enthusiasm. Ally along with the rest of the cousins couldn't wait to see what Grandpa left them. Steph, Ally, Zoey and Elle had been over last week to discuss the very subject and Grace was relieved to learn none of the girls wanted the bell.

She fidgeted in the chair as each one of Grandpa's belongings were read from the list along with the name of the family member who received it. She chewed on her bottom lip while pictures, dishes, rings, and even Grandpa's eyeglasses were handed out. Grace smiled as her dad's brother, Uncle Rick and Aunt Fran cuddled together on the sofa looking at the wedding picture of Grandma and Grandpa they'd just received.

"Breathe, Gigi," Andy whispered. "Ol' Grandpapa will pull through."

She turned and smiled. Andy knew she wanted the bell. She'd confided in him how much the heirloom meant to her.

"Gracie-girl." Dad glanced up and smiled.

She sucked in a breath.

"The memory bell."

Someone gasped, but Grace was too shocked to turn and see who it was. Grandpa gifted her the bell—the one she watched bring the family together for years. She stood, knees weak and legs shaking. The chatter in the room ceased as Grace leapt over the coffee table toward her dad almost toppling over her sister, Steph.

She glanced at Ally holding the heirloom, a solemn look upon her pretty face. Was she not happy? Did she want the bell? Grace's heart skipped. Impossible. None of the cousins cared about the bell. They used to make fun of Grace for the obsession she had with the ornament.

Ally held out the memory bell and plopped it into Grace's hands. A little too forceful maybe, but she was too overwhelmed to care. Her eyes watered. The bell she loved so much was now hers. Grace's chest puffed outward with pride, and her ears buzzed with delight.

"What a wonderful gift," Aunt Janice said in a dry tone from behind her.

"Wow, Gracie, you got the bell." Elle, Uncle Rick's daughter whispered.

Cheeks sore from smiling, Grace let out a giggle. Grandpa gave her the bell. She hugged the ornament to her chest. She'd keep it safe forever.

"May I see the bell?" Steph asked.

Grace didn't see the harm in letting her sister hold the bell, but before she gave it to Steph, Aunt Janice, Ally, Elle, and Zoey swarmed her.

"Oh, let me see it," Ally squealed with excitement.

"I want to hold it first," Zoey argued.

"You guys, it's the same bell that has been hanging on the porch for the last twenty years." Grace held the bell above her head so no one could touch it. She peeked over Steph's shoulder at her mom for help, but all Grace saw was the back of her mom's head as she talked to Aunt Fran. Grace scanned the room for someone—anyone to break up the excitement and let her move away from the prying hands that were now touching the bell. Andy had fallen asleep on the chair, and her dad and uncles were huddled by the liquor cabinet pouring drinks.

"Come on, Gracie, we just want to look at it." Elle rubbed her elbow into Grace's side as she reached for the ornament.

"I don't want it to—"

Aunt Janice moved at the same time Steph did, both stretching their hands upward. Grace stepped back into Elle but could not escape the onslaught of reaching fingers. The bell slipped. She squeezed her fingers around the ornament. Her hands were sweaty—clammy from nerves, excitement, and now fear. She tried again to step away from them, but they would not let her move. With no other choice, she brought her arms down to cradle the bell to her chest when Janice knocked the ornament from Grace's hands.

The white bell with the pink flowers cascading down the sides—the treasure she'd loved so much and rang every Sunday since she was a little girl—flew through the air smashing into the glass coffee table and shattered.

"No." She fell to her knees, ignoring the shards of glass from the table poking through her jeans and into her skin. Her hands smeared with blood as she pressed her palms into the carpet. A tear fell for every pinch from the glass embedded into her hands as Grace surveyed the broken bits around her. The bell. They broke it. She picked up a piece. Her vision blurred. Grandpa's gift lay scattered across the floor.

"Why?" she whispered.

"Grace?" Steph said.

"There is nothing left." Her lips trembled. "It's ruined." Grace's stomach twisted. She clenched her hands. Chest tight, she gasped, trying to understand—desperate to make sense of what had happened. She stared at the piece in her palm. The scream yanked at her vocal cords to scratch its way up her throat until it expelled from her lips, silencing any chatter within the room.

"It's just a bell, Grace." Janice lifted her nose.

She spun around to look at the family. "It was my bell." Spittle flew from her mouth as she sucked in another sob. "And now it's fucking broken."

"Grace Penner," her mom shouted.

Grace didn't care. She didn't give a damn that Mom was going to lecture her for the way she behaved. Nothing mattered now. The bell was in pieces on the floor. Throat thick, tears close to falling, Grace ran from the room and out the back door where she fell onto the grass. Her chest ached as sobs shook her body. The pain of losing the bell pierced her soul, puncturing it with tiny holes to bleed from her eyes. Knees sore, she pressed them into the ground, welcoming the pain as the muscles in her back tightened around her ribs and she gasped. Grandpa was gone, and the gift he'd given to her was broken. Grace pressed her face into her palms and wept.

CHAPTER THREE

"Hey, Dawson." Ben popped his head into the coroner's office. "You got anything on my vic yet?"

"A few things," the man said, not looking up from the bones on the metal table.

He didn't know Dawson well, but sensed honesty and kindness in the few moments they'd met. Unbeknownst to Ben, he trusted the man, which seemed foreign to him since he trusted no one. He pulled out his notepad and pen.

"I'm ready," he said.

The coroner glanced at him before he plucked something from under the jawbone and placed it into an envelope.

"What's that?" Ben asked.

"Not sure. I'll send it to the city lab and see if they come back with something. It will take some time, though."

Ben nodded. He was used to waiting. Sometimes it took months to get the results from a fiber found at a crime scene.

Dawson removed his rubber gloves and reached for the clipboard beside him. He handed it to Ben. "Your vic is a Jane Doe, and the first set of forensic reports I've gotten back show she was in the age range of sixteen to twenty-one."

Ben masked any emotion about the young life lost as he read over the report.

"When will we have a name?"

"I'm waiting for the dental records to be confirmed. Once I know, I will call you."

Ben handed him back the clipboard. "Thanks."

"There is one more thing."

He stepped closer.

"Her neck was broken."

Ben leaned over the decomposed body and squinted to get a better look at the area.

"Before we exhumed the body, I examined what I could. The hyoid bone was crushed." Dawson pointed to the bone under the jaw.

"Strangled," Ben said.

"Yes, and not gently either…"

"What do you mean? Aren't all strangulations brutal?"

"Yes, but this was done with such force it not only broke the bone but pressed it into a vertebra and lodged it there."

He flattened his lips while he peered at the two bones wedged together. "Someone she knew," Ben said, more to himself than Dawson.

"I'd say you're correct." The man blew out a heavy sigh.

"You okay?"

"Yeah. I haven't seen one of these in years."

"You're a coroner. You see dead bodies all the time."

"Sure, one's that are sick, or old, or passed from an accident, but not murdered. I know these are just bones, but when I look at them I see the young girl whose life was stolen. That's why I moved away from the city and came here. It all got to be too much."

Ben knew what he meant. He'd experienced the same thing, and it was one of the reasons he'd been placed on probation.

"Can you tell me anything else? Time of death?"

"Sorry, that's all I've got. I found a few bugs in the ground around the bones and sent them to the lab in Chicago. They will determine how long the poor thing had been buried there."

"Do you have a time frame for results?"

"Might be another week or two, maybe three. You know how they get in the big city."

"Thanks, Dawson."

"If I hear any more, I'll call you."

Ben left the room and walked out into the sunshine. He inhaled, allowing the fresh air to cleanse his lungs. What was he doing? The question haunted him since finding the body four days before. He should've let someone else take over. He'd left that part of him behind in Chicago, swore to himself he'd not do the job again until the investigation into his probation was closed. And yet here he was plucking away at another murder.

Sheriff Rhoads hadn't pulled him from the case, nor did he feel too inclined to do it himself. If Ben were to be honest with himself, he knew why he'd taken the lead. He was selfish. Solving murders was what he did, or used to do, and maybe in the back of his mind he knew he may never get to do it again.

He walked the short distance to the precinct, trying his best to forget about the reasons he should be doing patrol and not investigating a murder. He couldn't get the body out of his mind. The poor girl tossed away without a care. He hated dealing with the young ones—the lives lost before they had a chance to experience much of anything. With no identification, he'd have to wait to notify next of kin.

The girl was strangled, which in Ben's world meant homicide. But until lab results came back, they didn't know what had been wrapped around her neck, or how long ago the murder happened. There was no evidence of a rope, other than the few bits of fragments found on the girl's neck. It would make finding the assailant difficult, if they found him at all.

His cell phone rang, and he pulled it from the pocket of his suit coat. Kent James. He let it go to voicemail. Ben hadn't talked to his father in months and had no intentions of doing so now. The thought of rekindling any kind of relationship put a rancid taste in his mouth. As an only child, Ben grew up privileged. Money had never been a problem, and his father would rather give it to him than deal with any issues or problems he was going through.

He shoved the phone back inside his pocket. Whenever he thought of his father, memories of his mother followed.

He climbed the stairs to the front door of the precinct and pulled it open. At thirty-three he should sprint the steps, but today he felt far older than he was. The sour smell of carpets battered from years of being trampled on, and the remnants of soiled furniture greeted him. The station was old, never remodeled or updated. The white walls, no longer bright and welcoming, but were now stained yellow with creases of brown in the corners. He walked to the small cubicle farthest from the door and sat down. An empty frame stared back at him, and again he wondered why he'd brought the damn thing. The sorrow of what once was stirred inside his soul. Two smiling faces used to be pictured inside. Now all that remained was the glass and cardboard. A similarity to how his life was now. Empty.

He flicked the frame with his knuckles, knocking it over. Hell, he should be used to the loneliness by now. It'd been over a year. Ben placed his head in his hands, but he wasn't.

CHAPTER FOUR

Grace was heartbroken. She blinked back the tears as she sat at the kitchen table, a piece of the bell in one hand and a small tube of crazy glue in the other. Most of the family had left, with only a few lingering in the living room. Uncle Randy and Aunt Janice were the first to leave, almost immediately after the bell broke.

Grace clenched her jaw. Her gift from Grandpa was ruined.

She groaned.

Mom had said nothing to her about the outburst earlier, and Grace knew she'd have to apologize to the family, but she'd deal with that later. Mom was still in the living room cleaning up the mess. The coffee table shattered, spider webbing across the top first until it fell inward and onto the carpet.

"Is that the last one, Gigi?" Andy asked, taking a seat beside her at the table.

"Yeah, but there are still some missing."

"Maybe we didn't get them all?" Andy picked up the last muffin and began eating it. She smelled the lingering scent of marijuana and wasn't surprised when her brother dug into the baked goods on the table.

"I scoured the floor for an hour, making sure I got them all," she snapped.

"Could've missed some among all the glass from the coffee table."

"I didn't miss any. The bell is ivory, which is white, and the glass in the coffee table is clear."

"You sure lost your shit earlier."

She pressed her back teeth together.

"What's the big deal about the bell anyway?"

Grace held her hand suspended, the piece of glass pinched between her forefinger and thumb. "It's a family heirloom."

"Yeah, I get that, but why did Janice and everyone want to see it so badly?"

"Because they're jealous." Jules entered the kitchen and leaned against the doorjamb. Their eyes met, and he winked. Jules was her favorite out of all the three brothers her dad had. He was funny, caring, and always up for a good time. He was closer to Grace's age than her dad's. The seven years between them meant they'd grown up with similar likes and dislikes in culture, music, and politics. Jules was more like a friend than an uncle and she cherished the relationship.

"I don't believe that," Grace said.

"You need some Visine," he said to Andy, who shrugged in reply.

Jules's statement was absurd. Why would the family be jealous over the bell? A small family gem that no one gave two shits about for as long as Grace could remember.

"Well, believe it, Gracie." Jules popped a toothpick into his mouth. "They're vultures, and the bell has been in the family for years. Maybe it's worth money. We all know what money does to people." He looked at Andy again. "Seriously, kid, go put some damn Visine in those eyes or Dave's gonna beat your ass."

This time Andy listened, pulled the small plastic bottle from his jean pocket, and squeezed two drops into both eyes.

"Jan is the worst of them all. She can't handle it if anyone has something better than Ally or Mike," Jules continued.

"Aunt Jan can be abrasive at times, but I don't believe she didn't want me to have the bell."

"You sure about that?"

Grace nodded.

"Well, I'll go back to my first thought... money." He smirked.

"Come on, Jules. The bell is worth no more than my underwear." Grace carefully glued the sides of the piece she held before placing it into the small hole. "There. I have put everything back."

"Doesn't look like it." Jules stepped toward them. He placed his elbows onto the table and squinted. "There are three holes remaining."

Grace groaned. She'd seen them, too.

"You're telling me the bell is worth money?" Andy asked, still fascinated by what Jules said.

"I didn't say *is*, kid. I said *could* be. Two different things."

She wished the two of them would just shut up. There were three pieces missing and it wouldn't ring the same if she didn't have them all. Her eyes watered.

"Makes sense why they all wanted it," Andy said.

Grace turned toward her uncle and glared. "They didn't *want* it the way you both think. They *wanted* to look at it. Two different things." Grace mimicked her uncle.

"Funny, but like it or not, I could be right." Jules winked.

"If what you're saying *could* be true, why would Grandpa hang it on the porch all these years?"

Jules shrugged. "No idea, Gracie-girl."

"I call bullshit."

"Call it what you will, but money does awful things to people, and like ol' red-eyes over here said, it makes perfect sense why they wanted it." Jules stood and stretched his muscled arms high above him. "I better go. I've got a long day tomorrow at the shop."

"You still working on that soft tail?" Andy asked.

Jules's passion was working on motorbikes, and his shop specialized in them. Grace's dad didn't care for Jules's way of life, often telling him to get a real job.

"I am. You should swing by and have a look at her."

"I bet it looks sweet."

Grace rolled her eyes. She never understood Andy's fascination with bikes. Then again, she didn't understand much of anything Andy liked. She figured the motorbikes were a way for him to get close to Jules. Dad never showed much interest in anything Andy did, but Jules always gave her brother his time.

"It does." Jules leaned down and kissed Grace on the top of the head. "Don't fret about the bell."

She tensed. Fret was an understatement for how she was feeling about what happened. Her cheeks flushed, and she bit her lip.

"G'night all." Jules exited the back door, closing it softly behind him. The sound of his Harley rumbled into the house as he drove away.

"Do you think he's telling us the truth?" Andy asked.

"I don't even care. The bell's broken. Three pieces are missing, and it won't chime like it used to."

"What does it matter?"

"If it doesn't ring the same, it won't call them all together."

Andy laughed. "Gigi, you cannot tell me you still believe in the tall tale Grandpa told us when we were young."

Grace nodded, and before she could stop them, tears flowed from her eyes. She clenched her jaw keeping the sob locked inside.

Andy grabbed her hand. "We were kids. You have to know it's not true."

"But it is true, Andy. I saw it time and time again when I rang the bell." She wiped her cheeks. "They came. It was magic."

"Oh my gosh, Gigi. Do you know how ridiculous that sounds?"

Grace wanted to go home to lie on her couch with Zeke snuggled in close and let go of all the emotions running rampant inside of her. Grandpa was gone, the farm would never be the same, and the bell was broken. Unable to hold in her frustrations any longer, she laid her head on the table and cried.

Andy's chair scraped the floor as he pushed it outward. He reached his long arms around her back and hugged her. Her disappointment was hard on him, but knowing he would always be there for her made the ache a little less painful.

She pushed herself out of Andy's embrace, and when he didn't move, she realized he'd fallen asleep on her back. Perfect.

"Andy?" She bumped her shoulder into his chest. "Wake up."

"Huh?" He stood, and Grace escaped.

"Good job, bro. Here I thought you were giving me an extra-long hug." She picked up the mended bell and placed it gently onto the table.

"Sorry," Andy said, giving her a lopsided grin.

"You need to cut back on that shit, especially when you fall asleep standing up." She reached for her hoodie and threw it over her head.

He shook his head. "It's all good. I'm not chronic."

One arm in her sweater, she rolled her eyes at him. "Who are you trying to fool? You smoke weed all the time."

"What's that?" Dad asked, stepping into the kitchen with a garbage bag full of glass from the coffee table.

"Nothing," Grace and Andy said in unison.

Dad looked at Andy. Grace watched as his eyes narrowed, and his lips thinned into an angry frown. The black garbage bag whined as Dad's large hand clenched the plastic.

"Well, Daddy, I've got to go." She stood in between Andy and her father, gave him a hug, feeling him soften under her embrace.

He gazed at her. "You okay?"

"I'm good." She lied.

He kissed her forehead, something he'd done since she was a little girl, and Grace held back the surge of sadness. Dad had so many similarities to Grandpa.

She smiled up at him.

"I better get home." She grabbed the bell from the table. Andy had left. He'd seen his cue to disappear when Grace distracted Dad with a hug. He was no dummy. That she was sure of.

"Drive safe, Grace," Dad said, before he stepped out the back door, garbage in hand.

Chapter Five

"How would you like your eggs?" Grace asked the man sitting in the corner booth by the window. He'd been indecisive about his breakfast all morning, first ordering pancakes, then French toast, until deciding on the eggs and bacon.

"Scrambled please," he answered, without looking up from the paper he was reading.

Grace wrote it down on her notepad and walked away. She'd worked at Jay's Diner since she was sixteen with Ally. They'd applied on a whim, not thinking either of them would land the waitressing job, but Donna, the owner, liked their enthusiasm and hired them both on the spot. Grace didn't know what she wanted to do with her life, and so there was no point in leaving Oakville. With her tips and wage, she made enough to move out and buy a car. Plus, she loved the people she worked with, especially Ally.

"Did table ten finally order?" Mel asked, strolling beside her toward the kitchen.

"Yeah. I didn't think he ever would." Grace glanced out the window. Ally was late for her shift. Again.

She tore off three orders and clipped them to the ticket holder, then spun it toward Jose in the kitchen.

"You have three orders, Miss Grace?" Jose asked while reading them.

"Yup, I do."

He smiled and nodded before going back to prepping the meals.

Grace glanced at the front doors. Still no Ally. She reached inside her apron and pulled out her cell phone.

Where are you? She texted her cousin.

"She'll be here," Mel said, while pouring two cups of coffee. "Don't worry about it. Do you want to take Crazy Carl's order, or should I?"

She tossed her phone back into her apron pocket and smiled.

"I'll do it."

Carl White was a regular in the restaurant and most of the girls disliked serving him, but Grace didn't mind. On most days Carl was a little disorientated, and reeked of stale booze, but those weren't good enough reasons to not show him some kindness. Carl was lonely. At eighty-two, he had no family left, and no friends. Her dad said Carl was married once, but his wife left a few years into their marriage and never returned. Grace's heart broke for the old guy, and against her dad's wishes, she'd driven him home a few times after her shift.

"Morning, Carl. Coffee?"

Carl nodded.

She ignored the smell of liquor, and told him the breakfast special, even though she knew he wouldn't order it.

"I'll have a slice of apple pie." He positioned his fork in the center of the white napkin, plucked two packets of sugar from the glass container on the table and set them beside his empty cup.

"I'll be right back." She walked to the beverage counter and retrieved the coffeepot. "Did Ally get here yet?" she asked Mel as the waitress strode by.

"Haven't seen her. Maybe she was out last night and drank a little too much."

Grace shrugged. It was a possibility. They didn't hang out together all the time, and Ally had other friends.

The black apron tied around her waist shook as the phone buzzed inside the pocket.

Very sick today. Won't be in. Ally texted.

Okay. I'll cover for you.

Luv u

"Well, looks like it's just you and me for the breakfast rush," Grace said.

Mel propped the tray full of coffee, soda, and a dish for creamer onto her shoulder.

"We can handle it." She winked at Grace before heading off into the busy dining room.

Ben sat down in a booth at Jay's Diner and stared out the window at the rain. He'd started his shift an hour ago when Dawson phoned. The man gave him a name to his Jane Doe and an approximate timeline. The murder took place twenty-five to thirty years before. Ben had gone to the address the coroner told him, but no one was there. He decided to get a coffee and maybe a piece of toast to settle his stomach and go back later. The diner was a few blocks east on the main road and looked like a good place to wait.

"Morning, I'm Grace. What can I get for you?"

The girl tapped her pen on the notepad while she waited. He stared around her to see how busy the diner was, and why she seemed so impatient. To his surprise, the place was full.

"I'll take a coffee and toast," he said.

"White, brown, rye, or flax?"

"Brown."

"Sure thing." She smiled at him and sauntered away.

Ben glanced at his own notepad. He hated this part of the job. The truth swam in the back of his mind causing his eyes to focus in and out. It wasn't his job anymore. The reminder was like a kick to the groin. He closed his eyes and clenched his jaw. He didn't need to do this. No one commanded it of him. He was just a regular cop here in Oakville. He stared at the paper and the name written on it. He could've given the case back to Rhoads and walked away. He grunted.

Hell, the sheriff seemed to forget about the dead body, not mentioning it at all yesterday when Ben walked past him in the hall. He clenched his left hand. He couldn't walk away. Maybe it was years of taking charge and solving cases that pushed him to run with this one. He wasn't sure, and he didn't care. Truth and honor ran in his blood, and he'd hold true to the testimony until the day he died.

He glanced at the paper. The name called out to him. Again, the notion to flee filled him. He'd had to tell many families about the discovery of a loved one back in Chicago. It never got easy, and each time he was lightheaded and nauseated until the words exited his mouth. This would be no different. Circumstances were still the same: a murder, a body, someone's daughter.

Ben's stomach turned.

"Here you go." The waitress placed the coffee and a small dish full of creamers on the table.

He took the cup and dumped one cream and a spoonful of sugar into it. Ben looked up to see a frail old man stumble from the washroom. Grace rushed over to help him into a booth. It was obvious she knew him, but he wondered if they were related the way she took the time to make sure his feet were tucked under the table before she moved quickly to refill his coffee.

The old man would need more than a few cups to get sober. Ben smelled the liquor from where he sat. He assessed the elderly fellow and noticed the signs from years of drinking upon his face. The red nose, ruddy cheeks, glossy eyes, and slumped shoulders were all indications of a life devoted to alcohol. The man's gray hair looked like it hadn't been washed in days, and his beard was matted and uncombed. How did the girl tend to him without turning away in disgust? His own stomach wanted to revolt at the smell of the man, yet she stood mere inches away as she helped him sit upright and get the first few sips of coffee down.

Another waitress walked by and handed Grace a plate. Ben watched as she placed the piece of pie on the table in front of the old man. She hurried past Ben to return a minute later with his toast.

"Can I get you anything else?" Her voice held a comforting warmth to it.

"Do you know that fellow?" He tipped his head toward the drunken man.

"Sure. Everyone knows him."

"Is he always like that?" he asked, while spreading peanut butter on the toast.

"You mean drunk? Yeah."

"You say it like there is nothing wrong with a man walking around town inebriated."

She shrugged and her brown hair fell from her shoulders down her back.

"He's been this way all my life."

"Is he a relation to you?"

She raised a brown eyebrow before shaking her head.

"You seem to care an awful lot for him," Ben said.

She glanced back at the elderly man.

"Compassion is something everyone should receive whether or not they're a drunk." She moved away to serve another table, leaving him with those words.

Ben bit into his toast. The peanut butter stuck to the roof of his mouth, and he took a drink of coffee to wash it all down. He thought about the caring waitress. Not that he didn't think she was right. He just didn't see much kindness in the people he dealt with and if the truth be told, he didn't think there was much left in the world. He finished the piece of toast, wiped his fingers on the napkin, and pushed the plate to the side.

The wind blew, shaking the door, and he watched as leaves and bits of paper flew around in the rain. He'd wait for the storm to pass before venturing back out.

Sheriff Rhoads sauntered into the restaurant, spotted Ben, and made his way toward the table.

"Morning, James."

"Rhoads."

The sheriff took a seat at the empty table next to him.

Ben wasn't much for small talk, and so he took a sip of his coffee.

"Sorry, I couldn't help you with the missing person's reports last week. We just don't have any in these parts." The man shifted in the seat. "It's best to leave this one. The likelihood of solving it is slim."

Rhoads was in his mid-sixties, and Ben figured he'd been Oakville's sheriff for some time. His easy stature and careless manner didn't sit well with Ben. He'd seen it before. Comfort and repetition in a position made it easy to let things slide or to miss important details in a case. In a peaceful town like this one, he understood how Rhoads had gotten relaxed in his job. Ben figured he was paid well, and something told him the wealthier ranchers slipped him a bill or two to let them do things they weren't supposed to.

In the short time he'd been here, he'd witnessed farmers burning their waste. Household furniture and garbage blazed almost daily in their yards. Black smoke billowed into the air, and Ben wondered why no one was taking any notice of the obvious situation.

"You know about the farmers burning waste on their land?" he asked, more to get a sense of the sheriff's demeanor than out of curiosity.

Rhoads thanked the waitress when she placed a coffee in front of him. He didn't answer Ben right away. Instead, he took his time pouring cream and sugar into the cup.

"I know about it."

"And they still do it?" He didn't really care if they did, but he wanted to see Rhoads's reaction to his statement.

"People have been burning their garbage for years. Ain't no big deal."

"They're breaking the law."

"Far worse things they could do."

It was how he figured. The sheriff ran the town the way he wanted and possibly by how much the locals put in his wallet. He'd bet his house the man thought a lot of things weren't a *big deal*.

"Can you tell me who the drunk is?" Ben pointed at the man leaning to the left in the booth. He looked like he had passed out.

Rhoads didn't even look in the man's direction.

"Carl White. He's harmless."

Ben didn't need to know if he was a threat. He could see for himself the older fellow wasn't confrontational, but that didn't mean things wouldn't change when he told him it was his daughter they'd found two weeks before.

Ben took a deep breath to steady his nerves. Forgetting all about the sheriff, he pushed his coffee away and stood. He swallowed down the toast that wanted to come back up and wiped his forearm along his brow.

He made his way to the booth where Carl White sat.

Bloodshot eyes stared up at Ben, and for a moment he was transported back to when he was a young boy and the only memory he had of his grandfather.

"Mr. White?" Ben asked, even though he knew who he was.

A clumsy nod, followed by a hiccup.

"I'm Detective Bennet James. I'm here to talk to you about your daughter, Claire White."

Carl's red-rimmed eyes focused on him, and he straightened. The man seemed to sober up, or at the very least he did a good job of pretending.

"May I sit?" Ben asked.

A spotted, wrinkled hand motioned for him to do so.

"Thank you."

Grace returned with a pot of coffee and filled Carl's cup. She narrowed her eyes at Ben.

"He's not harming anyone, so don't make it your business," she whispered.

Ben's lips turned upward into a small smile at the girl's caring nature.

"I've no intention of doing so."

She turned her back to Carl and faced Ben. The scent of vanilla filled his nostrils, and he refrained from leaning into her.

"What is your intention?" she asked, with one hand on her hip and the other still holding the coffeepot.

"I'm a detective. I have business with Mr. White."

"Is he in some kind of trouble?"

"No, and I can't tell you more."

She nodded, glanced at Carl, and placed her small hand over his creased one.

"If you need anything, just holler." She winked at the old man before leaving to serve another table.

"Mr. White…"

"Carl. Just Carl." The man's voice was deeper than Ben expected. His outer appearance was that of a frail old man, and he thought the voice would match it. He'd been wrong. Carl's tone was rational, not slurred, and strong.

"Carl. A body was found." Ben never knew the right way to say it. He inhaled. "It was identified as Claire White, your daughter."

The man's thin bottom lip shook, and his veiny eyes filled with tears.

"When was the last time you saw your daughter?"

The old man shook his head but said nothing.

"Can you tell me why there was no missing persons report on her?"

Carl's gray head trembled, and he averted his eyes. A single tear dripped onto the table, followed by another one. Ben waited while Carl processed their conversation. He wanted to reach out and place his hand on the old man's like Grace had done, but he knew it wouldn't be appropriate. It didn't matter how many times he'd said the same thing, how many mothers, fathers, brothers or sisters he watched break down, the reality of what life could be like hit him square in the gut, and lately he found it difficult to breathe.

Carl lifted his head and met Ben's stare.

"She didn't come home," he whispered.

"I know it's been a long time, but can you recall the last time you saw her?"

"I knew something happened," he said. "No one believed me." He broke down again.

Ben offered him a napkin, and the old man took it and wiped at his eyes.

"Who didn't believe you?" Ben asked.

"It doesn't matter." Carl rocked back and forth. "None of it matters now."

Throwing all caution aside, he reached across the table, grabbed the weathered hand, and felt it quake beneath his hold.

"It does matter."

Dark eyes stared back at him, and for a moment Ben saw into Carl White's soul. Anger, hurt, guilt, and sadness. A lot of sadness.

Carl pushed himself out of the booth and fell to the ground before Ben could help him.

Grace was there and placed her hands under the old man's arms to help him stand.

"Are you all right?" Concern folded her brows.

Carl turned toward her and smiled.

"I'm fine, Gracie," Carl said.

She nodded.

"I want to go home."

"My shift is over soon. I can take you."

Carl shook his head.

"Okay, I'll help you to the door." She slipped her arm around his waist and helped him out of the restaurant.

Ben stared after them. He knew Carl was in his eighties and a fall like that could've broken a bone. He'd swing by his house later to check on him.

After getting Carl on his way, Grace returned to stand inches from Ben, red-faced, and with a glare that penetrated right through him.

"What did you say to him?"

"None of your business." Ben couldn't tell her anything. Well, he could, but since she assumed the worst of him, he'd keep it on the down low.

"It is my business when you're harassing one of my customers."

"How long have you known Mr. White?"

"All of my life. Why?"

"How well do you know him?"

She shrugged. "I guess not well enough to say what his favorite color is."

Ben figured the girl didn't know Carl other than to see him in the diner and wandering about town. He tossed a few bills on the table.

"Thank you," he said, and left.

The rain had stopped, but the sky was still a milky gray. A light breeze messed his hair. He needed to get it cut. It'd been weeks since he heard the hum of a razor at the back of his head. He'd even grown to like the longer locks of hair. Lana would've disapproved, but much of what he did back then never pleased her. He grimaced. She'd been a part of his life for so long that on some days he thought she was still in it. Ben ran his hand down the front of his face. He pushed all memories to the back of his head, got in the car, and drove to the Oakville Police Department.

***

Grace shut the door of her 2005 Volkswagen Beetle. She tossed her purse onto the already cluttered passenger seat and blew out a long sigh.

Without her cousin there, the morning shift had been horrendous. Two hockey teams at lunch, the seniors meet and greet, and then there was the incident with Carl and the detective. She was on her feet for over nine hours. Reluctant to stay longer than she already had, Grace offered to help until the teams were finished. Thank goodness Mel stayed to work the extra hours, too. The other woman was a godsend when it came to the diner. In the years Grace worked there, Mel never missed a shift. She couldn't say the same for her cousin.

Ally seemed distracted, and work wasn't important. She asked the other girls to take her shifts, and today she was sick. Grace meant to discuss this with her cousin. Maybe there was something going on that she wasn't aware of, or it was because Uncle Randy and Aunt Janice paid for all of Ally's things and the need to work wasn't a priority. With the time they spent together, Grace should know, but her cousin was keeping something from her, and it bothered her that Ally didn't trust Grace enough to say.

Her cell phone buzzed.

The message was from Andy: *Got interview. Need ride.*

"Ugh."

She wanted to go home, fall onto the double bed, and sleep until the next day. Grace placed the keys in the ignition, started the car, and drove toward her parents' place.

***

Grace pulled the car into the driveway and hit the horn. She kicked off her shoes, lifted her feet toward the vent, and turned the heat on. The warmth blowing from the car did little to ease her tender, sore limbs.

"Hey, Gigi," Andy said, dropping into the seat beside her. "Thanks for coming to get me."

Her mood lightened, and she smiled until the heavy scent of marijuana filled her nostrils.

"Do you think going to an interview high is smart?" she asked.

Andy shrugged. "It relaxes me and I'm nervous."

"Where's this interview at?"

"Oakville Senior Home."

Grace had to keep from slamming on the brakes. "You have an interview there?"

"Yeah. Why are you so surprised?"

"I don't know. I thought maybe you'd reach for something a little more low-key, if you know what I mean."

"The job came up, and I applied."

"What did you put for work experience?"

Andy didn't have any, and she was curious about whether he lied on the application.

"A few things."

"Andy."

"Oh, come on, Gigi. What was I supposed to put there? Nothing?"

"Yes, bro. That's what you put. You've never had a job before. What if they call your references?"

"Well, here's the thing… I put you down as my only reference."

"What? Andy! What am I supposed to say if they call?"

"That I worked for Dad's construction company doing odd jobs."

"Damn it, Andy. If Dad catches wind of this, you and I are both in boiling water."

"I technically did work for Dad."

"Two hours doesn't count," she said.

Her dad fired Andy after he'd found him sleeping in one of the trucks. Now she'd have to lie to the people at the senior home if they called. She glanced at her brother. Chances were slim he'd get the job, and she wouldn't need to say untrue things about him, but the possibility of a miracle was also there.

"Steph wouldn't do it, and I didn't want to ask Jules."

"Why not? Jules would be happy to be your reference. You know that."

Andy said nothing while he stared out the side window. He was different today somehow, and Grace couldn't put her finger on what it was.

"How much weed did you smoke before I picked you up?" she asked him.

"Half a joint. Why?"

"You seem off today. Is something wrong? Was Dad yelling at you again?"

"Dad always yells, and no, I'm fine."

"I know he's hard on you, Andy, but Dad loves you."

He gave her a sideways look.

"You sound like Mom."

She groaned.

"And there is no love, Gigi."

Grace caught the sadness attached to his words, and a piece of her heart broke for him. She wanted to believe their dad loved Andy like he did her and Steph, but as the years passed on, Grace saw the differences between how Dad treated the girls to Andy. Her dad expected more from her brother, often belittling Andy for not meeting the high standards her dad placed upon him.

"Dad just wants good things for you." She tried to convince them both.

"Yeah, right."

She could see the conversation was depressing him and changed the subject.

"What's the job you applied for?"

"Janitor."

She nodded. It was reasonable enough, easy with low expectations—two things her brother thrived at. She pulled into the parking lot and stopped at the front doors.

"I'll park and wait for you."

"Nah, I'll be okay." He opened the car door, and before she could argue with him, he was gone.

Grace yawned. It was just as well. She was tired and who knew how long his interview would last. She'd head home, get into her pajamas and order takeout.

CHAPTER SIX

Grace knocked on the oversized wooden door to Ally's suite in the basement of her parents' home. She called in sick again this afternoon for her shift, so Grace brought her a bowl of Jose's chicken noodle soup and a piece of carrot cake. The front door unlatched and creaked open. Ally's red hair was pulled back into a ponytail, her cheeks flushed, and she was wearing a sundress.

Grace raised a brow.

"Sick, hey?"

Ally shrugged.

"Sorry, Grace. I was out with a few friend's last night and got carried away."

"We've all done it." Grace stepped inside.

A candle burned on Ally's kitchen table, the lavender scent filling the room with a warm welcome. The suite was clean, something Ally was not known for, and Grace figured the maid who cleaned the main house tidied things up for her cousin. She placed the package on the table.

"Were you expecting company?" she asked.

"No. Why?"

Grace eyed her cousin.

"What?"

"Your place is never this clean."

Ally rolled her eyes.

"It was nothing."

"It?"

"Just a friend."

Ally picked up the Styrofoam soup container, popped off the lid, and slurped from the rim.

"Spill the beans. Who did you have over?"

Her cousin smirked.

Grace plopped onto the stool beside the counter and grinned.

"What's his name? Where did you meet him?" She leaned closer to her cousin. Ally had dated no one since Riley Bishop, her high school sweetheart, who had broken her heart three years before.

"Settle down, cousin. It was a one-night kind of thing. It's not going anywhere."

Grace's shoulders fell.

"Oh. Well, maybe it will turn into something more."

Ally glanced at her over the carrot cake she was biting into and rolled her eyes.

"That is unlikely to happen."

"Why? You've got to put yourself out there. Not all guys are like Riley."

The mention of Ally's ex put a frown on her beautiful face, and Grace immediately regretted her words.

"I didn't mean anything by it. I just want to see you happy, that's all."

Ally sighed, and Grace knew she'd been forgiven. Over the years they'd had plenty of disagreements, but none lasted too long, and Grace was always the one to apologize. She didn't like confrontation, and she hated when people were mad at her. It was why Josh broke up with her. He was tired of Grace's relentless apologizing and never standing up for herself. He just couldn't be with someone so weak. His words replayed in her mind and she blinked, holding her eyes closed. Tears formed behind her lids and she waited for them to pass before opening her eyes to see Ally staring at her.

"Are you okay, Grace?"

"I'm fine."

"He wasn't worth it," Ally said, and placed her arms around Grace.

"It's been almost two months. Why does it still bother me?"

"Because you cared for him."

Grace nodded.

Ally was there for Grace when Josh broke it off. She'd taken the time to help Grace pack up a few of the things he'd left at her place and even offered to drop them off so she didn't have to see him.

The relationship didn't last long, ten months to be exact, but Grace loved him. She blinked back the tears and pushed out of Ally's embrace.

"Don't forget about our girl's night next week."

"How could I forget? We do it every month." Ally laughed.

It was true. When Steph got married and moved to Chicago two years ago, Grace and the cousins missed her so much they planned a monthly girl's night where they sipped wine, visited, and watched movies in the comfort of their pajamas. The evening was always held at Grace's since she was the only one who didn't live at home.

"Did you by chance take any of the pieces of the bell the other night?"

"No, why?"

"I'm missing three of them and I've asked everyone else and they don't seem to have them either."

"Maybe they got thrown out?"

"I don't think so."

Ally dipped her finger into the cream cheese icing on the cake before putting it into her mouth.

"Is your mom upstairs?"

"Yeah. Why?"

"I want to talk to her about the bell." Grace opened the door and walked up the stairs into the main part of the large house.

"Uh... Grace," her cousin said, trailing behind her.

"Yeah?" She continued into the living room with the vaulted ceiling. She never liked the home. It was big, with too much space making it cold and uninviting.

"I don't think you should discuss the bell with Mom."

She stopped, swiveled on her heel, and faced Ally.

"It's still a sensitive subject around here."

"Why? It was an accident, Ally."

"Let's just say Mom isn't too keen on the topic." Ally pulled on Grace's sleeve.

"You're being silly. It's not like I'm accusing her of breaking it."

"No, but..." Ally's voice trailed off.

"Come on." Grace grabbed her hand and tugged her along. They entered the spacious white kitchen where Aunt Janice sat with a cup of tea.

"Hi, Mom." Ally placed a light kiss on Janice's cheek.

Not one wrinkle was on her aunt's skin, and at forty-five she still held the beauty of her youth.

Janice smiled at her daughter before saying in a frosty tone, "Grace."

"Hi, Aunty." She sat down and pulled the chair closer to the table.

"What are you girls up to today?" The question was directed to Ally, so Grace didn't bother to answer.

"Not much. Grace just stopped by and brought me lunch." Her cousin didn't mention she'd not shown up for work yesterday or this morning, and so Grace kept quiet.

Janice nodded.

"Grace wanted to come say hi, so we ventured up," Ally continued.

"Were you able to restore the bell?" Janice asked.

Grace didn't expect her aunt to bring it up since Ally said she was still sour about the whole thing. Which made little sense to Grace since the broken bell was an accident.

"No, I'm missing a few pieces." She pressed her palms together, nervous about the response she'd get from Janice when she asked her about them. Grace was used to the icy welcome, and even now as an adult she felt the distance between them like a cold winter storm.

"Stands to reason. It broke," Janice said, nonchalantly.

"Is it..." Grace wrung her hands together. "Is it possible you may have taken one of them by accident?" Why was this so difficult? She'd outright asked the other girls, but with Janice it was different. The woman made Grace feel inadequate, and she always questioned her words even after she'd spoken them.

"One of what?"

"The missing pieces." Grace regretted her words when Janice's green eyes slanted into thin slits as she glared at her.

"Are you accusing me of taking a piece on purpose?"

"No... no, I would never do that," she stammered, trying to avoid a confrontation.

"Then what is it you're saying?"

Grace took a breath and tried again.

"I can't find three of the pieces. I've searched Mom and Dad's, but to no avail. I've asked the other girls and they don't have them. I thought maybe one shard landed on your clothing, and you took it home." It was the best she could do without causing a fight.

"That is the most absurd thing I've ever heard." Janice stood and placed her cup on the kitchen island. "I can assure you if a piece did land on me, I'd not be taking it home."

"I just figured since you wanted to hold the bell, that, you—"

"Oh, please. Let's be honest, Grace. I thought Ally should've gotten the bell."

Grace chewed on her bottom lip to keep from saying more.

"Ally deserved the bell." Janice placed a hand on Ally's shoulder. "Even though I thought it wasn't worth more than a can of soda. The prettiest granddaughter deserved Grandpas treasured bell."

"Mom," Ally groaned.

"Well, if not the prettiest, the smartest," Janice continued. "And the one who is going to do something with her life."

"But Grandpa gave the bell to me," Grace whispered.

"Yes. We all know, but it doesn't mean you should have it, Grace."

She couldn't believe what was coming out of her aunt's mouth. Janice was always offish and sometimes strict, but never hurtful. Unsure of what to do, Grace stood to leave.

"Mom, we've talked about this," Ally said. "Grandpa gave the bell to Grace. Just let it be."

"If your grandmother were still alive, she would've given it to you," Janice said. "We all know Grace got the bell because she believed in that cockamamie story Charlie always told."

Grace didn't know what to think. Did Grandma not love her like she loved Ally? Not once in all her years growing up did Grace think either grandparent favored one grandchild over the other. What was Janice talking about? Her mind raced with moments of her childhood out at the farm. There was always love, even when they were disciplined for walking across the creek in the springtime. Grandpa passed three weeks before. Why would Janice say anything bad about him? It wasn't right. Grace hugged her stomach.

"I'm going home," she said to Ally.

Janice sipped her tea and Grace couldn't bring herself to say goodbye to the woman as she left the kitchen.

Ally followed her to the front door. "C'mon, Grace. You know my mom. She's always been this way."

Grace continued toward the front of the house without saying another word to her cousin. She heaved on the thick wooden door until it opened and stepped outside. The bright afternoon sun dried the tears wanting to fall.

"Grace." Ally grabbed her arm. "Don't be so silly. You're acting like a child."

"The bell was important to me, Ally." She opened the car door. "No one seems to understand that."

"I do, but…"

"But what?"

"You're taking it too far. It's a bell. That's it."

"It's my bell." She got in her car and drove away. Not one person in the family understood Grace's love for the memory bell, or the desperation to put it back together. Why couldn't they see how important it was to her? Grace squeezed the steering wheel. The bell was broke. If she didn't put the bell back together, how would the Penners remain whole?

She blew out a long sigh that moved the wisps of hair hanging down her face.

Grace didn't want to fight with Ally—she didn't want to fight with anyone. She hated unrest and confrontation more than anything, which seemed to be prevalent among some of her family ever since the bell broke.

Ally was never wrong. Her cousin didn't take the blame for anything, even when it was her fault, and Grace wasn't a fighter—for anything. She looked the other way, rolled over, or apologized.

She pinched her lips together. Where were the three pieces? It's not like they were small bits. All of them were big enough to be seen on the floor or placed into a pocket. Someone took them. She was sure of it. She just didn't know why.

If Janice took the pieces, there was only one reason why. It was simple and harsh—because Ally should've gotten the bell, just like Janice had said.

Janice wasn't the aunt Grace could go to for anything. She kept you at arm's length. No one got too close, unless you were one of her city friends. Janice came from a very wealthy family, which according to Grace's mom was one reason Jan had always looked down on them. Not that the Penners didn't have their own wealth, they did, but not the kind Janice grew up with.

Both Ally and her brother Mike could do no wrong according to Janice. When it came to family gatherings, her mom often complained about her aunt showing off the medals, honors, and homemade crafts the kids made for Grandma and Grandpa. Grace had always known Janice didn't care for her, but it didn't make the words she'd said hurt any less.

She drove past the diner and turned onto Main Street. The outdated buildings stood tall on either side of the wide road. She spotted Carl's bike perched against the red brick building of the bank. Her dad told her that forty years earlier Carl's house was actually on the outskirts of town. Over the years Oakville grew, and soon buildings surrounded the small, green-stained home behind the main road into town.

Grace thought she should check on him. After his fall the other day at the diner she wondered how the old man fared. What if he was hurt, or worse, had broken a bone? She should've gone to see him after her shift yesterday. Grace would never forgive herself if Carl was injured. The old man seemed frazzled and unnerved. What did Detective James tell him? Grace wanted to know and decided she'd ask the lawman if she saw him again.

She parked beside the bank, leaving her car to retrieve Carl's bike. A brown bag sat in the basket, and she didn't need to look inside to know what it was. How could Carl keep going on like this? All of Grace's life she'd never known him to be sober. The liquor had to be taking a toll on the old man's body by now. She leaned the bike against the porch, plucked the bag from the basket, and walked to the door.

"Carl? It's Grace." She knocked.

The door swung open and Detective James stood there.

"What are you doing here?" she asked, peeking around him to see Carl.

"I could ask the same of you."

She pushed past him and walked into the dark home. The two-bedroom house reeked of stale booze and rotten food.

"I came by to see if Carl was all right," Ben said behind her. "I don't think he needs any more liquor." He pointed to the bag she held.

"I didn't buy him any. It was in the basket of his bike and I brought it inside." She placed the bag on the counter.

Carl was passed out on the sofa, a picture clutched to his chest. She gently pried it from his sleeping hands. A young woman in her teens stood beside a younger version of Carl. Grace had never been in his home, only having driven him or walked him to the door. She stared at the picture. The woman looked too young to be his wife, and the way they stood next to each other, not embracing, Grace wondered who the girl was. Long blonde hair parted in the middle hung straight down past her shoulders. A smile turned the corners of her mouth upward. Carl beamed as he stood beside her. Grace stared at his face. She'd never seen him so jovial before. A pang of sadness pierced her heart at how time had changed the man in the picture.

"Do you know the woman?" Ben asked.

"I'd like to say it's his wife, but I have my doubts."

"Did you know his wife?"

Grace put the picture back in Carl's hands and moved to the small kitchen. She opened the window beside the table, searched the cupboards for garbage bags, and found the box under the kitchen sink.

"I didn't know Olga," she finally answered. "My dad told me she left Carl years ago." She threw the empty bottles, half eaten food, and any other thing that looked to be garbage into the bag. It surprised her when Ben grabbed a dishcloth and stepped behind her, wiping the kitchen table and counters. Once the room was clean, she placed the full garbage bag beside the door to take outside when she left.

Loud snores filtered in from the living room as Carl slept, and Grace made a pot of coffee for when he woke up.

"The woman in the picture is his daughter, Claire," Ben said, now sitting at the kitchen table.

"He has a daughter?" she said, more to herself than him. She poured the water into the old coffeemaker and turned it on.

"He *had* a daughter."

She faced him, leaning her hip against the counter. Carl's daughter died? How sad. She watched Ben tap his pen onto the table and stare at the little black book in front of him. The realization as to why he was here hit Grace like a cement truck.

"That's why you're here."

He looked up, and his brown eyes said it all.

"Two weeks ago, a body was found west of town at the grain elevators."

"I'd heard." She brought her hand up to cover her mouth.

"It was Carl's daughter."

"When did she die?" All her life Grace never knew he had any children. Carl was always a loner.

"We figure about thirty years ago."

She blew out a breath unable to hide the relief of knowing whoever had murdered Claire was not the same person breaking into the homes in town.

"I never knew," she said. "All the times he was in the diner, never once did he mention he had a daughter."

Ben wrote something down in his book.

"How did she die?" She didn't know why she asked how Claire White passed, but something in her needed an answer.

"Grace, she was murdered."

She sat down across from Ben.

"Poor Carl. No wonder he drank." Grace's heart sank for the man she'd always known as Crazy Carl, the town drunk. To have a child die was bad enough, but murdered was inconceivable. Now she understood why he had done nothing to improve his life. Why he roamed the streets picking empty bottles from garbage cans. He had nothing left to live for, or so he must've thought. Grace blinked away tears.

"How come I never knew?" she whispered.

"Most people don't talk about bad things, and if it doesn't affect you directly, these things get forgotten."

She nodded, absorbing his words.

"I hope you catch whoever did this," she said.

"Well, with no missing persons report to go off of, I am going to need to hear the accounts from Carl, and anyone else who lived in Oakville at the time."

"I'm sure you'll get your answers. Most of the older residents have been here all their lives."

"That helps. Thank you. But it's likely we may never find out."

"How do you investigate something like this?" She paused, uncomfortable with the way he was looking at her. "That happened so long ago?" She went to check on the coffee.

"Let me put it this way. Time is not on my side."

She took two coffee cups down from the cupboard and filled them. Without asking him, she placed a cup in front of him.

He smiled. "Thanks."

"Poor Carl. How much did he tell you?" She was concerned for the old man. It wasn't like he was in good health with all the drinking he'd done over the years.

Ben took a sip of the coffee before he leaned back in the chair.

"Not much, but he was drunk. Once he sobers up, I'm sure I'll get something from him."

"Carl is never sober." She regretted her words immediately. It wasn't like her to speak so badly about others.

"That may pose a problem, but I've got to try."

"Do you think it's worth it to investigate?" she asked. "I'm going based on Carl's age and his health."

"I do."

She nodded.

"Claire didn't deserve to die. Carl didn't deserve to live his life without his daughter, and for those reasons, it's worth it."

She sensed anger behind his words.

"How long have you been a detective?" she asked, curious about who he was, and deflecting him from the previous question.

He didn't answer.

"Were you a regular cop before?" she asked, desperate to keep him talking.

"Yeah. Something like that." He tapped his pen on the table.

"Does your job ever get to you?" She sipped her coffee and frowned. She'd forgotten to put sugar in it.

"It has its difficulties." He pushed the sugar bowl across the table toward her.

She tilted her head.

"Your face said it all." He smiled.

"Thanks." She scooped up a heaping spoonful of sugar and dumped it in her coffee.

"There are times I wonder why I do it, but every family I bring closure to makes up for the doubts."

Grace could never tell someone his or her loved one had died. She wasn't strong like that. She had a hard enough time standing up to her family and friends, and most times she didn't, allowing them to take advantage of her.

The cell phone in her purse rang, and she pulled it out.

Got the job. Need a ride tomorrow. Andy texted.

Great, it was just like her brother to assume she'd have nothing better to do tomorrow but drive him to a new job.

"Doesn't look like you're too impressed with whoever just texted you," Ben said.

She shrugged. "My brother. He drives me crazy sometimes."

He nodded but remained quiet.

She put her phone away after replying she'd do it.

"Do you have other siblings?"

"A sister, Steph, who is a little too forward sometimes."

"What about aunts and uncles do they live around here?"

"Yeah, my dad and his brothers Rick, Randy and Jules all still live here with their families."

Carl stirred in the other room, and before they got to him, he'd knocked over the lamp on the table beside the sofa.

Ben jumped up to help him off of the ground. Grace retrieved the lamp, but the glass had broken and she reached for the broom leaning against the wall.

"Come on, Carl. We've got a pot of coffee in the kitchen with your name on it," Ben said to the old man as he ushered him into the other room.

Grace stayed to clean up the mess in the living room. Once the place looked somewhat presentable, she placed the lamp by the garbage bag she'd put at the door earlier and ventured into the kitchen where Ben was with Carl.

"Can you tell me anything from that day, Carl?" he asked.

She didn't want to interrupt, so she stood off to the side.

The old man shook his head, and with trembling hands lifted the coffee cup to his lips and slurped.

Ben sighed and put his pen down.

Grace sat beside Carl.

"How're you feeling?" She placed her hand on his shoulder.

He smiled at her, but his eyes were glazed as he was still drunk.

"Carl, do you remember Detective James?"

He shook his head, spilling the coffee he held.

Grace took the dishtowel from the table and wiped up the mess.

"He's here to help you."

Carl looked at Ben, then back to Grace. He shook his head.

"If you can't tell him, tell me." She smiled. "You've known me all my life."

He stared at her, and she knew he understood what she'd said when his eyes misted with tears.

She waited.

Carl took another sip of coffee, and when he moved the cup from his face, a large tear lay below his lower lashes. Grace fought the urge to cry and instead offered encouragement by squeezing his shoulder.

"I… I don't remember," Carl said.

"Why not tell us what you can remember," Ben said.

Carl looked at Grace, and she smiled.

"Claire was our joy." His words were strong and clear. "She adored her mother…" Carl stopped, and more tears fell from his eyes. He took the dishtowel Grace gave to him earlier and wiped his face.

"When did your wife leave?" Ben asked.

"I don't remember."

Grace could see Carl's cup was empty. She got the pot and poured more for him and Ben before coming back to sit beside him.

"I… I knew she didn't run off. Claire wasn't like that." Carl coughed and more tears fled from his eyes. "She was a good kid. Had her entire life ahead of her." He tossed the coffee cup he was holding across the room. A heart-wrenching moan turned into a growl, and within seconds Carl's arm flung out and cleared the table of its dishes.

Scared of what he'd do next, Grace pushed the chair away from him. Ben was up and standing next to Carl before she was able to get out of her chair and to the other side of the room. Horrified, she watched as Carl thrashed his ageing body against the detective. Loud wails reverberated off the walls, and Grace felt the tears stream down her cheeks. Her soul ached for the man and what he'd lost.

CHAPTER SEVEN

Ben held onto the old man's arms as he struggled, a mix of rage and sorrow in his eyes. Ben felt sorry for the man. For eighty-two, Carl was stronger than Ben gave him credit for. Low muffled groans escaped from the old man's mouth, and Ben stood with Carl leaning into him.

"It's all right," he whispered.

"Get out," Carl growled.

He wasn't surprised to hear the words. The time passed was too long. Carl couldn't deal with what happened, and Ben believed him when he said he didn't remember. Guilt was sure to be the reason for the outburst, and as much as Ben needed Carl and any information he had, there would have to be another way for him to get it.

Carl lunged for Grace, who stood off to the side, and Ben held onto him.

"Get out of my house!" he screamed at her.

She jumped back and stared at Ben.

"Get out! Get the hell out!" Carl shouted.

"You need to go, Grace," Ben said. "I'm sorry."

She nodded, reached for her purse on the counter, and with moisture-filled eyes stared at Carl one last time before she fled the home.

When the door closed, Carl slumped back into the chair, laid his head onto the table, and sobbed.

No matter how many times he'd seen the same display, Ben was never prepared for how he reacted. His throat worked, and his chest ached with remorse for the man before him.

He knelt beside Carl.

"Where's my rum?" The old man asked, his head still on the table. "I need my rum."

Ben blew out a breath. The man couldn't cope without the liquor. It'd been his crutch for years, helping him get through each day, and now sadly he couldn't go five minutes without it. He walked to where he'd seen Grace place the bag. He pulled out the bottle and put it on the table.

"Mind if I look around a bit?" he asked, knowing Carl didn't care now that he had his booze.

He opened the bottle and took a long drink. Ben left him to search the house. He stepped into the living room and was surprised how fast Grace had cleaned it. When he'd arrived, the house was a mess. Garbage littered the floors, and every table in the kitchen and living room was covered with more dishes. She'd done a good job ridding the home of most of the mess in the hour she'd been there.

Ben's eye stopped on the old AM tabletop tube radio. The thing had to be from the forties. He wondered if it still worked. The relic sat on top of a sofa table with four small drawers. He opened the one closest to him and rummaged through the pictures inside. Black and white photos stared back at him of a young Carl and his wife. He flipped through more pictures of people, a barn raising, and a wedding. He closed the drawer and opened the next one.

Papers filled a small box, and Ben pulled them out, hoping to find something that might help in the case. He rummaged through mortgage and loan papers until he came across something interesting. It was a sizeable amount paid onto a mortgage in 1991. He grabbed the original papers he'd come across. Carl owned the house back then, but he'd taken out a second mortgage against it in 1986. Nothing on the paper said why, or to whom the money went, just that the amount was twenty-five-thousand dollars. He looked at the second paper where the loan was paid in full.

Ben took out his phone and snapped pictures of both papers before placing them to the side. He scanned the other documents, but there was nothing within them. He closed the drawer and looked into the next one. It was empty and so was the other one beside it.

He peeked into Carl's bedroom. Clothes and more empty liquor bottles were strewn across the floor. A hostile scent ravaged his nostrils, and he coughed, gagging into his hand. There was vomit on the bedding. Ben retreated, closing the door behind him.

Carl sat at the table, the bottle of rum almost gone. Ben gathered his papers and placed the coffee cup in the sink.

"Thank you, Carl," he said. "I'll be in touch."

"Bah!" he spat, waving his hand in the air. The chair slid back, and Carl's body teetered on the edge of the worn cushion. Ben waited to see if he'd fall, but the old man steadied himself on the edge of the table and regained his balance.

Ben left, unsure if Carl even retained all he'd told him today. The routine of drinking all day would catch up to him. Ben was surprised it hadn't already. It was sad. The man was lonely—anyone could see that—and besides Grace, Ben had yet to see anyone stop by or even talk to the man.

Once outside, he inhaled deep into his lungs. The fresh air was a welcome greeting to what he'd just smelled, and he took two more revitalizing breaths. He hadn't surveyed the backyard when he arrived—he'd been too concerned about Carl—and decided to poke around before he left. What was laid out before him was more like a small dump. Why didn't the town require the old man to clean up the yard all these years? It was an eyesore. The businesses surrounding the home couldn't be happy with the state Carl kept his place in. Boards were scattered about the uncut lawn. Old bike parts lay next to the shed, and two lawn mowers that probably hadn't run in years sat in the middle of the yard.

He made his way to the shed. The structure seemed to be built around the same time as the house. The wood leaned to the left, and Ben was hesitant to open the door. The roof boasted two gaping holes in it, and he wondered what wildlife would greet him when he ventured inside. He stood away from the building, lifted the metal latch that held the door closed, and carefully swung it open. It creaked, and dust fell from what was left of the roof, but the four walls remained in place, so he stepped inside.

The room was no bigger than his bathroom at home. A window over a workbench offered a bit of light and Ben spotted ropes on the counter beside what looked like empty reels and a turned over empty bottle of rum. He stepped closer and his heart sank.

A noose lay across the table.

He picked it up. Two knots were tied. The old man thought about killing himself, but must've been too drunk to finish tying the knots. A thick layer of dust sat on the rope. Carl probably forgot the noose was in here. An old newspaper lay under the empty bottle, and Ben pulled it out. A picture of Rhoads getting elected Sheriff of Oakville was the first story on the page.

Did Rhoads have something to do with Carl's missing daughter, or was it just poor policing? Ben didn't know—he had no leads—but something told him he'd need to look into the sheriff. He took the large shears hanging on the wall and cut the noose in two, grabbed the newspaper in case there was more information inside of it, and left.

Ben made a mental list of things he'd need to check up on, and the bank was at the top of it. He needed to see if there were any files dating back to the time Carl took out the loan and someone paid it off. Sheriff Rhoads needed to be interviewed, and Ben thought it best to search for Olga White. If she were still alive, maybe she'd be able to shed some light on Claire's disappearance. Before he got into his car, he thought about checking on Carl one last time. As he made his way up the steps, he heard the old man shuffling around inside. A quick peek through the window on the door displayed a scene that would haunt Ben for the rest of his life. The soft tunes of the AM tube radio played an old song. Carl, wearing a suit coat, danced in the kitchen while clinging to a wedding dress.

Ben wanted to weep for the old man and all he'd lost. The love he had for his wife showed in the sway of his hips and the way he clung to the dress, squeezing the garment to him. To have a love like the one Carl had for Olga was all Ben ever wanted, and instead his heart had been trampled.

Why did Carl's wife leave? Was it because of the drinking? Did Claire's disappearance tear them apart? Did she not love him? Ben couldn't help his dislike for the woman. She'd been heartless as far as he could see. She left her husband at a time where they should've stuck together. He'd seen it many times. Losing a loved one often tore families apart.

He turned from the tragic scene, feeling more alone than he'd ever been before. He understood Carl and why he leaned on booze as his crutch. He related to the old man and the sorrow he suffered at being left alone. He too, was dealt a similar hand. He loved Lana more than life itself. She was everything to him. In return she'd broken his heart, ripped his soul from his body, and left him cracked and broken. He'd never be the same, and he'd never find love again. Not because it wasn't there, but because he refused it. No one would hurt him like Lana did. Ben ran his hand down his face, the ache still picking away at his soul.

He wanted to die when she left—wanted to crawl into a bottle like Carl and let go of everything he'd worked for. There were times when he succumbed to the heady scent of the amber liquid, drinking himself into oblivion to wake with Malcolm picking him up off the floor. Shame didn't even touch on what he'd gone through those next days, and instead of apologizing, he'd distanced himself. Worked on being better. Getting better. But there were still nights when the loneliness crept in, robbing him of the serenity he'd worked so hard to achieve, stealing his breath and puncturing his heart once more.

Ben placed his head on the steering wheel and waited while the agony washed over him. It'd been a year, and on some days the past seemed like yesterday. He wanted to forget it all. Pretend it never happened. But there was no way life would allow it, and the damn past continued to torture him. Now he was on probation, with no friends, and wondering why he still existed.

What was life all about anyway? Did one just get by until it was their time to die? There had to be something more—something worth living for. Or maybe there wasn't. Maybe his path was to solve crimes and nothing more. He groaned. Life wanted to sink him, he was sure of it. Happiness wasn't in his cards, and so he'd play the shitty hand he'd been dealt and maybe, just maybe, he'd get by okay.

Ben let out a long breath. Crime didn't stop. Evil continued to rear its ugly head and lives continued to be taken as if they were nothing more than a mere whisper in the dark. It was his job to solve those crimes—to bring justice to the mourning families. He'd been a detective for over eight years, promoted from a constable who drove a cruiser giving out misdemeanor tickets. He never thought it'd happen so fast, and neither did some of his colleagues. He worked hard. Did his job well. He solved the Davidson case, which was what got him noticed.

Life on the beat was definitely less stressful, but it was unfulfilling, and Ben's desire to do more and to be more, pushed him to work extra hours helping the detectives crack the case. Henry Davidson was a serial killer who tormented Chicago for years, preying on women working the streets. Ben remembered the day they arrested him and the pride he experienced at being a part of something that affected the city. He'd never forget the hugs, tears, and gratitude from the victims' families.

He gained the same pride with every criminal he'd brought to justice since. It was in those moments he felt satisfaction in the person he'd become, and it was no thanks to his father. Ben could look in the mirror and see a man. But now when he looked into the mirror, all he sensed was shame. He rubbed his eyes. What was his purpose now? Where did he fit in? It sure as hell wasn't here in the old town, miles from the life he'd left behind.

Would the Claire White case be too much for him? What if he couldn't solve this one? How would he tell Carl? What would the old man do then? He gripped the steering wheel. Most times he formed a bond with the family, but what he thought of Carl was far more than anything he'd experienced for any other family in the past. He knew getting too close might risk messing things up, but he couldn't shake the overwhelming need to make sure the old man was okay.

***

Grace perched on a stool at the island of her mom's kitchen. She'd stopped by to pick up Andy for his new job and came early to talk to her mom about the ordeal with Aunt Janice yesterday. The whole thing still bothered her. It wasn't so much the way Janice treated Grace that had her up in arms because she was used to that. It was the blatant disregard for the gift Grandpa gave her.

"I just don't know why she thinks Ally should have the bell," Grace said.

Mom sipped from her cup of lemon chai tea while standing across from her.

"It's who she is, Gracie. Leave it alone." She placed the cup onto the counter.

Mom didn't like waves. Confrontation of any kind was not Vera Penner's thing. When she and Dad fought, she submitted to avoid any major blowouts. It must be where Grace got her submissive attitude. She wished to be more like Steph, or Ally. They spoke their minds sometimes when they shouldn't, but you always knew their stand on things. With Grace, she just gave in to whoever she was arguing with, even when she was right.

"You've got the bell," Mom said. "Nothing else matters."

"Yeah. A broken bell," Grace mumbled.

"I know you're upset, and rightfully so, but nothing will come from you pushing this."

"How can you say that, Mom? It wasn't your gift that broke."

Mom laid a hand over hers.

"No, it wasn't," she sighed.

Grace knew her mom was right, and she should just leave it alone, but she couldn't. Just because someone else wanted the bell didn't mean they should have it.

Grace plucked a grape from the bowl and popped it into her mouth.

Mom lifted the dishtowel to reveal a pan of brownies. She pushed them toward Grace and smiled.

"Jules thought maybe the bell was worth money, and that's why everyone wanted to hold it." Grace pulled a piece of the chocolaty treat from the pan.

"I don't think so." Mom dismissed the idea and poured more boiling water from the kettle into her cup.

"But why were they acting so crazy about it?"

She placed the kettle back onto the counter and looked at Grace. "Because it wasn't given to them."

"That makes no sense."

"Think about it, honey."

"Hey, Gigi." Andy sauntered into the kitchen with his backpack slung over his shoulder. He was glossy-eyed, and his hair was a mess.

"Hey, bro."

Andy opened the fridge and pulled out a can of Coke. He cracked the top and guzzled half of it before letting out a loud belch. Grace knew he was high. He pushed buttons when he was stoned. On any other day, he'd never burp like that in front of Mom.

"Andrew!" Mom slapped his shoulder.

He smirked, but never apologized.

"Nice," Grace growled.

"What? Can't a man burp?" Andy said.

"What time do you need to be at work?" she asked, even though she knew.

"I told you. Four o'clock."

Grace glared a silent reprimand at him for going to work stoned on his first day.

Andy returned her glare with a wide smile.

She rolled her eyes.

"Are you coming down with something?" Mom asked him.

Her mom really had no clue what was wrong with Andy, or his penchant for smoking weed 24-7. In fact, none of them knew why he did it. He enjoyed his pot, and maybe that was why he had no drive to do anything with his life. Dad seemed to think it was from Mom coddling him too much, but Grace thought it was something more. Something deeper. She wasn't sure what.

She eyed Andy. He had no cares. Life was simple for him because Mom and Dad made it that way. A tinge of jealousy took root in Grace's stomach, and she pushed the notion aside. Andy would get it together soon enough, and the new job would help.

"I've got a sewing class to get to," Mom said, kissing them both on the cheek. "Remember what I said, Grace. Let it go."

She nodded, but it wouldn't be as easy as Mom thought. The bell was hers and she treasured it. The thought of never having it back together again made her head spin with anxiety. Grace frowned and pulled another brownie from the pan.

"Why so down?" Andy asked. "Still stuck on the bell thing?"

No one seemed to get how much the bell meant to her.

"You need to give up, Gigi. Those pieces are long gone."

"No, they're not. Someone took them. I know it."

Andy laughed a little too long, and she chalked it up to him being high.

"Yeah, someone stole three pieces of an old porcelain bell. Come on."

She nodded.

"Why would they take it?"

It came to her then what Mom said.

"So I don't get to put it back together." She clapped her hands. "That's it. The reason the pieces are missing. They don't want me to put the bell back together."

"Are you high?" Andy asked.

Grace focused on him.

"That's your department."

"Damn right it is." He smiled. "But seriously, the bell is back together."

"No. It's not whole until I have put all the pieces in place."

He ran a hand through his shaggy hair.

"Whatever, Gigi. It's stupid. Just hang the bell the way it is."

Grace didn't want to hear it. She pressed her palms into the counter to keep from lashing out at her brother. Why was it so difficult for everyone to see what the bell meant to her—what it did?

Even now when she recalled the times Grandpa let her ring the bell, it was as if she were right there on the porch with him. The sound of the tiny metal ball clanking against the glass caused her arms to litter with goosebumps and her stomach to flutter. Nestled on Grandpa's lap, she'd wait, her eyes scanning the fields and long driveway for any sign of them—just one glimpse and she'd know it was real. Grace's small body would wiggle off of Grandpa's lap to stand at the edge of the porch and peer out into the distance. She held her breath, suspended at the back of her throat, immobile in her lungs. Just when she was about to give up, Grandpa would jump from the rocking chair. "*Look, Gracie-girl.*"

She'd spin around, braids whipping her cheeks, and see them come. The gravel kicked up a dust cloud a mile away. Grace jumped up and down as her aunts, uncles and cousins arrived. The memory bell had called to them just like grandpa said it would. *"It is as I've told you, Gracie-girl. The bell sings within their hearts and calls them home."*

She was a part of the bell—of what it signified—of what it did. No matter where they were, the chiming of the bell would always call the Penners home. The story fascinated her as a child and into adulthood. She'd seen the magic the bell had time and time again, and no one would take that away from her.

Grace ran the back of her hand across her wet lashes.

Andy came out of the pantry with two boxes of crackers, a bag of chocolate chip cookies, and three pieces of licorice.

"Really?" she asked.

He shoved it all in his backpack.

"You need all of that?"

"I'll have most of it eaten before we get to the lodge."

"Did you know the body found was Carl White's daughter?" she asked him, changing the subject.

Andy didn't look up from the piece of brownie he was trying to cut out of the pan. "Crazy Carl doesn't have a daughter, dumbass."

"Yes, he did."

Andy shoved the massive piece of brownie into his mouth. "How do you know that?" he asked while chewing. Bits of the cake flew from his mouth.

"Detective James told me. She was killed around thirty years ago."

"Detective James? Who's he?" Andy grabbed another hunk of the brownie.

"The detective on the case, *dumbass.*"

"How do you know his name?"

"He came into the diner to talk to Carl." Andy didn't need to know she was in Carl's house yesterday. Her brother was famous for blabbing his mouth when he was high, often telling their dad things she'd told him in secret. Mom wouldn't be too happy about it either. A young girl alone in the home of the town drunk.

"Doubt they'll find anything," Andy said. "It was too long ago."

Grace shrugged. "They've got forensics now. So, you never know."

"Yeah, that's true."

She glanced at the clock. Three thirty. They better go if Andy was to make it to work on time.

"Ready?"

"Yeah. I'm gonna hit the bathroom before we go."

"I'll be in the car." Grace grabbed her purse from the chair and stepped out the back door.

Andy jumped in a few minutes later, the smell of weed oozing off him.

"Was it necessary to smoke up again?" She sighed. "You can't go to work fried."

"Back off, Gigi."

"No. You're going to lose the job before you even start it."

He ignored her and opened the box of crackers.

"Damn it, Andy. Dad will be pissed if you get fired on the first day."

"Dad doesn't need that as an excuse to be pissed." He munched on a cracker.

"Why do you need to get high all the time? Can't you just be normal like everyone else?"

Andy turned toward her. "Are you going to drive me or not? Cause if all you're going to do is lecture me, I'll walk."

"But—"

"Gigi, shut the hell up!" He tossed the box of crackers onto the floor by his feet.

"Andy—"

"Just shut the fuck up."

She held her lips closed and pulled the car out of the driveway. Andy was the last person she wanted to fight with. All she wanted was the best for him. He'd never yelled at her before, and she didn't know how to take it. Sure, they had their disagreements over the years, but never once were they cruel to each another.

The drive to the old folk's home was quiet, and Grace relaxed her shoulders when she pulled into the parking lot and Andy jumped out.

She lowered her head onto the steering wheel. The tears were close, but she refused to cry. She wasn't weak like Josh said. She was strong, and damn it, she wouldn't break down. Andy would be fine, and in a few days they'd be back to their normal banter. The murder of Carl's daughter would be solved, and Grace would find the missing pieces to the bell. Everything would fall into place. She chanted the mantra over and over until she believed it to be true.

CHAPTER EIGHT

Ben sifted through the papers on his desk. One by one, he flipped past reports. After he left Carl's, he drove back to his office and dug out all the police files from 1985 to 1995. Since he didn't have an exact time of death, he'd span the ten years hoping to find something on Claire. So far all he'd read were accounts of minor offences and a fire on the east part of town. Ben picked up the picture he'd taken of Claire with Carl. The photo was grainy, as were most pictures taken back then, but the joy could still be seen on both of their faces. There was no such thing in Carl's life now—hadn't been for years—and Ben couldn't stop the remorse as it crept up his spine.

He massaged his face, rubbing his tired eyes. He'd made a silent promise to the old man to find out who killed his daughter. Carl placed himself somewhere in Ben's heart, and the determination to solve the crime ate away at his sanity.

"Hey, kid."

Ben looked up from his desk to see Malcolm. The familiar broad smile and mischievous brown eyes greeted him like a morning hug, and he remembered how much he missed the man. He hadn't seen his friend in months, and if he were to be honest, Ben stayed away on purpose. After his probation he wanted to hide, partly due to shame, and partly due to his pride.

"Hey, Gramps. What brings you this far out of the city?"

Malcolm and his wife, June, practically raised Ben from the time he was twelve into his adult life. When his father was gone on business, Ben spent his time at their home. Malcolm was already in his fifties when he began tutoring Ben, so calling him and his wife Gramps and Gram seemed appropriate.

"Why, you of course." Strings of white brushed through the man's black curly hair, and the corners of his face creased from age.

Ben didn't know what to say. He knew Gramps would come to check on him eventually, but now that the old man was here, his neck ached with guilt.

For seventy-nine, Malcolm still got around well. Gram, not so much. She stayed in most days, and Ben made sure they were in the best retirement home Chicago offered. He used his father's money to pay for it and didn't feel one ounce of remorse.

He should reprimand Gramps for traveling the hour to Oakville, but he knew his lecture would fall on deaf ears. Malcolm was independent and no one, not even Ben, would take that from him.

"Got time for lunch?" Ben asked.

"Ahh… you always know how to make an old man happy." He slapped a large dark hand onto Ben's back and laughed.

"How'd you get down here?" He grabbed his suit coat and phone.

"Oh, I drove."

"You what?" Ben stopped to stare at him.

Malcolm didn't have a license. He'd lost it a few years before, after too many infractions and speeding tickets.

The old man laughed so hard he leaned into the wooden cane he held.

"You haven't changed a lick. I can still get you."

"Old bugger. I thought I'd have to arrest you."

"Nah. You'd do no such thing."

Malcolm was smart. Ben could never do it.

"Did you take a cab all the way here?" The cost would be absurd, and he'd make sure to reimburse him.

"Lou's granddaughter lives here, so I caught a ride with him."

Lou was Malcolm's friend from years past. Ben liked the elderly fellow. He'd taught Ben how to play Gin when he was young.

"How's Gram?" he asked. The old woman was sweet and kind. She'd never tried to replace Ben's own mother, but always showered him with love and affection.

"As crotchety as ever!"

"Stop it. You love her."

"Damn right I do. Ain't nobody in the world I love more. That's why I can say that!" Malcolm took small steps down the hallway.

"How is the retirement home?"

"It's a prison."

Ben laughed.

"The other day we weren't allowed to go outside. Do you believe that?"

"I'm sure there was a reason. Luxury Living is one of the most lenient homes around."

"Yeah. They said a water main broke, but I think they ran out of food."

"They didn't feed you all day?"

"Oh, they fed us. Prison food."

Malcolm always had a story to tell. They walked to the restaurant next door, a quaint soup and sandwich eatery Ben was sure Gramps would love.

"Oh, I almost forgot," Malcolm said after they sat down. "I got one of these." He pulled out a cell phone from his pocket. It was the newest edition with touchscreen and all the bells and whistles.

"Why did you get that?" Ben had given them an old flip phone when they moved into the retirement home years before to keep in touch. It eased the task of teaching them how to text.

"The lady said it was the best thing a going." Malcolm frowned. "Except I can't figure out how to use the damn thing."

Ben groaned.

"You're going to need a whole tutorial on it. They're like a computer."

"You don't say?"

"Yeah, and that's why you should've kept the old phone I gave you."

"It stopped working."

"Why didn't you let me know? I would've got it fixed."

Malcolm gave him a look—the same one he gave when Ben pretended not to know the answer on one of his exams.

"Boy, you're never around. Jane and I haven't seen you in months."

Guilt settled on his shoulders, and he slumped forward. Malcolm was right. Not that he didn't want to see them—he did—but after Lana and then his probation; he didn't know what to do. The thought of placing his fears and anxiety on the old couple made his stomach turn.

"I know. I'm sorry."

Malcolm was quiet while his dark eyes assessed Ben. "It's not like you to up and leave the way you did."

It was the truth. He'd sat outside the retirement home for over an hour on the day he left, but was too much of a coward to go inside.

"Son, you've got to let things go."

Ben looked away.

"I know she done and hurt you, but you can't stop livin'." It was just like Gramps to say what no one else wanted to.

"I'm fine."

"Yeah, yeah, you're about as fine as me knowing how to use this damn phone."

He smiled.

"She was no good for you. I knew it from the moment I laid eyes on her."

Ben raised a brow.

"Oh, you were blinded by love, but I saw. Oh, yeah, I saw all right. She always wanted more. Nothing you did was ever enough. Hell, she even made you buy her a bigger ring."

He thought back to the time he'd proposed. Lana's face lit with excitement, until she'd seen the ring, a half carat diamond solitaire. At the time he'd dismissed the flicker of disappointment in her eyes and told himself she was over the moon, just like he was, but two days later she was complaining how a bigger diamond would look much better on her hand.

"You were too good for that woman. Time's past for you to pick up and move on."

He knew what Malcolm said was true, but he wasn't ready, and the old man didn't know half of what happened. He couldn't even think about loving another woman the way he loved Lana, even though she was more maintenance than most. And what if he fell in love again? Would he always wonder when the hammer was going to drop, and she'd break his heart, too? No. He didn't want to live like that.

He nodded but said nothing. How could he when Gramps expected him to be okay?

"Betrayal is hard to overcome, son, but you'll be stronger for it."

"I disagree."

"Tsk, tsk. Now that's where you're wrong."

Ben averted his eyes.

"Life is full of lessons. Some teach us love, some empathy and compassion, and others give us strength."

"Can we just disagree on this one?" Ben didn't want to discuss Lana or what happened.

"How's work going?" the old man asked.

"I'm sure you already know I'm on probation."

"It took a bit of digging, and a hell of a lot of phone calls, but I finally got an answer where you were."

He didn't know what to say, so he waited for Malcolm to continue.

"Boy, what is going on?"

"It's a long story, Gramps."

"Well, I've got the time." He sat back and folded his arms across his chest. "So, get to tellin' it."

Ben inhaled a deep breath. He hadn't spoken about it since he'd given his statement to the board. Now he'd have to let the one person he admired above all else know he stooped to a criminal's level.

"I lost my temper, and I hit my captain," he blurted out, keeping the rest to himself. "I could lose my job because of it."

Malcolm was quiet.

"I know what you're thinking, and I know I was wrong, but damn it, the bastard deserved it."

"Son, you don't know what I'm thinking, and since when do you lift your hand to anyone?"

Ben hung his head.

"Why did you hit him?"

He didn't want to say—didn't want Gramps to know the full truth. "It all seems stupid now," he mumbled, wanting to forget about that awful night.

"Hmmm."

He couldn't tell if Malcolm believed him, and Ben figured wherever the old man's conclusion fell, it would come with a lecture.

"I don't know what got into me." He stared at the table. Half-truths were no good for anyone, and the way Gramps eyed him, he saw right through Ben's story.

"That's how it is then?" the old man asked.

Ben nodded. The facts were against him, especially since the entire department had seen Ben hit his captain. He knew why he snapped that day, but he'd not admit it.

"I'm working on a case here." He picked up the paper menu and scanned it, trying to dissuade Gramps from the subject of probation.

"A murder?"

Ben nodded.

"And Lou said nothin' ever happens out here."

He held in a sigh of relief when Gramps went along with the turn of conversation.

"Well, it does, but this one seems from years past."

"How many years?"

"No exact date yet, but approximately twenty-five to thirty years ago."

"Must make things difficult."

"Very, and the father of the deceased girl is a drunk. Can't remember much and doesn't want to."

"Puts a burr in your backside, doesn't it?"

"I understand his resistance, and the alcohol has dimmed his memory, but if I knew anything about the girl it'd help."

"Where's the man's wife?"

"Left after the girl had gone missing. I've got to run a check on her name. I'm not even sure if she's still alive."

"Sounds peculiar."

"My gut tells me she is innocent, but I have to rule it out like everything else."

"Sure."

Ben remained quiet.

"Seems to me you've got a dilemma on your hands in more ways than one."

Yeah, he did, and Gramps was no fool. He figured it out.

***

Grace jumped onto the couch in between Steph and Elle, spilling popcorn all over them.

"Gracie, what the hell!" Steph giggled while picking a piece of popcorn from her shirt and dropping it into her mouth.

"You have no idea how much I needed this," Grace said, reaching for her soda on the coffee table.

"Well, I'm happy to be here, even if we are missing two of the gals," Elle said.

Zoey was down with the flu, and Ally had other plans or something of the sort. Grace was a little down about the missing cousins, but if she were to be honest, after her argument with Ally a few days before, she was happy to have the space from her.

"I'm thrilled to get a full night's sleep," Steph said. "Finn is up at least twice during the night."

"Tell Tom to get up with him," Grace said.

Steph rolled her eyes. "Please, he has to work in the morning."

Grace hoped there wasn't trouble brewing for the newly married couple. For as much as her sister was difficult, she had a big heart. Grace knew without a doubt Steph loved Tom more than anything. She smiled as she watched the girls pass the popcorn back and forth, tossing pieces in the air and catching them in their mouths. They always had fun together, no matter what was going on in their lives. It was something Grace wanted them to keep forever.

"Who's hungry?" she asked.

Elle and Steph raised their hands without stopping their game.

"I'll order pizza."

"I love pizza," Steph yelled, and missed the piece of popcorn. "Damn it!"

Elle cheered and tossed popcorn into the air to act as confetti as she gloated about being the winner.

Grace's phone rang, and without looking to see who it was, she answered. "Hello?"

"Gigi? Can you come get me?" It was Andy.

"Are you okay?" she asked.

Steph and Elle stopped their conversation to listen, and Grace left the room so they wouldn't hear.

"Yeah. I just need a ride."

"Where are you?" she whispered.

"I'm on ninety-five. A few miles out of town."

A car raced by in the background.

"What the hell are you doing there?"

"Can you come get me or not?"

"Yeah, I can."

"Thanks, Gigi." He hung up.

Grace stared at the phone. Why was Andy way out there? She walked back into the room to grab her purse.

"Who was that?" Steph asked.

Grace didn't want to tell her sister. Steph didn't get along with Andy and her opinion mirrored Dad's.

"I'll be right back," Grace said, grabbing her keys from the counter.

"Gracie, who was it?" Elle wanted to know.

"Andy. He needs a ride." She closed her eyes, waiting for the outburst from her sister.

"Damn it, Grace. When are you going to stop chasing after him?" Steph grumbled.

"I don't chase him. He needs a ride. I'd do it for either of you."

"Yeah. But he uses you. Just like he does everyone else."

Elle remained silent, and Grace knew she didn't want to get involved. Uncle Rick and Aunt Fran raised their daughters to stay out of other people's issues. Smart, Grace thought. She wished her sister would do the same.

"No, he doesn't," she said. "I won't be long."

"It's not the point of how long you are, Grace," Steph said, and there was an edge to her voice. "Stop doing everything he asks you to do. He has to get his shit together on his own without you or Mom holding his hand."

"You know as well as I do, Steph, that Andy is treated differently by Dad. He's got some issues from it. He'd be there for any one of us."

"Yeah. If there was something in it for him," her sister replied.

There was no point in arguing. Steph wouldn't see her point.

"I'll pick up pizza on the way back," she said, before closing the door and racing to her car.

***

Twenty minutes later, her headlights shone on a figure standing on the side of the road. It was Andy, and she pulled her car to a stop beside him.

"Took you long enough!" Shivering, he hopped in and pulled his arms into his shirt.

"Yeah. You're welcome," she growled. "What in hell are you doing way out here?"

"I got lost." Andy snickered.

She clenched her jaw and sat upright.

"Knock it off. Tell me why you are way out here."

"Ugh. Come on, Gigi. I'm tired. Just drive." He lay his head back, closed his eyes, and bounced his legs up and down.

What was going on with him? He'd ripped her head off the other day when she'd lectured him about the weed, and now he wasn't telling her anything. They used to be so close.

She peeked at him, not sure she knew him anymore.

"I drove all the way out here. Don't you think I'm owed an explanation?"

"I was at a party and my ride left, okay?" He kept his eyes closed.

"Where?"

"The grain elevators."

"Andy, why would you guys go out there?" Claire's body was found there two weeks before. It wasn't right.

"Oh, stop being so uptight with everything."

"I'm not being uptight."

"Yeah, you are."

"Who were you with?" Andy had few friends, and most of them were just as lazy as he was.

"The usual," he said.

He wouldn't tell her a thing and, frustrated with the lack of information he was giving her, Grace gripped the steering wheel.

"Drop me at the farm," Andy said. "Jules is there."

"Does he know you're coming?"

He was quiet.

"Andy?"

"Yeah. Geez, Gigi, you need to relax."

Jules was staying out at the farm until the place sold. She made a left at the stop sign and drove west. Grace hadn't been out there since Grandpa passed, and she wasn't looking forward to the emotions of seeing the place would dredge up.

Five minutes later, the Penner ranch came into view and she turned the car down the long driveway. Grace sucked in a breath, relieved to see the lights on in the white farmhouse. She prayed Jules didn't have company, especially a female friend. That would make for an uncomfortable visit, and he wouldn't be pleased to see them. She didn't need anyone else angry with her tonight.

She stopped the car beside Jules's truck. Andy jumped out, sprinted to the front door and, without knocking, walked in. Grace followed at a slower pace behind him.

She shivered in the brisk evening air. A sweater would've been a good idea. She pulled her hands into her long-sleeved cotton shirt to keep warm.

The wheat fields were mere shadows in the dark, but Grace knew they were there. She made out the shape of the barn and the buildings beside it. The place was so familiar she could walk around it with her eyes closed. Her chest ached as memories flooded her mind. Running barefoot through the field, hiding in the barn, and... ringing the bell. She swallowed past the tears and walked up onto the front veranda.

Grandpa's rocking chair still sat in its same spot next to the small wicker table he'd placed his coffee on. The stool she'd sat on when she was a little girl and listened to his stories was also there. The ache in Grace's chest intensified, and she turned away from the reminders of a past she would forever cherish.

Not yet ready to go inside, she leaned against the railing and looked out into the darkness. The door opened behind her and the light from inside lit up the porch.

"Evening, Gracie," Jules said.

"Hey." She didn't turn to face him.

"How're you doing?" He stepped beside her.

"Great," she squeaked, unable to hide the emotion in her voice.

Jules put a muscled arm around her shoulders and squeezed her to him.

"Yeah. I figured," he said and kissed the top of her head.

It was just like Jules to know what was wrong without her telling him. It was one of the many things she loved about him.

"You haven't been out here since Grandpa passed."

She shook her head.

"Makes holdin' it in much more difficult when you're faced with the reminders."

Grace sniffled.

"It's tough some days." Jules sighed. "I swear the old bugger is still here."

"Really?"

"Oh yeah. Once in a while I smell his cologne, and just the other day I could've sworn I heard the chair on the porch rocking."

"No way!"

Jules nodded.

She leaned into him. "He was such a big part of my life. I feel like a piece of me is missing."

"I know. He was the glue that kept us all together."

She nodded.

"Any luck with the bell?"

"No, and I'd rather not talk about it."

He said no more.

"Andy wanted to come here. I'm sorry if you were busy."

"He's high," he said in a matter-of-fact tone.

"Isn't he always?"

"On weed, yes."

She pulled from his embrace and faced him.

"What do you mean?"

Jules's dark eyes softened, and he smiled.

"Don't worry about it, Gracie. I'll take care of him."

"Jules? Is Andy doing other drugs?" Grace's stomach twisted at the thought.

He said nothing. He didn't need to. His expression said it all. Grace's shoulders fell. Andy on other drugs? It can't be true. Why would he? Questions filled her head, and she squeezed her eyes shut.

"I'm guessing he's got some things going on," Jules offered.

"Yeah, but why? How did I not know?"

"Maybe this was the first time. Maybe it wasn't. I'll talk to him in the morning and see if I can't get him to open up to me."

If there was anyone Andy would spill his soul to it was Jules, and Grace's shoulders relaxed a little more knowing her uncle was there to help.

"We will keep this between us for now," Jules said. "No sense in Dave finding out."

Grace agreed. Her dad would kick Andy's butt if he knew any of this. As it was, Dad guessed that her brother smoked weed, but never found any when he searched Andy's room.

"He seemed a bit off in the car, but I just thought he was annoyed at me asking questions."

"It's difficult to see if you don't know what you're looking for."

Jules dabbled in the drug scene when he was younger, but Grace didn't know much about that time—she was ten—and the family didn't talk about the past. She remembered Jules missing from family gatherings. When she'd asked where he was, Mom told her he'd gotten into trouble and was sent away. Later on, through snippets of conversation, she'd put things together on her own. Jules had gone to jail.

It was one reason her dad wasn't close to his youngest brother. A Penner did not go to jail. If there was anything Dad instilled in her when she was growing up, it was to be proud of the family name—to know where you came from and who brought you there, and to never ruin it. She guessed that was just another reason for Dad to be angry with Andy. Her brother wasn't doing any profound deeds other than lying on the couch all day.

"Do you think he might be in some sort of trouble?" Grace asked. She knew nothing about what went on with drugs and the people who associated with them. All she knew was what she saw on those crime shows, and it scared the hell out of her to think Andy could be tangled up in the mess.

"I think he's experimenting."

"You mean like a phase?"

"Yeah, kind of." He hugged her to him. "Don't worry, Gracie. Everything will work out."

She wrapped her arms around him and took comfort in his embrace. Jules would figure things out with Andy. She trusted him.

"Thanks."

"You want to come in and warm up? You're freezing."

She remembered Steph and Elle back at her house.

"Shit. I can't. The girls are at my place. I've got to go." She placed a light kiss on his cheek before racing down the steps to her car.

"Drive safe." He waved at her before disappearing into the house.

She'd been gone over an hour.

She groaned, knowing what she'd face when she got home.

CHAPTER NINE

The morning air was crisp and dense. A light fog tickled Grace's nose and clung to her lashes. Her head pounded and her stomach turned. The effects of two bottles of wine the night before. She was sure the temperature was below zero as the cold seeped through her clothes. The hairs on her arms and legs stood, and she hugged the long sweater to her.

Awoken to the ringing of her cell phone, Grace thought about letting it go to voicemail, but on impulse she answered. Regret caused the muscles in her temples to pound, as she stood in the early morning hours freezing. Ally hadn't shown up for her shift, and Donna needed Grace to cover. Her cousin's continuous absence at work was annoying her. Unable to let Donna down, Grace jumped out of bed, got ready, wrote a note for Steph and Elle, and headed out the door.

The Volkswagen ran on diesel and would take time to warm up. She should've started it a half hour ago, but she assumed since it was still September the weather would be warm. Instead, there was a thin layer of frost on the windshield and the grass sparkled with ice crystals.

An envelope was taped to the driver's side window of her car. She stepped closer, staring at the typed inscription.

"What a tangled web we weave when first we practice to deceive," she whispered.

What did it mean and why was it taped to her window? She shivered. Hesitant to pull it off, she scanned the neighboring condos on either side of her place and out into the street. No one was around. She ripped the envelope from the window, got into her car, locked the doors, and blew a sigh of relief as the hair on the back of her neck rose. Something was inside the envelope as she examined it again. A small lump pressed into her thumb. She slipped her index finger into the small opening at the corner and, like a knife cutting butter, sliced open the envelope.

Grace gasped.

A piece of the bell sat nestled inside. She tipped the packet until the tiny shard fell into her palm. Why had the piece come to her this way? She read the quote again. Grace had heard it somewhere before. She pulled out her phone and typed in the words. It was from a play she'd studied in school.

She tipped the envelope upside down to see if the other pieces were there. It was empty. Anxiety knitted a path through her veins and caused her heart to beat erratically. Grace blew out a shaky breath. Her hands shook. She hadn't experienced the sensation since she was a little girl and Andy didn't come home for supper. Mom had grown frantic as the hours went by and each phone call to friends turned up empty. Two days passed before he was found in the forest bordering Grandpa's land. He'd been exploring and got lost.

Grace closed her eyes and inhaled through her nose, blowing the air slowly out of her mouth. The cold air relaxed the muscles in her throat and calmed the restless beast from stabbing at her heart. A feeling of desperation followed with the faint touch of misery. What did the words mean? Was someone being deceitful? But who, and about what?

Grace dropped the piece back inside the envelope and started the car. The thought of a dark secret buried in her family set her stomach to spin and her face to become flushed, even in the chilled morning air.

She was being silly. The Penners held no secrets, nothing of the worrying sort, anyway. It was just too impossible for her to comprehend. Grandma and Grandpa raised their boys on love, and they showed the same values to their children and other people around them. Grace thought of Andy and Dad—well, maybe not so much there—but she believed Dad loved his only son. Maybe Andy was being too sensitive.

Grace didn't know, and she hated to speculate how Andy felt, or why Dad treated him differently, but she hoped things changed between them soon. Especially if what Jules said was true and Andy had a problem.

She wondered if whoever left the piece had the other two as well.

Grace pulled out of the parking lot and headed to the diner. On most days she was happy to go to work, but today was different. Being overworked was probably the reason, and she couldn't stop the feelings of resentment toward Ally for not showing up again for her shift. She could've said no when Donna called, and it was something Steph told her to work on, but she just didn't have it in her.

Grace groaned. She was always picking up everyone's slack. She needed to learn to stand up for herself. Tension bothered her—every muscle in her body coiled up so tight, causing her back to ache and head to spin. It was how she felt anytime someone was angry with her. It was so awful, Grace often resolved the situation with an apology, even when she wasn't in the wrong.

She placed her hand on top of the envelope. She should be elated one of the missing pieces had been returned. Soon she'd have them all and the bell would be intact.

"Everything will work out," she said.

All would be well, and life would resume, but she wasn't so convinced.

***

Ben stirred his coffee with a flimsy plastic stick he'd found beside the machine. He was on his second cup since arriving at eight-thirty this morning. Rhoads was late and Ben wasn't surprised. It was another one of the sheriff's annoying habits. Did the man do anything by the book? Hell, if he couldn't even show up on time, especially when he knew Ben was waiting for him, then how could he run the department?

Unable to sit any longer, he stood. The walls were plastered with Rhoads's plaques. How had the man deserved any of the accolades when all he did was sit back and let the town run itself? Ben observed Rhoads's desk, fingering the papers and files placed on top. He picked up a picture of the sheriff in his uniform with the mayor. Ben guessed the District Superintendent wasn't aware of the relaxed way things were run in Oakville.

He scoffed.

Why did he even give a shit? It wasn't like he'd be here much longer. He'd be smart to look the other way like everyone else. Don't be a whistleblower and just keep his nose out of it.

He frowned. Being on the right side of the law was in his blood, and to uphold those values and morals meant the world to Ben. Seeing the sheriff so indifferent about everything irked him, but then again, who the hell was he? A detective on probation and possible termination. He had no grounds to dictate how Rhoads ran the precinct.

"Excuse me," Ben called, just outside of the office to the young deputy he'd spoken with the day he found Claire's body.

"Yes, sir?"

"What's your name?" He'd been told at some point, but to hell if he remembered it now.

"Trent Enders."

"Could you do a search on Olga White for me?"

The deputy nodded.

"Oh, and if you've got any files on the victim, I'd appreciate them, too."

"Sure thing, sir." Enders took off down the hall.

Ben wanted to put the deputy to use, and with a bit of guidance and constructive criticism, the man would do well at his job.

"Mornin' James." Rhoads sauntered into the room, placed his metal coffee cup onto the desk, and sat down.

Ben didn't think it was wise to remind the sheriff he was an hour late and cut right to the chase of why he was there.

"I'm not getting anywhere with Carl, and I need to talk with some of the people who were around back then."

Rhoads nodded, leaned back in the leather chair and rested his hands on his protruding belly.

"I know you were in the department thirty years ago. Is there anything you can tell me that you haven't already?"

"I'm not sure what else needs to be said."

"I need to know everything about Claire."

"Well, I only know what I saw."

"And what was that?"

"She was a bit wild, if you know what I mean... promiscuous. Liked to flaunt her body in short-shorts and low-cut shirts. Carl didn't like it, but the boys in town did, and she was with a new one every week."

Ben wrote what Rhoads was saying.

"Carl was strict with the girl, but it did very little to influence her. She'd take off and be gone for a few days, and he'd be worried sick."

"Did Carl come and report those incidents?"

"Yup, and we'd send out a car to go lookin' for her. We'd never find her, and a few days later she'd just turn up."

"Carl reported her missing the last time, too, right?"

"He did."

"And what happened then?" Ben already knew the answer.

"We ignored it."

He understood why. The girl was constantly running off.

"Why didn't you get on it when she didn't turn up after a month?" Ben asked.

Rhoads reached for his cup.

"Carl was drunk damn near every day."

"That does not answer my question."

"Couldn't get nothin' out of him."

"But you arrested him?" Ben read the file where Carl was arrested two months after Claire's disappearance.

"He tried to light our building on fire."

Ben knew that. He placed the pad of paper and pen onto his lap and stared at Rhoads.

"Here's how I see it. You thought the girl finally left for good, and so you weren't concerned. It wasn't until Carl pushed you to get information, but he didn't make it easy being drunk most of the time. And then you dropped the case completely because, well, it was just too damn hard. Carl got pissed and in a drunken rage tried to light the department on fire."

Rhoads's beady eyes squinted, and the edges of his lips curled.

"While Carl was in jail, you put the case to bed, telling him Claire ran off and there was nothing you, or he, could do about it."

"Go to hell, James," Rhoads growled.

"I'm close, aren't I?" Ben didn't give a shit if Rhoads was pissed, or if he'd embarrassed him. A girl was murdered in his town, and he'd done nothing but assume the answer instead of doing his damn job.

"You better watch yourself, *Detective*." Rhoads's reminder that Ben was no longer a detective, but now at the bottom of the barrel, was like a knife to the stomach.

He should walk away, leave it be, but he couldn't and leaned closer. "Call me what you will, but I made damn sure to always do my job. You on the other hand, have not."

"I can have you run out of here, so tread lightly," Rhoads countered.

"Is that a threat?" he asked, between clenched teeth. The sheriff didn't intimidate him, and there was no way in hell he'd back down now. "Don't think after a thorough investigation into your office, Internal Affairs won't find out how you've been taking money on the side from the farmers to look the other way when they are breaking the law." He was going on a hunch, and when Rhoads averted his eyes, Ben knew the bastard was exactly what he thought of him.

"They are minor infractions," Rhoads said, his tone lighter.

"It won't matter to them what they are. A sheriff breaking the law he is supposed to enforce doesn't look good, especially if he's taking a wage from it."

"Seems to me you did the same thing, and what's saying they'll take your word over mine?"

"The difference is I have nothing to lose, but you do."

Rhoads fiddled with the button on his shirt as he pondered what Ben said.

"I've told you damn near everything," he whined. "I've given you access to all our files. What more do you want?"

"Do you know anything about Carl taking out a loan at the bank for twenty-five thousand dollars in 1986, then in 1991, and two months after Claire was missing the amount was paid in full?"

Rhoads shook his head.

"Did Carl have money back then?"

"No. Not that I know of. He and Olga lived a very simple life."

"Who would have that kind of money to pay off the loan in full?"

"The only people in this town that wealthy are the Penners."

"Do they still live here?"

"Charlie passed on a month ago, but his sons all live nearby."

"Did Carl know Charlie?"

"Oh, yeah. They were the best of friends back then."

"I'll need the names and addresses of all the sons."

Rhoads nodded.

Ben stuffed the pad of paper into his pocket and reached for his coffee.

"Dave Penner and Claire were the same age. You might want to start with him," Rhoads said.

He nodded.

"Sir?" Enders stood in the doorway. "I've got some information on Olga White for you."

"What did you find?" Ben took the papers from the deputy.

"Not much. Just a few things from when she used to live here."

He examined the first report in front of him. It was a restraining order placed on Olga White by Charlie Penner.

"Want to tell me about this?" He tossed the paper onto Rhoads's desk.

The man picked it up and without even reading it said, "This was a long time ago."

Ben wanted to put his hands around the sheriff's neck.

"This was three months before Claire went missing. Explain."

Rhoads let out a breath and the button on his shirt popped off. He didn't pay any mind to it, and placed the paper back onto the desk.

"She was infringing on Charlie and Anna's marriage."

"What in hell does that mean?" Ben was tiring of the damn circles the man was running in.

"She was sweet on Charlie." Rhoads said in a lazy tone.

Ben picked up the paper and read it in full. According to Olga, she and Charlie had a fling, and the woman wasn't over it.

"How much were you paid to keep quiet on this one?" Ben demanded.

Rhoads stood.

"I've had just about enough of your accusations."

"How much?"

"Get the hell out of my office!"

Ben grabbed his briefcase, and without another word left the room. Every muscle in his body tensed and his jaw ached from clenching his teeth together.

"Sir?"

He turned to see Enders racing after him.

"If there is anything else you need? I'd be honored to help you."

The deputy wanted to be a good cop, not a lethargic piece of shit like his commander, and Ben admired him for it.

He patted the man's shoulder. "I may take you up on the offer."

Enders nodded, and his wavy blond hair bounced on his head.

Ben gave the man his card. "Call me if you have any more information."

He gripped the handle of his briefcase. He needed some air and headed outside. The front doors of the precinct were heavier than usual. He pressed his weight into them until they flew open and he walked out into the sunlight. He flexed his hand, desperate to diminish the urge of smashing his fist into Rhoads's face. The man was incompetent and a bloody liar.

The cell phone buzzed in his suit pocket.

"Hello?" he barked.

"Ben?" The voice stopped him dead in his tracks.

Lana.

"How are you?" she asked.

"What do you want?" He couldn't keep the irritation from his words, and he didn't want to.

"What have you been up to?"

He suppressed a growl.

"I… I'm calling to invite you to come for dinner."

He remained silent as his heart broke all over again.

"No."

"It's been a long time, Ben."

"Not long enough."

She laughed, a strained pull of the vocal cords.

"I have to go."

"Please consider it. We are—"

"Don't say it, Lana," he growled, the sound so menacing it surprised even him.

"But…"

He hung up. Lana's face stared back at him on the screen. He hadn't removed it, or her number. Memories from the past ran across his mind, and for a moment his heart soared at the recollection of what life was like back then. Just as quickly as the emotion came it disappeared, and the truth slammed into him sucking the air from his lungs. The ache in his soul lingered, drawing out the sorrow—the pain and the bloody agony of what she'd done to him.

"Damn it." He flung the phone into the air. Chest heaving, he waited for the normalcy to return—for things to somehow be different—for a life where laughter came easily, and love was more than an emotion that hurt like hell. But it never came, and it never would.

"Shit." He ran his forearm across his brow. "Shit," he said again, when he realized he might have broken his cell.

The phone sat on the sidewalk half a block away. Ben picked it up, praying it'd still work. The screen was cracked and there was a small chip on the top corner. He pressed the button, and the screen lit.

"Those things cost money," a voice said beside him.

Ben hadn't noticed the two kids standing there. No older than twenty, both looked like they hadn't showered in days. The one on the left smirked and his eyes were so red Ben wondered how much marijuana the kid smoked.

He said nothing and put the phone back in his pocket.

The other kid fidgeted from one foot to the other. His hands were jammed into the green coat he wore, and the black baseball hat sat lopsided on his head. His pupils were so dilated the color of his eyes were black. Ben watched the boy's features for any other signs as to what he may be on.

"If you can go flinging a phone like that around, you can afford to lend us some cash," the vampire-like kid said.

"Or maybe I arrest you for loitering on a public street." He flashed his badge.

"I was just messin' around," the boy said, holding his hands up and stumbling backward.

"Are you okay, kid?" he asked.

"Yeah, I'm fine." He continued to walk backward.

Ben considered following them. He'd seen firsthand what drugs did to a person, and these kids were well on their way to that kind of destruction. It was sad where society had gone, and how young the kids became addicted.

He watched the boys until they disappeared down the alleyway and headed to Carl's place a few blocks away and see how the old man was doing.

Oakville was a good-sized town with all the amenities one would need. He had paid little attention the past month, but now that he was walking the streets, it was easy to see the town functioned more like a small city. What had life been like in the little town thirty years before? He'd bet it was a heck of a lot smaller and safer, too. It would've been difficult to kill someone and bury a body with no one the wiser. Which made sense that somebody had to know something. In most cases, that was how it happened. A secret kept for years and years out of fear, or a disbelief of what they saw.

Was that what happened here?

He walked past the diner and saw Grace through the window, a tray in one hand and a coffee pot in the other. She had empathy for Carl. There weren't too many young adults he ran into with the same genuine kindness and giving nature he'd seen in Grace. He wondered how old she was, and if she had a boyfriend. Not that it mattered if she did.

He shook his head, unsure where the thought even came from.

He moved along, leaving any judgments of Grace back at the diner, and turned the corner toward Carl's home. If memory served him right, the old man's house was behind the bank on a road that didn't exist anymore. Whoever thought up the idea to build around Carl's place was an inconsiderate ass. The weathered wooden structure stood off the alley, tucked in between commercial property. The only way to get to it was through the backstreet. You'd miss it if you didn't know it was there.

"Nothing like stomping all over the man's pride."

Carl's bike lay in the middle of the road. Ben picked it up, noticing the bent basket in front and the worn seat and handlebars. It had to be older than him. Duct tape wound around the metal bar that attached the seat to the bike, and the gears were missing.

"The damn thing has no brakes," Ben whispered, still examining the cycle.

Carl needed a new one, and when this was all over Ben would buy it for him. He pushed the bike into the yard and leaned it against the porch. Empty bottles of liquor were strewn on the too-tall grass and in the corners of the entranceway. A yellow piece of paper was stuck to the door, and he pulled it off to read it. A warning to tidy up the yard or the town would issue a fine. The notice served no threat in Carl's life. He didn't care if he got a ticket. He didn't care if he lived. Anyone with eyes in their head could see that.

What harm would it do for someone to help the man out? He's lived in the town long enough to have formed relationships with people. Why didn't anyone offer to clean up the yard, or his home?

He knocked on the door.

Ben shouldn't jump to conclusions. For all he knew someone asked, and Carl turned them away. Drunks could be unpredictable, and he'd seen the old man get angry when he didn't remember much about Claire.

He knocked again.

Someone shuffled around inside the house. He tried the doorknob and was not at all surprised when it turned and the door opened. The television was on and Carl sat on the couch watching it.

"Morning, Mr. White."

The old man glanced at him, then back to the TV. Ben couldn't tell if he was drunk, or halfway to sober. The curtains were drawn closed behind the couch, and a lamp in the corner lit the small room. A musty scent hung in the air, and Ben figured it was from lack of fresh air. The place sure smelled better than the first time he'd been here. He noticed Carl kept the counters and tables clean since Grace tidied them.

"Mind if I sit down?" Ben made his way into the living room.

"Why are you here?" Carl asked, without looking at him.

"I just came by to see how you were getting along."

Carl laughed, a phlegmy chuckle.

Ben noticed the old man was wearing the same clothes he had on three days before.

"Have you eaten today?"

Carl ignored him.

"I know you like the diner's apple pie. My treat, if you feel up to it." He was hoping the man would take the bait.

Instead, he was met with silence.

Ben waited.

Minutes passed before Carl stood and walked to the door. Ben followed, watching as the old man got on his bike and rode in the diner's direction.

***

"Grace, do you have table ten?" Ally asked from behind her.

"Uh… no. I haven't taken it yet. Before I forget to ask, can you take my shift tomorrow?" Grace reached across the vacant table for the empty coffee cups and silverware, placing them on the tray she held.

"Sorry, I have plans." Ally took the tray of dishes from her and walked away.

Grace pressed the rag onto the table and scrubbed until her arm hurt. She shouldn't be surprised Ally said no, it was to be expected. Grace couldn't remember the last time her cousin worked a shift for her. She moved to the booth by the window when she saw Carl on his bike and Ben walking beside him.

"Who's he?" Ally asked, following Grace's line of vision.

She wasn't in the mood for her cousin's inquisitive bull crap, so she ignored her.

"Grace, who's the guy?"

She shrugged.

"What's your problem, Grace?"

"Detective James," she said, to avoid a fight.

"Yummy. How do you know his name?" Ally placed the tray of clean silverware on the table and focused all of her attention on Ben.

Grace tried to hide her irritation by picking up the forks and knives.

"He was in the other day," she whispered, not wanting Ally to hear.

"Looks like he's coming in today, too. I hope he sits in my section."

The bell over the door rang as they entered, and Grace tried her best not to look until they were seated.

"Ew. He's sitting with Crazy Carl."

It was just like her cousin to scoff at Ben for sitting with someone she considered to be beneath him.

"They just found his daughter." This time she didn't keep the irritation from her voice.

"I don't care. He's gross, and he stinks."

Grace was shocked at how shallow her cousin had become. Janice's judgmental attitude rubbed off on her daughter, and soon Ally would be just like her mother, if not worse.

"That isn't very nice."

"Oh, come on, Grace. Stop acting like he doesn't bother you."

"He doesn't." It was the truth, and the look on Ally's face said she didn't believe her. "Carl's done nothing to me, so why should I judge him just because he smells?"

"Because he's an alcoholic, Grace. Ugh." Ally's brow wrinkled and her full lips frowned.

"It's not a reason to dislike someone." The table was dressed, so she picked up the tray and headed to the kitchen.

Ally followed.

"I don't get you."

"What do you mean?"

"Carl is not worth anyone's time. He's drunk 24-7, Grace. Yet, you still feel sorry for him?"

"Yes, I do."

"Why?" Ally folded her arms across her chest. Her blond hair was pulled back into a high ponytail, offsetting her peaches and cream complexion. Her cousin was beautiful, and Grace had the urge to run her hands through her own hair.

"Don't you wonder why he drinks? Have you never thought what happened in his life to cause him such despair?"

"Not really."

"People don't just wake up one day and say I'm going to be an alcoholic, Ally. Something caused Carl to turn to liquor, and maybe it was his missing daughter."

"How do you know that?"

Grace rolled her eyes. It was clear all Ally wanted to do was argue with her.

"I'm done with this conversation. Are you taking their table or not?"

Her cousin looked toward the men. "No. My stomach is a little off today and smelling Carl will definitely make it worse."

She clenched her jaw to keep from saying another word. It was better to walk away than get into it with her cousin. The outcome would have her apologizing like she always did and trying to fix things between them. She grabbed the coffeepot from the burner and left. Grace placed a smile on her face before she approached the table.

"Good morning, Carl. Detective James."

"Call me Ben," he said.

He had kind eyes. They were a rich brown surrounded by thick black lashes, but she was more attracted to the easy, reassuring, sexy smile he displayed. She placed two menus in front of them.

"Coffee?" she asked.

"Yes, please." He slid the empty cup toward her.

Grace sensed his stare like the sun on a warm June day, and she licked her lips. She filled both cups, even though Carl never said he wanted any.

"I'll be back to take your order."

"I… I'll just have toast, and Carl will have his usual." Ben smiled.

Grace's cheeks flushed. His smile lit up his entire face, and it didn't matter that he was unshaven either. She spun on her heel, positive she'd turned thirty shades of red, and fled to the kitchen.

"That was quick," Ally said, sliding two plates from the kitchen window toward her.

Grace sliced a piece of apple pie and put it on a small plate for Carl. She kept her head down so Ally didn't see the glow illuminating off her skin.

"He is cute, and I hardly blame you."

Too late, damn it.

Her cousin took a fry from the communal plate the waitresses shared.

Grace tapped her toe while waiting for Jose to put the toast up in the window.

"He looks older than you, though."

"So what?" she snapped, unsure if it was the lack of sleep, the fact Ben was here, or her conversation with Ally earlier that caused her eyes to slant with anger.

Ally shrugged.

"Just sayin'." Her cousin popped another fry into her mouth, put two plates on the tray, and walked to her table.

It was going to be a long day if every time she came back to her station Ally was there to drill her. A small plate of toast glided across the counter, and she put it on her tray next to Carl's apple pie.

Grace inhaled deep into her lungs and exhaled through her mouth. A few more breaths calmed her nerves, and she headed for their table.

"Here you go. Toast and pie." She set the dishes in front of them.

"Thanks," Ben said.

"Can I get you anything else?"

He shook his head, and Carl ignored her.

She guessed Ben was close to thirty if not a bit older.

"Grace?"

She'd been staring at him, and he'd caught her. Crap. She swung around to walk away and slammed into Andy.

She groaned.

"Hey, Gigi. Can I borrow some cash?"

"No, hi how are you, or thanks for taking me to Jules's place the other night?" She scowled. What was wrong with her brother? Maybe it was the new job? When Grace was his age, she'd gone a little crazy with going to the local pubs, and more than a handful of times she and Ally trekked into the city to the bars.

"I don't need much," he said.

She grabbed his arm and dragged him to the corner of the restaurant, away from any listening ears.

"What do you need money for?"

Andy's face was gray, and his eyes were hollow.

"Are you sick?" She placed her hand to his forehead.

He stepped away from her.

"I haven't gotten paid yet, and I need it for a few things." He chewed on his fingernail, a habit she'd never noticed before.

"You don't look well. Are you sure you're okay?" She reached for his forehead again, but this time he swatted her hand away.

"I'm fine, Gigi. Can you help me out or not?"

"How much?"

"Eighty dollars."

"Eighty dollars, Andy?" she shouted, and some of the patrons turned toward them. She lowered her voice. "What do you need that much for?"

"Stuff."

"What stuff?"

He shifted, and his eyes darted from one corner of the room to the other.

"I have a date. I want to get a haircut and get cleaned up."

"Ask Mom."

"I can't."

"How come?"

"Dad says I'm cut off. I need to learn how to be responsible." Andy made a face.

"He makes a good point."

"I got a job, didn't I?"

"I suppose."

He smiled.

"So, you have a date?"

He nodded.

Grace didn't know what she thought about it. She was unsure whether she was happy he'd found someone, or sad because he hadn't told her before now.

"Please, Gigi."

"Fine. But I want it back when you get paid." She pulled out her tip money from the morning and handed him the cash, leaving herself a few coins.

"Thanks." He stuffed the bills into his pocket and left without another word.

Grace watched him go, praying he was okay, and that Jules had talked to him. Andy did have a date, and that cheered her up. Maybe he was on the road to better things.

She made her way back to Carl's table. The old man finished his pie, and she took the plate. Ally walked by and Grace plucked the coffeepot from her tray to fill their cups.

"More coffee?"

"Who was that?" Ben asked.

"My brother."

"Older or younger?"

Grace raised her brow.

"Younger."

"Does he have a job?"

"He just got hired as the janitor at the old folk's home in town."

"Do you always lend him money?"

She finished filling his cup and stared at him.

"What's with all the questions?"

"Your brother's got a problem."

"Excuse me?"

"How long has he been using drugs?"

Grace did not want to have this discussion with him. What happened in her family was their business, no one else's.

"By giving him money, you are not helping him." Ben took a drink of his coffee and she regretted filling his cup.

"I'm not sure what problem you're referring to, and what I do with my money is my business." She turned to walk away when his words stopped her.

"Is that what you'll say when he overdoses?"

She spun around and her long ponytail slapped her in the face.

"He smokes weed. That's it. You can't overdose on weed."

"He is not high on weed."

"Really? And how do you know that?" Did she have blinders on? Jules saw the same thing the other night and now Ben, too. She'd admit Andy was acting strange, and he didn't look well, but she figured it was from the new job and the embarrassment of asking for money.

"Look at his face. His pupils are so dilated you can't see the color of the iris. His pasty skin, the messy clothes, poor hygiene. Those are all signs of an addiction."

Rage boiled inside of her. How dare he say Andy was an addict? He knew nothing about him.

"My brother is not an addict."

"How long has he been borrowing money from you?"

Grace thought about what he said. In the past two months she'd lent Andy almost four hundred dollars, but he always paid her back. Before he'd started working, she'd let a few instances slide, but last month he'd given her back the hundred he'd borrowed plus a few extra dollars in thanks. Andy was not an addict. She'd know if he were.

"It doesn't matter."

"You are enabling him." His words slapped her in the face.

"Stay out of my life, Detective," she said through thinned lips.

Ben threw a twenty onto the table.

"No problem." He helped Carl out of the booth before leaning into her and whispering. "The next time your brother stops me on the street to ask for money for his drugs, I'll arrest him."

CHAPTER TEN

Grace reached over her mom to pluck a piece of bacon off the turkey she'd just pulled out of the oven. The room smelled delightful, and her stomach growled in anticipation of the dinner she'd soon devour.

It was a tradition Grandma and Grandpa upheld before Grandma passed away—a family feast on the fourth Sunday of every month. Since then, Dad had asked if Mom would take it over, and she'd agreed. Grace loved the dinners. It was another excuse to be with her extended family. She stretched her neck. The argument with Aunt Janice replayed in the back of her mind. Grace swayed from one foot to the other. How would today go, especially since she'd gotten the envelope last week?

With the family lounging in the front room and dining area, she'd taken refuge in the kitchen away from her aunt. Ally hadn't shown up yet, and Zoey and Elle were in a deep discussion with Jules over which actress he should date if one ever showed an interest in him.

"Is Steph not coming?" she asked her mom.

"Finn is sick with a terrible cold, so her and Tom stayed home today."

Mom slapped Gracie's hand when she tried to pull another piece of bacon off the turkey.

"Gracie..."

"But it's so good." She reached again, and this time her mom didn't stop her. "Where's Andy?" She hadn't seen him either and wondered if he was working.

Mom didn't answer, and that usually meant she didn't know, or she knew and would not say.

"Is he coming?" Grace asked.

"I believe he is."

Great! She couldn't wait to ask him how his date turned out the other day.

"Something smells wonderful." Aunt Fran floated into the room, her long blond hair combed perfectly away from her pale face. Grace always admired the older woman and the way she looked at life with a Zen-like demeanor. Fran didn't worry or fret about things. She was calm and relaxed, just like her faded blue jeans and loose tops. Dad often said she was a free bird, a hippy of the modern times. Grace loved every part of Fran.

"It's good to see you." She hugged Grace.

"Aww, Aunty… I love you."

"Right back at ya, Gracie-girl."

"Franny, would you mind taking what Jan brought out of the box and placing it onto a plate or platter?" Mom asked.

Janice never cooked, and when asked to bring something to dinner, she either got Uncle Rick to make it or she bought it at the store.

"What did she bring this time?" Fran opened the box. It was always a surprise, and most times a pleasant one. Janice wasn't cheap by any means, and she never cinched on the food she brought either.

"Cherry cheesecake from the bakery," Grace said, peeking over Fran's shoulder to have a look.

They smiled in anticipation of how good it would taste after dinner.

"Any luck on the pieces of the bell, Grace?" Fran asked.

She looked at her mom for approval on discussing the topic, but she was busy basting the turkey before she put it back into the oven.

"Someone returned one piece the other night."

"You never told me that," Mom said.

"You didn't want to talk about the bell, remember?"

Mom looked at her after she'd closed the oven door. "I thought we'd exhausted the bell issue, but this is interesting."

"Where did you find it?" Fran pulled out a stool and sat down.

"Someone taped it to my car window with a note."

"Who taped a note to your window?" Dad asked as he came into the kitchen with Rick, Randy, and Jan.

Grace didn't want to discuss it in front of everyone. She opened the fridge, ignoring the question.

"One of the missing pieces of the bell was returned to Grace the other day," Fran said.

Damn it. Grace closed the fridge and faced them. Every muscle in her body tense, she chewed on her bottom lip.

"Returned?" Uncle Rick asked, as he put his arm around Fran.

Grace froze. Her tongue thick, heart racing, she fidgeted with the hem of her shirt.

"You said there was a note," Dad said.

She didn't miss Janice's lips thin, or the way her mascaraed eyes glared at her. Grace wanted to throw herself into the pot of boiling potatoes. All eyes were on her, and she didn't know what to do. She knew by telling them about the piece and the note they'd assume she thought one of them had it, which wasn't far off, but she'd rather keep that part to herself.

"C'mon, Gracie. Spill the beans." When did Jules come into the kitchen?

Elle and Zoey stood beside him.

"I… I… the envelope was taped to my car window with the piece inside," she rushed out in one breath and turned to leave.

"Really?" Dad and Rick said in unison.

She swiveled on her heel, nodded, and peeked at Randy who stood with Janice, both solemn.

"What did the note say?" Zoey asked, in the same soft voice as Fran's.

Grace's entire body trembled like a terrified rabbit surrounded by a pack of wolves, and she looked to Mom for help. Instead of finding a way out, her mom nodded she wanted to know, too.

"It wasn't a note," she said, trying to discourage them from wanting to know more.

"Well, then, what was it?" Dad asked.

"A quote," she whispered.

"A what?" Rick turned to Jules. "What did she say?"

"What was it, Gracie?" Fran asked.

"A quote," she said louder.

"What kind of quote?" Elle asked.

"What a tangled web we weave when first we practice to deceive," she blurted.

No one said a word. Grace felt their stares, heard their silent accusations. If there was a moment when she wished to be transported elsewhere, now was the time.

"Sounds like made-up bullshit if you ask me," Randy finally said.

Dad gave his brother a look. "Maybe if it was your daughter, you'd see it a bit differently."

"It should've been our daughter," Janice blurted.

"Oh, for shit sakes, Jan, leave it alone," Jules said. "Gracie got the damn bell, not Ally."

"Grace, are you sure that is what the note said?" Dad asked.

"I've got it in my purse. I can show you."

He nodded.

She walked to the counter where her purse was and pulled out the envelope. Before she showed them, she removed the piece of the bell and placed it into her pocket.

Dad examined the words while Mom leaned over him. Once he was done, he passed the envelope to Rick. The rest of the family gathered around him to see it.

"Kind of creepy if you ask me," Fran said.

Mom nodded while she opened the gravy packets and dumped them into the pot of water on the stove.

"I could see returning the piece, but why leave the message?" Jules asked.

"Someone is probably messing around." Andy came into the kitchen, his eyes bloodshot, his pupils huge.

Dad's nostrils flared.

Grace stepped toward her brother, but with the family surrounding her, she couldn't move.

"Where the hell have you been?" Dad asked him.

"Around." Andy stayed where he was, a good distance from Dad.

Jules shook his head, disturbed by what he saw.

"Are you saying one of us wrote that note?" Janice asked, turning the conversation back to the bell.

"No. I… I," Grace stammered.

"Because you've already accused me of taking the missing pieces," Janice whined.

"I didn't accuse you. I asked if you may have taken them by accident. I asked the girls, too." She glanced at her cousins, who smiled and nodded.

"Oh, please. You outright blamed me."

"Is that true?" Randy asked.

Grace shrank into herself.

"I didn't blame or accuse Aunt Janice of anything. I asked if the piece had stuck to her clothes."

"You've got to be kidding! What the hell kind of question is that?" Randy exploded, and Grace didn't miss Janice smirk as she stood beside him.

"Hold on. That is not an accusation." Dad had an edge to his voice.

"It sure as shit is," Randy yelled. "And now this damn note. I think Grace has made the whole thing up for attention."

"I agree," Jan said. "Ally would never do this if the bell was given to her."

"Gracie isn't like that." Fran sighed.

"No one asked you, Fran," Janice snapped.

"And Ally wasn't gifted the damn bell, Jan," Rick said. "So, drop it already."

"Who would've left it then?" Jules asked.

They looked at one another.

This was not going well, and Grace needed to deflect the situation.

"Maybe it was a joke, like Andy said." She smiled, and no one returned the sentiment.

"Do you think whoever left it has the other pieces?" Rick asked.

She wished they would all just shut up.

"It would make sense," Dad said.

"Did anyone here take the pieces?" Andy bit into a bun and chewed it with his mouth open.

"Aren't you one to ask?" Randy scoffed.

"What does that mean?" Andy's eyes were dark, and his jaw sat crooked.

"Look in the mirror, kid. You're completely out of it."

Oh, no. Grace looked from Dad to Mom to Jules.

Dad lunged for Andy.

Jules stepped in front of him.

"Not like this," he said in an even tone, but Dad shoved Jules out of the way and reached for Andy, who was jumping up and down in the same spot with a crazed look on his face.

"David," Mom growled and rushed around the island to stand between them. "Not here."

"Randy's right. Look at him. He's higher than a bloody kite," Dad yelled.

"Pathetic," Jan said, loud enough for everyone in the room to hear.

Grace glared at her aunt.

"Dave, leave it until later," Mom said, and Grace knew she was suggesting when Andy wasn't high.

Dad remained where he was, jaw clenched and glared at her brother.

Andy seemed oblivious to the anger directed toward him.

Jules stood to the left of him, just in case.

"Aunt Janice, maybe it was Ally who took the pieces," Andy said, and Grace wished he'd just shut up.

"That's absurd and you know it," Jan said.

"Why?" He took another bite. "Why is it absurd?"

"No one wants to even listen to your rambling."

"Conveniently, she isn't here."

"Kid makes a point," Jules said, and Grace knew he agreed with Andy to piss Jan off.

"Makes perfect sense," Andy crowed. "Ally's always been jealous of Gigi."

"Andy," Dad growled.

"That's untrue and you know it," Grace said. "Ally and I are best friends."

"You won't be for long. Isn't that right, Aunt Janice?" Andy smiled, grabbed another bun and left out the back door.

Grace sighed with relief at the same time Mom did.

Elle and Zoey stood behind their dad while Fran stirred the gravy on the stove.

"A drug user and a liar," Jan said.

"No one needs your opinion," Jules snapped.

"Look at him." Jan pointed a red fingernail at the back door Andy had just left from. "He's a disgrace to this family. A loser. How can you be proud of that?"

"Leave."

Everyone in the kitchen turned toward Mom.

"Get out of my house, Janice. Now," Mom hissed through gritted teeth.

"I'd be happy to and don't expect me to come back either." She exited the kitchen with the same amount of arrogance she always had.

Dad was quiet, but Grace could tell he didn't agree with Mom. After all, he'd thought the same thing of Andy.

Randy followed his wife without uttering a word to any of them. The house reeked of tension, and no one moved. Mom was the first to leave, and Grace was sure she fled to her bedroom to cry. Aunt Fran followed her. Dad and Uncle Rick escaped into the dining room and opened a bottle of whiskey.

Grace looked to Jules.

He winked at her before cutting himself a piece of Janice's cheesecake and slapping in onto a plate. He held up a fork, and she grabbed it. They both dug into the dessert at the same time. The cake tasted bitter, telling of a future filled with a disaster she'd not be able to control. Grace set the fork down and pressed her palms into the counter. Everything was falling apart. The bell needed to get put back together before it was too late.

Elle and Zoey placed their arms around Grace's waist. Their silent comfort did little to change what just transpired, but it warmed her heart to know they were still there for each other. She laid her head on Zoey's shoulder as a tear fell from her lashes.

***

Grace turned the bell within her hands. Two holes remained. She was careful not to touch the glue from the piece she attached a few minutes before as she held the porcelain memory up to the light hanging over the table. The glass was thin enough to see through. It was amazing the thing hadn't broken before now. As she inspected the chime, she noticed the metal wire attached to the stone. Grace carefully flicked the pebble with her finger. The glass made a clinking sound as the rock hit the inside wall.

She blew out the breath she'd been holding when nothing happened. Too scared to do it again in case the bell broke, she spun the ornament within her hands. Blue and pink flowers cascaded down the sides in a waterfall of faded colors, and Grace wondered where the chime came from.

If Grandpa gifted the bell to someone else like Ally, the family would still be together. No disagreements. No arguments. No fights. Tranquility and peace would remain, and the bell would be intact.

She sighed.

Uncle Randy and Aunt Janice thought their daughter deserved to have it. Grace was not worthy of such a gift. Why did they see her as undeserving? What had she done to make them hate her so? She placed the bell back inside the box and put her head in her hands.

The urge to cry washed over her like a brush on a canvas, each stroke tempting the emotions within her. She blinked away the wetness. The desire to have Randy and Jan see her as an equal hurt Grace to the core. Jules would tell her it didn't matter what they believed. She'd done nothing to deserve such outright malicious behavior. Now they were no longer welcome in her mother's home, and it was unlikely they'd come knocking, anyway.

How had it all gotten out of hand?

Dad stuck up for her, but not for Andy, and that bothered Grace. There was tension between father and son, but she'd never allowed herself to see how much until the other night when Dad didn't say a word to Janice in Andy's defense. There was no closeness there, and she wondered if that was why her brother lived a life of carelessness.

She was disappointed in Dad, and it bothered Grace to feel such an emotion toward her father. He'd taught her how to fish, brand a cow, and change her oil. They had a simple relationship with love and respect. Now when she thought of Dad, her stomach turned at the obvious differences between Steph and Grace to Andy and how they were treated. She didn't understand why Dad favored the girls to his only son. All these years she'd made excuses—let things slide, brushed them off—but she couldn't allow tonight to go unnoticed. She couldn't blink and pretend it didn't happen. Mom had gone against Dad a few times when it came to Andy, but not enough for things to change.

Apprehension settled itself in Grace's chest and squeezed. She leaned forward to ease the ache there. What if she asked Dad? Her ribs compressed. A potential conflict might ensue, and Grace didn't do well with those. She could ask Andy, but knew she'd get the same story he'd always told; Dad just didn't love him.

No explanations. No reasons. It was black and white to Andy, but not to her. Now she wanted to know. Grace massaged her cheeks as the guilt at letting it go on for so long ate away at her insides.

The table vibrated, and she grabbed the cell phone sitting beside her.

Heard about today… glad I wasn't there. Ally texted.

Wished you were. Could've used the help.

I hate having to apologize for my mom, but it sounds like my dad was to blame too.

It's fine. Don't worry about it.

Love you.

Love you too.

Grace let her shoulders fall, relieved Ally didn't share the same opinion as her parents. She picked up the box with the bell inside, brought it into the bedroom and placed it on the nightstand.

"Two more pieces and everything will go back to the way it used to be."

She crawled into bed, turned the bedside lamp off, and amidst the darkness surrounding her, Grace wondered if the magic still existed within her broken heart.

CHAPTER ELEVEN

Ben chewed on the tip of his pen while he read the papers Deputy Enders had given him that morning. The bank loan Carl had taken out was for the purchase of land west of town. Unfamiliar with the surrounding farms, he pulled out the map and searched for the section Carl had bought.

If there was one thing he hated, it was a map. He could figure out roads, miles from one destination to another, but with sections of land and quartered parcels, he had no clue what he was looking at.

"Enders, can you come here?"

"What's up?" The deputy made his way toward Ben from the front desk where he'd been deep in conversation with the blond at the counter.

"Can you show me where this piece of land is on the map?"

"Sure thing." He glanced at the paper, walked to the map, folded it into four sections until it was the size of a brochure, and pointed. "Right there."

Ben leaned in to have a better look.

"How do I get there?"

"Oh, that's easy. It's the land next to the Penner's farm."

"Charlie Penner's farm?"

"Yeah."

"Show me on the map where the Penner farm is."

Enders unfolded the map, and with a red pen sectioned out a sizeable chunk of paper.

"He owned all of that?"

"Still does… well, his kids do. Until it sells, that is."

"Why don't they want to keep it?"

The deputy shrugged. "Jules is the only one interested. The others want their cut, and he can't afford to pay them out."

"Makes sense." Ben stared at the outline showing the Penner farm. "It's a shame to let the land go to a stranger."

"It's a soft spot for Jules. He's staying out there now until it sells."

"I bet the tension in the family is high."

"At the Penner's? Nah." Enders swatted the air. "They're one family that is like glue."

Ben had his doubts. Every family had disagreements, and in most there were a few bad seeds. "Even glue wears over time."

"I've yet to see it."

Enders was young. He didn't pay attention to body language like he should. Ben would bet money not all was what it seemed with the Penners.

"Can you take me out there?"

"Sure. I enjoy a pleasant country drive now and then."

The boy was kind with a desire to learn, but Ben wondered how he survived in the world with such a naïve outlook. Life wasn't easy, and unfortunately Enders would see it soon enough. He just hoped the boy didn't have too much invested when it all toppled over.

"I want to go through a few more of these papers before we go," Ben said. "I'll meet you out front in an hour."

"Sure."

"One more thing. Where did you get these documents?"

The deputy smiled. "The bank."

Ben sat back in the chair. A newfound respect for the young man took hold.

"You went to the bank with no one telling you?"

"That's right."

"How did you know to go there?"

His eyes averted Ben's stare. "I read the file."

"The White file?"

He nodded.

Ben was impressed. Being a deputy in a small town didn't warrant much learning. It was rare to be dealing with a homicide. The kid was probably used to reporting on a stolen bike or other small misdemeanors.

"Did you go through these?" He held up the thin stack of papers.

"I did." Enders put his hands out. "I'm sorry. I know it's confidential, but I—

"What are you sorry for?"

"Well, Rhoads said to let you do your thing and stay out of your way."

"You're a cop, Enders. I asked you to let me in on anything you find, and that was an invitation to go digging."

"Well…" the deputy hesitated. "I'm sure you'll find it once you start reading, but there's a document in there that shows who paid off Carl's loan."

"In here?" Ben looked at the papers.

"Yeah."

"Well, who was it?"

Enders leaned in.

"Charlie Penner."

Twenty-five thousand dollars was a lot of money thirty years ago, and for someone to hand it over raised questions. What motive did Charlie Penner have to do such a good deed? He'd been sleeping with Carl's wife, so maybe it was out of remorse, or perhaps because they were friends and Claire had gone missing. Charlie could have just been helping Carl out and nothing more.

Ben's brow folded.

He didn't buy it. There was more to the payout than just a kind gesture. He wouldn't get to ask Charlie Penner, and that was a shame. Ben needed to talk with his sons and anyone else who may have known the man. Not waiting the hour to go over the papers, Ben packed up his briefcase and grabbed his suit coat.

"There's more," Enders said.

Ben raised a brow.

"Carl's bank statement shows not only was the loan paid off, but a deposit of another ten thousand dollars was put into the account the same day by Charlie Penner."

"Thirty-five thousand dollars?" Ben whispered to himself.

"That's right."

"Let's take that drive now."

"Great!" Enders tossed the car keys he'd been holding into the air and caught them.

***

Ben looked out the window at the wheat fields passing by. The pale-yellow grain was seen for miles. He asked Enders to take him to the piece of land Carl had bought first. The deputy pulled the cruiser onto a narrow dirt road. The graveled driveway stretched twelve yards into the field and ended. Nothing else was there, just wheat, or so it seemed. Ben got out of the car. He pulled a long piece of the dried stalk. It seemed no one had tilled the crop, and now it was dry and going to seed.

"Who farms this land?" he asked.

"No one anymore."

"Who used to farm it?"

"Charlie Penner."

"When was the last time he cultivated the ground?"

"Last year."

"Had he become ill? What was the reason for not harvesting the crop?"

"He got sick and didn't have the energy to work the land anymore. Most of the crops had gone to seed, except the ones closest to the house. Jules farmed them on his days off."

"What does Jules do?"

"He's a mechanic. Owns the auto shop off of main."

"What about the other boys? What do they do?"

"Dave runs a construction company. Rick is the coach for the varsity football team, and Randy works in the big city for a financial company.

"None of them could help their father with the land?"

"Well, Randy isn't the type to get his hands dirty, if you know what I mean, but the other two did from time to time."

Ben thought on everything Enders had said when it hit him.

"Charlie didn't pay off the debt as a gift," he said, more to himself than the deputy.

"I beg your pardon, Detective?"

He faced the other man. "Charlie wanted this land, but Carl bought it. What I can't figure out is if Charlie was so well-to-do, why he didn't purchase the land before Carl did?"

"You didn't read the papers, did you?"

Ben glanced back at the car where the documents sat tucked in his briefcase. "No."

"The land was sold to Carl by Charlie."

"What?"

"Charlie was the original owner."

Ben tried to piece things together in his mind. Why in hell would Charlie sell Carl a section of his land only to buy it back five years later? Was he in financial trouble? He stared out across the field to a stand of trees a hundred yards away. None of it made sense. And it wouldn't until he sifted through all the papers and talked to a few folks.

A rusted old truck with a wooden tailgate pulled into the field and stopped behind the cruiser. A wide-shouldered man with biceps the size of Ben's head stepped out of the vehicle.

"Hey, Jules," Enders shouted, waving at the large tattooed man who walked toward them.

"Trent," Jules nodded, before training his dark eyes on Ben. "Jules Penner." He reached out his hand.

"Detective Bennet James." The man's handshake was firm, with no malice connected to it, and Ben decided he liked him.

"I was doing my morning drive when I spotted you guys. Thought I'd come check things out. What's going on?"

"Trying to piece together some things," Ben said. "Maybe you can help us."

"Sure thing."

"We know your father, Charlie Penner, owned this land."

"That's right." Jules's eyes softened at the mention of his father, and Ben remembered the man had passed a month before.

"What we are trying to figure out is how come he sold it to Carl White in the winter of 1986."

Jules laughed. "Dad loved cards and whiskey. From what I've heard over the years, Dad lost the land in a game of poker for, I believe, twenty-five thousand dollars." He sobered. "Dad didn't want to sell, and Mom was hopping mad over it, but a deal was a deal and Dad kept his word."

"Well, that makes sense," Enders said.

It sure as hell did, and why Charlie bought it back, too. Carl must've been in dire straits after Claire went missing and sold it to the man.

"Did he say why he bought the land back from Carl after his daughter vanished?"

"It was his land to begin with, and if you're thinking my father had something to do with Carl's daughter's disappearance, you're mistaken."

"I never said that." Ben took a breath. "I'm just trying to do my job."

"Carl got to drinking and Dad took the opportunity is my guess."

Ben nodded. "Can you tell me anything about the time Claire went missing?"

"I wasn't even one yet."

"You're quite a bit younger than the rest of your brothers."

"I was an accident." Jules smiled.

"Thanks for your time." Ben stared out at the surrounding field. "It's a shame the land had to go to waste."

"It's a big spread." There was regret in Jules's voice.

"If there is anything else you might remember, please call me." Ben handed him his card.

"Not sure what I'd remember being that I was still in diapers."

"Claire's death was thirty years ago. People talk over the years. If any conversation comes to mind, I'd appreciate a call."

Jules put the card in his pocket.

"Was the girl murdered?" he asked.

"Yup. Strangled," Enders spoke up, and Ben shot him a glare.

"Stuff like that doesn't happen around here," Jules said.

"It happens everywhere." Ben turned to leave.

"Poor Carl. Talk was all this time she'd run off, met up with her ma and the two were living a happy life."

The mention of Carl's wife had Ben asking, "Do you know if Olga is still alive?"

"No, I don't."

"Thanks for your time."

"I'm just sorry I couldn't help you more."

Ben waved at Jules before getting into the car. He was a good judge of character, and Jules was a decent person. The man hadn't lied to him once. With each day that passed, a piece of the puzzle came together in the case.

The phone in his pocket buzzed.

He glanced at the number and ended the call.

"Guess you didn't want to answer that," Enders said, as they drove back to town.

Ben ignored him. He didn't discuss his personal life with anyone other than Malcolm, and even then, it was a stretch.

"How long have you been on the job?" Enders asked.

"I've been a cop for fifteen years and a detective for six of those."

"I bet things are different in the big city."

"Things are the same everywhere. You just have more awful stuff in the highly populated areas."

"I get that, but we don't have a lot of crime out here."

"How do you like working for Rhoads?" He still didn't trust the lawman.

"It's all right."

"You don't sound so convincing."

"He's not into the job, if you know what I mean?"

"Oh, I know."

"I want to learn more, do more, but Rhoads would rather sit at his desk and read or go to the weekly men's card game at the lodge than do any policing."

It was all just as Ben thought, and it saddened him to see Enders not getting the chance he deserved.

"Well, I don't mind if you want to help me out a bit."

"Really?" The kid almost drove the car into the ditch he was so excited.

"Sure. I see your potential, and so far, you've given me no reason not to include you." Ben glanced at him. "There is one thing you need to remember. No one hears details of the case unless I say."

"I was wondering when I'd get called on that."

"As long as we understand each other."

"Yes, sir, Detective."

"It's Ben." The sudden reminder of what he'd left behind and worked so hard for pierced his chest. He hadn't heard a word into the inquiry, and he wondered if it'd ever be settled or they'd forget about him out here in the sticks.

Oakville was a few miles away, and Ben had a strong desire to stop at the diner. He hadn't been in since his argument with Grace the other day about her brother, and he felt terrible for leaving things on bad terms. Even though he didn't know her well, he considered their acquaintance a friendly one, and he didn't want to ruin it.

He wasn't interested in any romance or affair with the girl. She was far too young for him anyway, but there was no denying the attraction he had toward her. Beautiful in a simple sort of way, Grace was forthright, and had a kindness about her that drew him to her.

Instead of minding his own business, he'd butted his nose into her personal life, which he should've never done, and it resulted in bad blood between them. He'd seen the tragic endings of addiction many times and how it affected family members and friends. It wasn't something he wanted for Grace, and he was compelled to step in. She was naïve in thinking her brother was not involved in illicit drugs. The kid had the look all over his unwashed and unkempt body. It screamed at Ben and yet; she was silenced by it all. He knew why, too. She was in denial. Most people were at first, until it smacked them in the face, and they had to acknowledge it. He didn't want to see that happen to Grace. She was so delicate and soft. How would she react knowing her brother was an addict? And from what Ben saw, the kid was in over his head.

He wanted to protect her from all of it, but why? There were no feelings other than concern for the woman. He held no starry-eyed notions toward her. It was his nature and nothing more to watch out for others. The very reason he'd become a cop. Maybe he'd stop in for lunch and convince Enders to come with him. It was better to have a distraction from the five-foot-two brunette with the big blue eyes, but he also wanted to be alone with her to apologize and didn't need the distraction if he brought him along.

***

Grace placed the bill on her last table for the day. She'd been on her feet for most of her shift and again had worn the wrong damn shoes. Her toes and heels cried out with each step she took. It would be a miracle if she had any skin left on her feet once she took off the flats. She limped to the front door to flip the sign to 'closed' when the familiar face of Detective James stared back at her from the other side.

Grace jumped and gave a little squeal. Night shift wasn't her favorite, and this was just one of the many reasons why. She opened the door a crack.

"Sorry, we are closing."

Ben peered around her. "But there are people inside."

Grace glanced back. "They're just finishing up."

"I won't stay long. I just need a cup of coffee."

She hadn't seen him since their disagreement over Andy two days before and had caught herself scanning the streets for a glimpse of him. Even though she didn't know him well, she couldn't stand to think he was angry with her for the way she treated him.

"Fine." She opened the door to let him in. "You've got a half hour until I cash out."

"Thank you, Grace."

He'd said her name before, but this time there was something else attached to it. An apology perhaps? He had overstepped the other day, but did it warrant the regret she heard in his voice? Grace shrugged off the notion to ask him and headed toward the coffee station.

She stole a look at Ben while she reached for a cup. He sat in the same booth by the window. He was a man of habit. She liked that about him. Not one to hold grudges, she grabbed the last piece of apple pie out of the fridge and made her way toward him.

"Here." She placed the coffee cup and pie in front of him.

"I didn't order that," he said.

"No, but you look like you need it." She smiled.

He smiled back at her.

One simple curve of his lips had her wondering what they'd feel like pressed against hers. She averted her eyes, feeling awkward suddenly. Flustered and confused at her own reaction to him, she gathered the cutlery on the table. It wasn't the nightly routine, and now she'd have to clear all the forks and knives from every table, so she didn't look like a fool.

"Do you have time to sit?" he asked, taking a bite of the pie.

"I... uh..."

"Come on, take a load off. I'm sure you've been working all day." He glanced at the tables and chairs around them. "The place looks clean already. If you sit with me for a few minutes, I'll help you finish up."

Grace didn't know what to say. She'd never been this uncomfortable around anyone before. Ben made her second-guess herself. She had glanced at her reflection in the window several times already. The ponytail she'd placed her hair in was coming undone, and she was sure most of the makeup she'd put on earlier was gone.

When with Josh, she had been content in sweats and a hoodie, her usual attire. Their relationship was simple, familiar and secure. She peeked at Ben through her lashes. She needed to stop comparing everyone to Josh. He wasn't there anymore, and she missed the reassurance their relationship provided. She masked the sadness from her eyes and smiled.

"Okay, but only for a few minutes." She plopped into the booth.

"Did you work all day?" He dug the fork into the pie.

"Since noon. We close at eight on Sundays."

"Have you always wanted to be a waitress?"

"Are you asking me if this is what I want to do with my life?"

He smirked, and her insides warmed.

"I guess."

"No, but it's a job, and it's in town and close to family."

"Family means a lot to you, doesn't it?"

"Yes. Isn't it important to everyone?" she asked, not missing the way his brown eyes lost their shine.

"Nope. It isn't."

"Don't you have family?"

He pushed the empty plate away and took a sip of his coffee. "I don't."

"I'm sorry. Did they pass?"

"Unfortunately, no."

The way he said the words cut deep into her soul. He'd meant them. If his family hadn't died, what had happened to make him not want anything to do with them?

"I'm sorry. I didn't mean to make you upset."

"It's fine. My life has been this way for a long time."

Grace wanted to hug him. His shoulders slumped, his full lips turned downward, and in the glossiness of his eyes, she saw he still hurt from the past.

"What happened?"

He stared at her for a long time, and she wasn't sure if he'd say anything. In fact, she wasn't expecting more than a few short words on how she should mind her own business.

"My mother left when I was twelve years old. I haven't seen her since."

She pictured him, a small child yearning for his mother. A piece of her heart broke.

"Why did she leave?"

He shrugged. "I don't know. Maybe I wasn't a good kid. Maybe she hated my dad. Maybe she hated us both."

Grace couldn't stop her eyes from welling with tears. She blinked to cover the emotion. "I doubt that," she finally said. "Did your father ever say why she left?"

"Kent wasn't much for conversation. He wasn't home a lot, and when he was, we spent very little time together."

"What a shame," Grace whispered.

"He didn't want to be a father, and so I spent most of my time alone."

She reached across the table and placed her hand over his. "I'm sorry. That sounds terrible. You had no siblings?"

He shook his head, and his thumb caressed the inside of her wrist. "The only good thing my father did was hire Malcolm to tutor me."

She noticed the change in him when he spoke of the other man. "How long did he teach you?"

"All of my teenage years. He still mentors me from time to time."

"Mentors?"

"Gives me advice."

"This Malcolm sounds more like a good friend."

Ben smiled. "I guess you could say that. He and June are the only people I share my life with."

His story was sad, and Grace was a spoiled brat for thinking her family problems were anything to worry about when it came to what Ben had lived with.

"Do you see your father now?"

"I haven't seen him in a year, and I don't plan on to." He hesitated, opening his mouth as if to say more.

She waited, but he remained quiet, and she left it.

"How are things going with the case?" she asked.

"Good. I've been getting some leads."

"Great. How is Carl?"

"Has he come in lately?"

"No, I haven't seen him in a few days."

"I'd like to check on him tomorrow. Do you want to come?" He averted his eyes from hers. "That's if you don't work or anything."

Surprised he asked her, Grace couldn't keep the smile from her face.

"I'd love to. What time were you thinking?"

"Around noon. Want to meet me at the department?"

She slid out of the booth and grabbed his plate and cup. "Sure."

"Thanks for letting me come in after hours." He reached into his pocket to pay her when she held up her hand.

"No, it's on me tonight."

"Grace, I have to tell you I came in here to make amends for the other day." He placed his hand on her shoulder. "I'm sorry I interfered in your personal life."

No one had ever apologized to her before, and she didn't know what to say. A huge part of her wanted to tell him she was sorry, too, but she held her tongue.

Her sister would be proud. It was an unusual experience for her, since she'd always been the one to apologize, even when it wasn't her fault.

"Thank you, Ben." She leaned in and kissed his cheek. Before she realized what she'd done, it was too late to take it back. Her lips had touched his skin, inhaled his scent, and damn, he smelled good.

"What do you need help with?" he asked.

"Excuse me?" She squeaked, almost dropping the cup and plate.

He looked around the diner when she realized he'd offered to help clean up. "Oh, don't worry about it. I only have a few tables left to wipe down."

"I'll see you tomorrow then?"

She nodded.

"Have a good night."

She smiled, hoping he didn't see the twenty shades of red her face had turned, or the disappointment reflected in her eyes as he walked away.

CHAPTER TWELVE

Grace searched the cupboards in her mom's kitchen for a mixing bowl. She'd arrived earlier than the scheduled nine o'clock they'd agreed upon. Her plan was to get a head start on things before Steph and Finn arrived, but when she walked into the kitchen, her sister and nephew were already there. Mom needed help baking twenty-five dozen cookies for the church bake sale on Sunday, and both girls agreed to help.

"Let's get going. I've only got until eleven thirty," she said, lifting a bowl from the top shelf in the cupboard.

"Why?" Steph asked, pulling out two bottles from the diaper bag and placing them into the fridge.

"I just have to leave." She took the pans from their place beside the oven and slapped them onto the counter.

Finn started to cry.

"Damn it, Gracie!" Steph growled and took the baby out of the highchair he was sitting in. She bounced him on her hip until his crying subsided to just a whimper.

"Sorry. I'm just in a hurry to get things going."

Mom measured out the flour for the first batch and dumped it into the bowl. "You didn't need to come."

Grace sighed. Yes, she did. If she stayed home, Mom and Steph would have something to say about it. Besides, she always kept her word.

"Do you have to work?" Mom asked.

"No, it's my day off."

"Then why the rush?"

She shrugged.

"Have you been working a lot lately?" Steph placed Finn back in the highchair and put a handful of cheerios in front of him.

"A few extra shifts," she said.

"More like every day," Mom mumbled.

"I've been covering for Ally. She's been sick."

"I saw her yesterday at the grocery store. She seemed fine to me." Mom pulled the butter from the fridge.

Grace shrugged. She didn't want to hear it.

"Someone is being used," Steph added.

"Not everyone looks sick when they are," Grace replied.

Steph scoffed.

Mom wrinkled her nose.

Grace placed the baking soda down onto the counter and ignored them both.

"Have you ever said 'no' to her?" Steph popped a chocolate chip into her mouth.

Grace shook her head.

"Why not?"

"Because I'm usually not busy when she asks?"

"C'mon, Gracie, even you don't want to work every single day."

"I don't, but we help each other out. That's what friends do."

"When was the last time Ally worked for you?"

Grace thought on Steph's question. She couldn't remember. She'd asked Ally a few days ago, and the time before that was months ago when Grace was sick with the flu. Ally had told her no both times. Grace had to call in sick and leave the diner shorthanded for the day.

The reality of how much she'd done for her cousin pressed against her stomach. She'd worked countless hours and days for Ally, some of them being double shifts, but Ally hadn't repaid the favor once. Grace refused to answer Steph, too afraid of breaking down and crying. Instead, she dumped the baking soda, salt and sugar, into the bowl with the flour.

"I need the butter and eggs, please." She pointed to the ingredients on the counter.

Steph handed them to her, and Grace was relieved she didn't push the subject further.

"Gracie will figure things out when she is ready," Mom said with a smile.

"Where's Andy?" She hadn't seen her brother in days, and each time she texted him, he either replied with one-word answers or not at all. She hoped to see him today. Maybe he'd open up to her about what had been going on.

Mom continued to beat the ingredients in the bowl.

She glanced at her sister.

"Mom? Where is Andy?" Steph asked.

"I'm assuming he's at work." Mom didn't like to keep secrets, and she hated to lie, which made her behavior even more unsettling.

"You assume?" Grace said.

Mom dropped the bowl she'd been cradling onto the counter and met their concerned looks with one of her own.

"I don't know where he is. He came home a few days ago. He got into it with your Dad and we haven't seen him since."

"Have you talked to him?" Steph asked.

"Yes, I've texted with him and he says he isn't coming back here."

"Did Dad get physical?" Grace hated having to ask, but they all knew what Dad and Andy's relationship was like.

"Not really, just a push out the door and that was all." Mom wiped at her eyes with the apron she was wearing. "Andy wasn't himself. He was acting all weird. I didn't want him to go, but… well, you know how your dad can be."

"If you ask me, it's about time the little asshole got a taste of the real world," Steph said.

Andy needed to grow up, but he was going through something. Grace knew it. She needed to talk with him and see what it was.

"He's been living off you and Dad since graduation. I say good for Dad." Her sister could be harsh most times, and the frown on Mom's face told Grace that Steph had gone too far.

"Maybe he's staying out at the farm with Jules," Grace jumped in. "I'll call him later and see. I'm sure he's fine, Mom. He just needs some time."

"Why call?" Steph asked. "Let him figure things out on his own."

"What if it was Finn?" Grace spun things on her sister.

Steph's face lost all color. Good! Maybe now she would see things through Mom's eyes and not her own self-absorbed ones.

Grace didn't want her mother to worry, so she gave her a hug.

"It'll all work out. It always does."

"Thanks, sweetie." Mom kissed her cheek. "I'd been meaning to ask. Have there been any more envelopes?"

Grace groaned and shook her head. For the past several days she'd raced to her car in the morning, eager to see another envelope taped to the window. But nothing was there.

"I still can't believe someone did that," Steph said. She had the same reaction when Grace sent her a picture of it in a text a week ago.

They discussed who in the family might've done it, but neither had any idea.

"I wish I knew who it was." Grace sighed.

"Me, too, so I can throttle them." Mom still had a sore spot over the argument with the family the other night.

Still concerned over where Andy might be, Grace left the room to text Jules.

Andy there?

Hey, Kid. Yeah, from time to time.

Is he okay?

Depends on who you're asking.

I'm asking you.

No.

Grace's stomach twisted. *I'll stop by tonight.*

See you then.

"Maybe it is Aunt Janice," Steph said to Mom when Grace came back into the kitchen.

"I don't think so," Mom said with a frown.

"Well, I wish whoever it was would return the other two pieces so I can put the bell back together."

"What if you never get the other pieces back?" Steph asked.

Grace's chest tightened. "I will get them back."

Steph rolled her eyes. "You still think it holds some sort of magic?"

Why was it such a big deal to everyone how she perceived the bell? Grace had seen it work, and she believed the bell to be magical. She didn't dare tell Mom and Steph about the desperation she felt to put it back together either. They'd think she was dumb in assuming the bell would repair the family. Even Grace knew deep down how silly it all sounded, but she couldn't deny what she saw as a child, and how it made her feel. The family was a solid structure until the damn bell broke. Now they were a mess. The bell had to be put back together.

"Leave Grace alone." Mom pinched Steph. "If she wants to think of the bell in that way, who cares? I think it's cute."

Grace rolled her eyes.

"But Gracie, I don't want you getting upset when the bell is put back together and nothing changes."

"I won't, Mom." But it would devastate her.

Grace dumped the chocolate chips into the batter and stirred them with the wooden spoon. She stared at the little chocolate pieces being buried by the dough. Much like her life, she was suffocating from things she could not control. Grace did not know how to get rid of the feeling that something terrible was about to happen. She scooped a big lump of cookie dough and shoved it into her mouth. She loved the taste of the raw goodness.

"Gracie, you're going to get sick." Mom raised a brow.

Grace mimicked her.

"You're such a brat."

She laughed and took another scoop of batter.

Mom pried the bowl away from her and started spooning small pieces of dough into the pan.

Grace snuck a chocolate chip over to Finn. She giggled when his blue eyes grew big and he smacked his lips. He tossed the remaining cheerios onto the floor and whined for more chocolate.

Steph was busy scooping out the dough with Mom, so Grace gave him another chocolate chip. The smile he gave her was worth the trouble she'd be in when Steph found out.

***

"Dave Penner?" Ben asked, as a tall man with a worn jean jacket and dark hair stepped into the trailer.

He'd been waiting twenty minutes after being instructed by one of the staff loading the back of a pickup truck to go into the site office if he wanted to see the boss. Once inside, all he found were two desks, one empty and the other occupied by a redhead named Linda. After brief introductions, the woman volunteered to find Dave.

Ben rubbed his forehead. The start of a headache was taking root. Shit. He didn't need this right now.

"Yeah. Who are you?" Dave sat down at the desk in the corner of the room. He rummaged through blueprints; the papers rustled as he found what he'd been looking for and rolled it up.

Linda never came back, and Ben guessed she'd taken a break.

"Detective Bennet James."

Dave placed the rolled-up print on the desk and stared at him.

"Can I ask you a few questions about Claire White?"

He leaned back into the leather chair and placed his hands behind his head. "Go ahead, but there isn't much to tell you."

Ben sat in the chair on the other side of the desk. "How long did you know Claire?"

"Most of my life. We grew up in the same town. Went to school together."

"Can you describe the type of girl she was?"

"It was a long time ago."

"I realize that. But being as her body was found west of town, anything you might know would help me."

"Sure." He took a deep breath before continuing. "She was charismatic. Lived for the moment and didn't care about the consequences."

Ben took notes. "How close were you with her before she went missing?"

Dave shifted in his seat. Ben watched him.

"We were friends."

"What kind of friends?" He waited before adding, "How much time did you spend with her?"

Dave ran his hand through the dark hair and sighed. "Almost every day. Until Carl forbid her to see me."

"How come he did that?"

"Carl didn't like any of us Penners."

"Care to elaborate?"

"Not really."

Ben wasn't surprised with his response. The Penners had a reputation within the community, and if people knew Charlie had an affair with Olga, they'd look down on them.

"I know about your dad and Carl's wife."

Dave's brow folded.

"Your dad placed a restraining order on Olga. My guess is it was kept quiet, so no one knew, especially your mother."

"Mom knew. Dad made a mistake. He saw it afterward."

Ben was shocked Charlie's wife knew and did nothing. He wondered what mistake Dave referred to—the affair, or placing a restraining order on Olga.

"Carl had his suspicions, but Dad never told him. And since me and the boys were the only ones who knew," he paused and smiled, "it was easy enough to say Olga was crazy."

"The boys, as in your brothers?"

"Yeah, except Jules."

"And you guys made assumptions that Mrs. White was off her rocker?"

"She was. Showing up at the farm unexpected. Telling everyone she loved my dad. Mom was getting uneasy." He shrugged his wide shoulders. "We didn't need the trouble."

Ben nodded. The picture was becoming clearer. "And did Carl retaliate for what happened?"

"No, but their friendship ended, and Carl hated us afterward."

"Do you know why your dad stopped the relationship with Olga?"

"My guess is things became too serious." Dave smirked. "It wasn't meant to be like that."

Ben eyed the other man. Was he speaking from experience? Dave held himself with ease, but there was arrogance on the edges.

"Their relationship ended five months before Claire disappeared. Can you tell me anything about that?"

Dave's face changed from calm and serene to jagged and angry. "Not really, and if you're implying my dad had anything to do with Claire, you're barking up the wrong tree, Detective."

He changed directions.

"Did you see Claire the day she disappeared?"

"I saw her two days before. She snuck out to meet me."

"Where was that?"

He hesitated. His eyes shifted from Ben to the wall behind him.

"Dave, where did you meet?"

"The diner."

"Was she upset? What did you talk about?"

"I don't remember." He pulled the chair into the desk. "It was a long time ago."

"Were you working then?"

"Yeah, I worked on the farm, and the odd construction job."

"Was she dating anyone other than you?"

"I never said we were dating."

Ben remembered his conversation with Rhoads last week. He'd described the girl as promiscuous. This made finding the killer even more difficult, and there was always the possibility a drifter had ended her life, too. He squinted. The headache intensified across his forehead and down the sides of his face.

"How did she die?" Dave asked, and Ben couldn't tell if the man was concerned because she was his friend, or because he had something to do with it.

"She was strangled."

He grabbed the rolled-up blueprints on the desk. "Is that all? I've told you all I know."

"One more thing. How long after Claire disappeared did anyone notice?"

"I'm not sure what you're asking, Detective." Dave stood.

"Did you or anyone else notice she wasn't around, and when was it that you did?"

"A week, maybe. But talk was she ran off to look for Olga."

Ben's head shot up.

"Look for her mom?"

"Yeah, Olga had left Carl a few months before. She never came back."

"Has anyone seen her since?" Ben was under the assumption Olga had left a few months after Claire went missing, not before. Maybe Carl couldn't remember with all the alcohol he'd drank over the years. It was an honest mistake, yet one that he'd need to look into.

"Do you know where Olga lives now?"

"She passed away a while back. She lived in Riley. It's a town an hour's drive from here." Dave sighed. "I know what you're thinking. My friend's mother is a caregiver at the retirement home Olga was in."

"Thanks."

Dave nodded and without another word left the cramped trailer with the two desks and a water cooler.

Ben followed him out the door and squinted into the bright sunshine. He wasn't prepared to see Grace in the construction yard talking with Dave Penner. He flexed his jaw. The man was a person of interest. Did she know something about the case he didn't? He pounded down the steps, and the movement banged against the bloody ache in his head. He wanted nothing more than to go home, take some medication, lie down in a dark room and forget the world existed.

"What the hell are you doing here?" He grabbed her arm to pull her away.

"Hey—" Dave yelled.

"Shut the hell up, Penner. This is not your concern."

"Damn right it is when you're talking to my daughter!"

"Daughter?" Ben looked at Grace, whose blue eyes had darkened to the color of a stormy sea.

"What is the matter with you, Ben?" She pulled her arm from his grip.

"You're Dave Penner's daughter?" He still couldn't believe it. How had he not known? He re-played all their conversations in his mind. Her last name was never mentioned. Damn it.

"Yeah. Is that a problem?" She crossed her arms.

"Why didn't you tell me?"

"What the hell is going on here?" Dave asked, giving Ben a menacing look.

"Nothing, Daddy. It's fine." She faced Ben. "This is Detective Bennet James. He's investigating Claire White's murder."

"I know that, Gracie. I was just talking to him."

"Oh, why—"

"The detective wanted to know if I remembered Claire from high school." Dave gave Ben a threatening stare. He picked up on the warning. So, this was how the Penners got what they wanted. Intimidation worked well on others, but it didn't on Ben. He'd dealt with far worse. A farm boy didn't scare him.

"And Charlie Penner." Ben added and smiled at Dave.

"Grandpa? What did you need to know about Grandpa?" Grace asked him.

"Never mind." Dave ushered her away. He spoke in low tones and Ben couldn't hear what he was saying. Probably using intimidation or filling her head with lies. Dave Penner just placed himself at the top of Ben's list. There was something about the man he didn't like, and his instincts were never wrong. With no reason to be standing there, he left.

As Ben drove back to the department, he went over the conversation with Dave. The man's laid-back approach seemed to be a front, especially given how he'd reacted when Grace started questioning things. Ben couldn't say if the man was outright lying, but experience told him he wasn't being forthright. It was possible the man's demeanor was because of the reputation the Penners had and his wanting to uphold their name. People were funny with those types of things, especially in small towns.

He prided himself on solving all of his cases. But it wasn't about his pride. Hell, he could do without it. The victims left to deal with life afterward were what pushed him to go beyond the job. To work countless hours, lose sleep, and pour over every single document put in front of him. Ben thought of Carl, broken, desolate, and alone. The only solace he'd found was at the bottom of a liquor bottle. The man's life had been ripped apart.

Ben couldn't help his anger toward Charlie Penner for sleeping with Carl's wife. The man betrayed his best friend. Ben knew first-hand how devastated Carl must've been. Trust is difficult to repair once broken, and sometimes it never is. It must've been the reason he'd sensed a connection with the man. They'd both been hurt, tossed away without a care. He couldn't fix his own circumstance, but he'd try to mend things for Carl. He had to.

Chapter Thirteen

Grace waited for Ben on the bench out front of the Oakville Police Department. She hadn't been seated more than a few minutes when he walked through the front doors toward her. Dad's warning to stay away from the detective had done little to stop Grace from meeting with him.

It made little sense why Dad was so adamant about the man. He hardly knew Ben. She couldn't fathom the quiet detective being anything but kind and thoughtful. From what she saw, he was good at his job, so why did Dad feel so threatened by him? When she'd asked her father why Ben was there, he'd said it was none of her business. Which intrigued her more.

Grace wrung her hands. It wasn't unusual for Dad to forbid her from seeing someone. He'd done it with Carl and a few of the friends she had in high school. Grace hadn't listened then either.

Maybe Dad was just being protective. She was used to that. Dave Penner ran a tight ship. Rules were obeyed and if not, there were consequences. Not severe ones, like Andy had endured, but a lecture followed by a long grounding.

Grace didn't see any harm in checking on Carl from time to time either. As far as she could tell the old man had done nothing to merit Dad's stern warning for Grace to stay away. Still, she'd never tell him about the occasions she'd driven Carl home or been in his house. The more time she spent with the poor man, the more she saw how fragile he was, and for the first time in her life she was embarrassed of her family for talking about Carl the way they had. Grace didn't deny he was a drunk, but other than the one sad fact, he had always been kind to her.

"I was wondering if you'd show up," Ben said as he drew closer.

"Why wouldn't I?" She stood from her seat on the bench. She'd keep seeing the detective, and what Dad didn't know wouldn't hurt him. Besides, she wanted to know why Ben mentioned grandpa earlier and the only way she'd find out was by asking him.

"Your dad wasn't too fond of me when I left." He carried a brown leather briefcase in his left hand with ease.

"He's a good man, Ben. Just a bit over-protective, if you know what I mean."

Their eyes met, and she looked away before her pale cheeks changed color.

"Did you know Claire and your dad dated?"

"No. I didn't. Dad doesn't really talk of the past, unless it's farm stories or high school football rendezvous, but I'm not surprised."

"How so?"

"Oakville was smaller back then. Can't think there were too many girls to date."

"You've got a point."

"What did you need to know about Grandpa?"

"I probably shouldn't tell you." He slipped out of his gray suit coat and hung it over his arm.

"Is… is it a part of the case?" Grace's curiosity got the better of her, and she placed all apprehension aside to know more.

"It is." He kept walking,

"Let me guess. You can't tell me."

"I'd prefer you kept the memories of your grandpa, Grace."

What did he mean? Was Grandpa a suspect? What did Ben know?

"Well, that is kind of you, but I'd like you to tell me anyway."

"No."

She stumbled. No?

"I'm not a child. I can take whatever you tell me."

"I don't think you can."

She halted, but he kept walking, and she jogged to catch up.

"Tell me."

"No."

She grabbed his arm to stop him. He slowed his steps instead.

"It is my family. I have a right to know."

His brown eyes darkened. She glimpsed sadness within the stable depths. It wasn't the first time she'd witnessed the emotion, but she'd not seen it remain for as long as it did.

"That is exactly why I'm not telling you," he said.

"You make no sense." Flustered, she stomped her foot. "Just tell me." She'd settle for a small clue at this point. One word, maybe a sentence, but he remained quiet.

The streets were unusually busy this afternoon, and for a weekday. Grace watched the cars drive by while she followed Ben in silence for the next two blocks to Carl's house. The old wooden home came into view and Grace's stomach knotted. The last time she'd been at Carl's he screamed at her to get out. Even though he'd come into the diner with Ben once afterward, she hadn't spoken to the older man since.

She stopped.

"What's the matter?" Ben turned toward her.

"I… well, the last time I was here…"

Recognition reflected in his eyes. He smiled. "It'll be fine, but if you don't want to go, I understand."

She took a deep breath, lifted her chin, and forged ahead.

Ben grabbed her hand, and before she could contest his advance, he tugged her along behind him to the front door.

Flies hovered over the many garbage bags scattered across the porch. A rancid smell filled the small abode, and Grace crinkled her nose.

"He must clean it from time to time, otherwise it would get gross out here," Ben said, just before he knocked on the door.

"I wonder what time to time consists of in Carl's world."

He raised his eyebrow. "Cheeky."

She smirked.

They waited a few minutes, and when no one came to answer, Ben tried the knob. It turned, and they walked inside.

"Carl," he called. "Carl, are you home?"

The TV was on in the living room. Ben shut it off and continued through the room, stepping over garbage and empty bottles of liquor. Grace followed behind him. He halted, and she ran into his back.

"Sorry," she whispered.

He bolted ahead of her to the bedroom. Grace wavered, holding onto the wooden door frame. She blinked, deciphering what was before her. Carl was on the floor and Ben knelt beside him.

"Is he okay?" she asked. Her voice seemed far away, not her own. She repeated, "Is he okay?" a little louder.

"I don't know. I can't find a pulse. Call an ambulance."

Grace opened her purse and pulled out the cell phone. Her fingers shook as she pressed in the numbers.

"Oakville Emergency?" a woman on the other end said.

"I need an ambulance to Carl White's house."

"Who?"

"Carl White."

"I'm sorry what is the address?"

Grace ran outside to get the number on the house, but all she saw was worn chipped wood siding.

"I can't find an address." She scanned the area. "One block off of main behind the old brick bank in the alley. Please hurry." She hung up and raced back inside to the bedroom. Ben's shirt was untucked and his hair was disheveled as he pressed down on Carl's chest.

"The ambulance is on the way."

He didn't look up, but Grace saw the determination on his face.

"Is there a pulse?" she asked.

He stopped, placed his fingers on the man's wrinkled neck and waited. Time seemed to stretch. "It's faint, but there." He sat back on his heels and blew out a long breath. Shoulders drooped, he let his hands fall to the side. He looked so helpless. Grace remained across from him, standing in the doorway, but the urge to go to him pressed on every nerve in her body.

Needing to do something besides stand there, she pulled the blanket off the bed. The stale sheet almost made her gag, but she held back the reflex. She laid the quilt over Carl and knelt beside Ben.

She didn't know how else to offer him comfort other than to let him know she was here, and without another thought, she placed her hand over his and gave it a light squeeze.

"I hope he makes it," Ben said, his voice tired and scratchy from the CPR he'd done.

"Me too."

A knock on the door tore her hand from his, and she opened it to let the paramedics in. Two men in their early thirties entered and Ben directed them to Carl. Grace stood back and watched while they hooked the elderly man up to oxygen, attached a pulse reader to his finger, and put an IV into his arm. They loaded him onto a stretcher and into the running ambulance.

"Is there any next of kin we can call to let them know Mr. White is in the hospital?" the paramedic asked Ben.

"No, he has no family."

The words weren't supposed to affect her the way they did. She'd known Carl had no family, but somehow envisioning no one there when he woke up, and no one to lean on or to help him, tore a hole in Grace's heart, and she wanted to weep for the old man.

"Please wait." She raced down the steps toward them. "Call me. I will look out for him."

"Grace?"

She ignored Ben, took the paper and pen from the paramedic and wrote down her information.

"Are you sure, ma'am?" the paramedic asked.

"Yes. I will meet you at the hospital."

The man nodded and left.

Grace spun on her heel and ran back inside to retrieve her purse. She needed to get her vehicle and head to the hospital.

"Why did you do that?" Ben asked from behind her.

His words halted her steps, and she froze halfway to the door.

He stood in the middle of the kitchen, his shirt creased, his hair messed, and cautious of her answer.

She shrugged. "It's the right thing to do."

He crossed his arms.

"I didn't want him to be alone. It's not right, Ben. He should have someone there to wake up to."

The corners of his mouth curled upward, and he stepped toward her. The air between them seemed to disappear.

"You're something, Grace Penner."

She smiled.

He placed his hand against her cheek and ran the pad of his thumb across her lips. Her throat worked as she held his gaze.

"I'm going with you." He pulled away from her.

Grace shivered in the absence of his touch, but quickly regained her composure. She wasn't expecting him to come, but she was relieved he'd be by her side.

***

Ben sat beside Grace in the hospital waiting room. The air conditioning was broken, or it wasn't turned up high enough to emit the cool air needed for the stifling area. The outside temperature was well above ninety-five, and if he didn't get in front of a fan soon, he was going to be soaked right through his dress shirt. A quick glance at Grace told him she was roasting in the heat too. Her long chestnut locks, once down, were now tossed up into a messy bun on top of her head. She used the pamphlet on Diabetes to fan her face, but all it did was move the hot air around.

He'd been up to the desk twice to ask about Carl—and the air conditioning— and received no information on either.

Ben bounced his knee, vibrating the floor around them. Had Carl died? Was he alive and on life support? What was going on? Questions circulated through his mind as the heat invaded his clothes and penetrated his body. And what of the damn air conditioning? The bloody place was going to go up in flames soon if they didn't fix it.

He wiped at his face. How could the staff handle such conditions? He wasn't moving around like they were, and he was ready to throw his cell phone through the window.

"Do you always tap your leg when you're nervous?" she asked. There was an edge to her voice, from the heat no doubt, and he ignored it.

"Yup."

"How much longer are they going to keep us waiting?"

"No idea."

"You're a cop. They should give you details." She swiveled in her seat to face him. "Did you show them your badge?"

Ben rolled his eyes. "They don't care."

"He has no other family. Do they know that?"

"Yes, they know."

"We are the only ones here for him. Did you tell them that, too?"

"Yes, I told them."

"Maybe you should try again. You know, but with that detective no-nonsense attitude."

"The what?"

"Tell them you want information on Carl White now. He's part of an investigation. They will tell you."

"He's not part of an investigation, Grace."

"Sure he is. It's his daughter's death you're investigating."

"Right, but he's not the one being investigated." It was too hot to talk, and he sat forward, placing his head in his hands. The headache he'd gotten rid of earlier was forging a plan to return.

"Well, we can't sit here any longer. It's already been three hours." She moved the brochure faster. The paper slapped the air, creating no more of a wind than it had before.

"I know how long it's been."

"Great!" She threw her hands up and laid back into the chair before she sat upright again. "Maybe you could ask one more time."

"I'm not asking any more damn questions. They will come and tell us when they hear something." He tried to remove the irritation from his voice, but he hadn't succeeded. And when her blue eyes watered and she turned her shoulder to him, Ben felt like an ass.

He hadn't meant to hurt her feelings, but damn it, he was just as frustrated. He should apologize for yelling at her, but he couldn't quite bring himself to do it.

"Jerk," she mumbled.

"I've been told that a time or two."

She gasped and placed a hand over her mouth. "I'm sorry. I didn't mean to—"

"Grace, it's okay. I was an ass, and I deserved it."

"It may be true, but I shouldn't have said it. I am sorry." She tipped her chin.

"Why would you say sorry when you did nothing wrong?"

"It was mean," she whispered.

"It was the truth."

She didn't answer.

Ben observed her. He didn't know Grace very well, but from the time he had spent with her, he'd seen a reluctance to cause trouble—stir the pot. She gave into her brother on a whim, believing the bullshit lie he'd told her about having a date. He'd heard it all, even though she didn't think he had. She'd not rebutted Dave when he pulled her aside earlier today and began talking in low, threatening tones.

Grace Penner was a people pleaser. Easy to take advantage of and played for a fool. He wondered how many times it had happened.

She had a good heart, he could tell, but most people would take that and stomp on it. They'd drain every ounce of kindness from her until she was left empty of anything good. Ben's chest expanded with a profound need to protect her—to watch her back and make sure no one hurt her again.

"Grace?" He hooked his finger under her chin and turned her gently to face him. "You apologize a lot, don't you?"

Her eyes were fixed on the floor. She shrugged.

"For things that aren't your fault." He nudged her again. "Grace, look at me."

She lifted her eyes to his. A strong desire to hold her in his arms took hold and he couldn't shake it. He removed his fingers from her chin and sat away from her. Grace Penner was beautiful, fragile, and had a heart of gold. The last of the three he admired the most. It wasn't common to find someone with such traits, and he wanted to keep her for himself. She was a rare gem, but sadly she wasn't, nor would she ever be his. He was not interested in a relationship and not in the market for the broken heart that would come with it. He'd played that role and to hell if he'd let it happen again. But he didn't have to be rude or unkind to her.

One tear slipped from her lashes to fall onto the already damp cheek. He wanted to wipe it away along with all the reasons she'd ever apologized and didn't need to.

"I was mean, and for that I am sorry."

She smiled and leaned into him.

"Can you please tell me why you were asking about my grandpa today?"

He wasn't expecting the question and thought he'd made it clear earlier that he'd not tell her. Ben positioned himself away from her, and he knew she sensed his reluctance when her dark brows knitted, and she chewed on her bottom lip. He'd hurt her feelings again, but this time it couldn't be avoided.

He prided himself on the ability to read people, and Grace was genuine. One of the few he knew that were out there in the world. Her brother, father and grandpa, on the other hand, were not. Should he tell her what he knew about Charlie Penner and crush whatever fantasy the girl had of her grandfather, or keep it to himself, saving her from the humility of it all? He held a fast rule to never lie—nothing good came of deception—and in his line of work he'd seen enough of it. His intact morals didn't come without consequences, and sometimes that meant hurting those you cared about. Ben was not in favor of hurting Grace, especially in this circumstance. Damn it, he wished Malcolm were here. He could use the old man's advice.

"I can't." The words stretched from his throat to scratch at his vocal cords.

Face pale, eyes distant, she sat back in the chair.

He was an asshole. The worst there was considering he'd just finished telling her he was sorry for being mean. He'd shut her out of the one thing she had a right to know. Life sucked. It was a simple analogy. People hurt you. People fail you. People break your trust. Grace needed to see the reality of what life was like and that the family she'd known, or thought she'd known, was not perfect.

He sighed. But damn it, he wouldn't be the one to make her face it. He'd conceal the reality from her and allow the girl to have her fantasy, her image of perfection, and if another asshole broke that realm of semblance for her, he'd kill them.

Ben needed some fresh air and stepped outside. The sun had not ceased its relentless attack, and he didn't know which heat was worse, in there or out here. Reluctant to go back in just yet, he leaned against the wall beside the emergency doors. If Carl died, he'd never be able to tell him who killed his daughter. His shoulders sunk, his spine curved from the weight of the case and the people involved. Ben wasn't even close to solving things. Dave Penner was the only suspect who'd had a relationship with Claire. He'd been distant with Ben, which aroused suspicion. Ben needed to delve deeper into their family. See what secrets they had. He looked through the window at Grace, still sitting in the chair. He didn't want to do it, but she was the one person he could trust. She was his ticket inside the close monarchy that was the Penners. He flexed his jaw. He'd just purchased a ticket straight to hell.

Chapter Fourteen

Grace unbuckled her seatbelt as Ben pulled the car in behind her Volkswagen. They'd waited most of the afternoon at the hospital. Carl's liver was not good, and the doctor and nurses had worked hard to stabilize him. It'd be touch and go for the next little while because of Carl's age and his history of alcohol abuse. After a quick look in on the elderly man, they headed home, deciding to come back tomorrow. She had said little to Ben during their stay at the hospital after he'd refused to tell her anything about grandpa, so Grace decided she'd ask Jules when she was there tonight.

"Thanks for the ride." She opened the door, gave him a quick smile, and left before he replied. The keys jingled in her hands as she repositioned the strap of her purse back onto her shoulder and walked to her car. The minute she saw the envelope taped to the driver's side window, she lunged forward and ripped it off. Placing the keys between her lips, she read the typed message on the front.

"Family is precious, a special gift, except when deceit hides lurking in the midst."

She shivered.

"You okay?" Ben asked.

Grace jumped.

"Shit. You scared me." She fumbled with the envelope, dropping it onto the pavement. They reached for it at the same time, but he was quicker and snapped it up, reading the inscription on the outside.

"What's this?" There was no mistaking the detective in him now as his eyes took on a dark, cloudy demeanor.

"It's nothing." She reached for the envelope, but he held it away from her.

"There's something inside."

"Yes. It's a piece of my bell." She grabbed the paper from him and tossed it in her purse. She wanted to get home and glue the missing piece back in its place. Grace opened the car door to leave, but he shut it and leaned in so she couldn't reopen it. She pressed her lips together and ground her back teeth.

"Explain."

"Am I being investigated?"

"Maybe. Now get in the car."

Her pulse quickened. She licked her lips. She wasn't in any trouble. Why would she be? Grace opened the car door while he walked around to the other side and got in.

"Tell me what's going on."

"Grandpa passed last month. He willed me the memory bell, a family heirloom, but it broke, and there are three pieces missing. The envelope holds one of those pieces." She explained how the family had fought over the bell, how it broke, and that now she was receiving the strange messages with each piece.

"Do you think someone in your family is sending them?" he asked.

"Yes. They were the only ones present when it broke." She'd thought long and hard over why someone may have taken the pieces and still didn't know. Aunt Janice wanted Ally to have it. Jules thought the bell was worth money, and the others, well Grace wasn't sure.

"Do you have any idea why these messages are attached?"

"I don't." She shook her head. This recent note bothered her more than the other. She leaned forward and placed her head against the steering wheel.

"Deceit hides, lurking in the midst. What does it mean?" she whispered.

"Maybe someone is playing a trick on you." Ben handed her back the envelope, and she tucked it back in her purse.

She groaned. Why was someone tormenting her? If there was a lie being hidden within the family, why was the person choosing this way to have it come out? And if it was a joke, Grace wasn't laughing.

Her cell buzzed inside the purse still on her lap. She pulled it out.

"Hello."

"Gigi?"

"What do you need, Andy?" she asked with a sigh.

Silence.

"Hello? Andy?"

"Hi. Uh… sorry. Gigi, I need you to come get me."

Grace sighed. "Right now?"

"Yeah."

She glanced at the clock on the dash. Almost five. "Where are you?"

"At the police station."

She straightened. The bun on top of her head bounced, loosening the hair from the elastic to fall onto her face. She brushed it aside. "What? Are you okay?"

"Yeah, I'm fine. Just come get me."

"I'm literally parked out front. I'll be right in." She hung up the phone, shoved it back in her purse and opened the car door.

"Who was that?" Ben asked.

She'd forgotten he was there. "It was Andy. He's at the police station and needs a ride." She got out of the car, not caring at this point about goodbyes.

Ben opened the door and caught up to her on the sidewalk. "I'll come with you."

"You don't need to. It will be fine." She didn't know why Andy was there, and if it was something bad, she wasn't sure Ben should be with her.

"Maybe I can help, if he's in some kind of trouble."

"He is not in any kind of trouble," she said, with a hint of sarcasm in her voice. He assumed her brother was in deep water, and she didn't like it. Andy was her family, and that meant he was her problem. "I don't need you to come with me." She walked faster.

He matched her stride for stride. "I know you don't, Grace, but I want to help."

Ben sounded sincere, and she gave him a sideways glance. He looked truthful enough. She thought on it while she climbed the steps to the front door of the small police station.

"Let me do the talking," she said, and she stepped in front of him when she got to the front counter.

"May I help you?" the clerk asked, a blonde woman Grace had never seen before.

"Yes, I'm here to pick up my brother, Andrew Penner."

The woman typed Andy's name into the computer. "In order for Mr. Penner to be released, bail needs to be paid."

"I'm sorry, what?" Grace wasn't sure she heard the woman. Bail? What had Andy done?

"One thousand dollars, and a signed document that he will appear in court in a month's time." The clerk slipped a piece of paper under the plastic window.

Ben stepped around her and snapped up the paper.

"Hey, Bonnie. I'll sign off on the boy if bail can be waived."

"He will be your responsibility, Detective."

"Yeah, I know that."

Before Grace had a second to intercede, Ben had signed the papers and was given Andy's belongings in a brown paper envelope.

"What just happened?" she asked.

He turned toward her and smirked. "I got the bail amount lifted, so you didn't have to pay."

"I heard that part." She frowned.

"Oh, and Andy answers to me until he goes to court."

Grace growled low in her throat. "No."

"What?"

"No, Ben. Andy is not your responsibility. He is mine, and I don't need you coming in here taking charge."

"I was just trying to help."

"I didn't ask for your help."

"Okay. I'll have Bonnie print out another form and you can sign that one."

Grace nodded.

"We need another form, sorry. Miss Penner is going to accept full responsibility for Andrew."

Bonnie nodded, the blond hair shining against the fluorescent lights. "She will need to pay the bail first."

Ben stepped aside to allow Grace to pay the fine, except she didn't have a thousand dollars to spare. She needed the money in her account for rent and bills.

"What happens to him if I don't pay the bail?" She whispered so Ben wouldn't hear.

"He will be transported to county jail until his court date thirty days from today."

Grace swallowed. "What exactly did he do?"

Bonnie took the piece of paper she'd just handed Grace and read it. "He's been charged with possession of narcotics."

"Excuse me?" There had to be a mistake. "For marijuana?"

The clerk didn't reply, and Grace figured she couldn't say. What would Grace tell her parents? She chewed on her bottom lip. What was she going to do? Andy couldn't stay in jail for a month. She pulled the cell phone from her purse and with shaky hands dialed the one person she knew who had the means to help her.

"Hello," Ally answered, her usual cheery self.

"Hey."

"Grace! I was just going to text you. What's up? Thanks so much for covering my shifts earlier this week."

"Ally, I need your help, but before I say more, you must promise not to tell anyone."

"Yeah, sure, Grace. What's going on?"

"Andy got arrested and I need your help to get him out of jail. Bail is one thousand dollars."

Ally said nothing right away, and Grace was just about to ask if she was still there.

"What was he arrested for?"

"I'd rather not say."

"I'd like to Grace, but I can't. I'm sorry."

"Could you help me out with at least a bit of it?"

"I don't think so."

"Oh, okay." She tried to hide the disappointment from her voice. "Well, I better go then." Grace thought for sure Ally would have her back on this. They were like sisters, and Andy was family. All she asked was for some of the money, and she knew Ally had thousands in savings.

"Don't be mad, Gracie. I just can't hand over my money for bail."

"You will get it back."

"From Andy? I don't think so."

"From me, Ally. I'll pay you back. I just need the help right now. I've got bills and can't afford all of it up front."

"I'm sorry."

"But Andy will go to jail for thirty days if it's not paid."

Ally hung up the phone.

Grace stared blankly at the screen. Tears formed in her eyes until she was blinded by blurry images. She thought about calling Steph, but knew the answer she'd get from her sister. Abandoned and left to deal with this mess all on her own, she reached for the wallet inside her purse.

"Grace." Ben placed his hand over hers. "Let me help you."

She met his gaze. His face softened, and his eyes shone with sincerity. He was the only person willing to help her. How was that even possible? He wasn't even family. He was more of a stranger than anything.

"I'll call Jules."

"Why bother anyone else with this? I am here."

She didn't want to allow it, but she also couldn't let Jules come to her rescue when he'd done so much for Andy already. Grace ended the call before she pressed the send button.

"Okay, but I call the shots." She wanted to clarify that he did nothing with Andy without her say.

"No problem." Ben handed Bonnie back the paper he signed earlier.

The clerk rolled her eyes and began the process of release.

Ben ushered her to a row of wooden chairs with brown upholstery wrapped around worn cushions. Grace shook her head. Why didn't Ally help her? If her cousin didn't have the money Grace could understand her reluctance, but the girl had more money tucked away than anyone she knew and the use of Aunt Janice's credit card whenever she needed it. How could she just turn her back on them? Grace would've done whatever was necessary to help her or Mike if they were in the same situation. Her cousin knew her better than that. The ache in her chest intensified, and she leaned forward.

"I'm sorry you couldn't count on whoever it was you called." Ben sat down beside her.

Grace pressed her lips together, too afraid if she let go of the words, she'd release the truth she knew was there.

The metal door opened that separated them from the police and their prisoners. Andy shuffled out, holding his shoes.

"Thanks for coming, Gigi." He walked toward her. His skin was pasty with a gray tinge to it, and his hair was unwashed and matted. The clothes he wore were the same ones she'd seen on him days before.

She ran toward him and wrapped her arms around his small waist. "We need to talk."

He pushed out of her embrace, dropped his shoes on the ground and slipped his feet into them. "Just take me to Jules."

"No, Andy. I'm taking you home."

"No way, Gigi. I'm not going back there." He sniffed and wiped at his nose.

"Yes, you are. We need to tell Mom and Dad."

Andy laughed, a sad, miserable chortle. "I'm not telling them. They don't need to know."

"But Andy—"

"No. I don't need their help or yours." He left her there and walked out the doors.

She sent Ben a pleading look for help.

He darted after Andy. "Hold up a minute."

Dusk had fallen to lay murky shadows all around them, and a bright red sky lingered to the west.

"Who are you?" Andy asked.

"Detective James."

"Oh, right. You were going to arrest me the other day for loitering." Andy scoffed and turned to leave.

"I'm a friend of your sister, and I just got you released."

Andy looked at Grace.

"It's true. I couldn't afford your bail, and Ben got it waived on the condition he makes sure you attend court in a month."

"Don't worry. I'll be there, so you can go on your way," Andy said to Ben.

"That's good news, but first your sister wants to talk with you."

Grace examined her brother. He was different—void of any emotion. His eyes didn't hold the familiar spark she'd always seen in them. They were hollow, transparent to what was going on around him. The old Andy would want her help and be scared to death of Mom and Dad's reaction. Instead, he was a man she did not know, and it was frightening. How had she not seen this? The signs were all there to slap her in the face.

"I don't want to talk." Andy smirked. "Gigi, are you giving me a ride or not?"

Ben remained quiet, and she knew he was giving her the opportunity to challenge her brother.

"Not until we talk," she said, drawing strength from Ben of all places. She'd take what she could get.

Andy threw his hand in the air as if to dismiss her and started down the steps.

She raced after him. "What drugs were found on you?"

"None." He kept walking.

"Bull, Andy. The paper said narcotics. What did you have?"

"Leave it alone, Gigi."

"Cocaine," Ben said from beside her.

Grace sucked in a breath.

"Mind your own business, *Detective*," Andy snapped.

"Tell your sister the truth instead of being a coward," Ben growled.

"You're doing cocaine?" she asked, still shaken by what she'd just heard.

Andy was silent.

"And other drugs," Ben interjected.

"What do you mean?" Grace asked him.

"The paper says he was found with cocaine, Oxy-Contin, fentanyl, and marijuana."

Grace mouthed the drugs' names. Where had Andy gotten them? Her eyes lit.

"You were stealing from the old folk's home," she accused him.

"It wasn't much, and it's not a big deal." Andy stopped and lit a cigarette.

"When did you start smoking?" Grace didn't know if she could handle any more surprises from her brother.

Andy shrugged.

"It's always a big deal." Ben stood in front of him. "Do you know how addictive those drugs are? Not to mention how dangerous they are and what any of them can do to you?"

"Back off, man," Andy said.

"How often are you doing them?" Grace wanted to know.

"Doing what?"

"Stop it, Andy, and tell me. Is it every day?"

"Not much."

"Grace, from my experience with this kind of thing, I'd say he's doing it more than he's telling you," Ben said.

"What do you know?" Andy growled before he faced Grace. "You're not going to listen to him, are you?"

She scrutinized every inch of the brother she loved more than anything. Red nostrils, gray skin. Emaciated, short-tempered, and now arrested. Grace thought about the past month and Andy's behavior, but if she considered it further, she had noticed changes in her brother months before that. He was distant and absent from most of the family gatherings. She assumed it was because of his and Dad's relationship, but it wasn't. He was using drugs the whole time, and she'd been too caught up in her own life to see it. She took him at his word when he asked for money, needed a ride, or vanished for a few days. And all along he'd been lying.

Grace closed her eyes to stop the tears, but it was too late. They fell from her lashes one by one to soak her cheeks. Andy wasn't safe out on the streets. He'd just find more drugs, and more trouble, and maybe death. She paled, unable to comprehend life without her brother. No, it couldn't happen now that she knew. She had to do something.

"What do you think?" she asked Ben.

"You're asking him?" Andy shouted.

"He needs to be away from it, but also has to decide on his own."

It made sense. Andy couldn't be here. He needed to go away to rehab, or… jail. Grace inhaled, knowing what she was about to do was going to be tough. Andy was going to lose it, but there was no other way.

"Put him back in jail." She whispered the words, unsure if she should even say them out loud, but she knew it was the right thing to do.

"What? Gigi, are you serious?" Andy yelled, but before he bolted, Ben grabbed a hold of his arm and swung him around. He slapped the handcuffs on her brother before she had a chance to blink.

"Are you sure?" Ben asked.

"What the hell?" Andy wrestled against Ben. "Damn it, Gigi, I thought you cared about me. I thought you loved me. You're my sister!"

Every word he said sliced through her, to cut away at her heart. Andy continued his onslaught of insults until right before her eyes he changed to the little boy she remembered and loved. Down turned eyes and a full bottom lip quiver.

"Please, please don't make me go back in there," he pleaded.

Ben ushered him toward the doors.

"C'mon, Gigi. I'll do whatever you want. I'll stop doing the drugs. I'll stay clean."

Was she doing the right thing? He'd be so helpless in there. What if he got beat up or, worse yet, killed? She placed her hand on Ben's shoulder to stop him when Andy let out a scream and thrashed around.

"I hate you! Do you hear me? I hate you!" he spewed.

"Don't listen to him, Grace." Ben held onto Andy while he flailed his body into the big window, shaking the glass.

"But what if he gets hurt?"

"I'll see if we can't lock him up here for now."

She nodded.

"You're such a bitch!" Andy lunged at her.

She jumped back. "I promise it's for the best."

"You're dumb enough to think that!" he screamed.

"Kid, your sister is trying to help you." Ben pushed him through the door and back inside.

"What the hell do you know?"

"I know more than you think," Ben said.

Andy stopped his assault against Ben and went limp. He turned empty eyes toward her. "You're so stupid, Gigi, you don't even see what is right in front of your face."

"What are you talking about?" Grace stepped closer.

"Think about it."

"Ignore him," Ben said. "He's just angry."

"If you weren't so fucking dumb, you'd see everything isn't so perfect."

"What do you mean?" she whispered.

"The family isn't what you think."

"Andy?"

"You and that stupid fucking bell thinking it will bring everyone together. Fuck, you're dumb." He laughed.

"Shut up."

"Ally is the reason Josh broke up with you," Andy said, still laughing.

"You're just angry at me and lashing out." Grace refused to consider his words.

"You're so naïve. Poor Grace, too busy pleasing everyone to see when she's being screwed."

"That's enough." Ben gave her brother a shake.

Andy's chest moved up and down from his erratic breathing. He turned away from the detective toward Grace. "I've known all this time. I even dropped you hints, but you were too fucking stupid to pick up on them."

She placed her hand on Andy's shoulder.

He stepped away from her.

"What are you saying?"

"Ally is sleeping with Josh, you idiot!"

"What?" Grace touched her lips with trembling fingers.

Andy smiled.

"Sucks, doesn't it? Your best friend and cousin screwed you, but that's what Penners do… they fuck you."

Grace's head spun. She grabbed the back of the chair beside her. Knees weak, she leaned to the side. Her mind raced over the last few months. Ally had taken more time off of work and spent less time hanging out with Grace. She even missed their girl's night. She focused on Andy, shoulders slumped forward, a cocky grin creased his face.

"You knew?" she whispered. "And you didn't tell me? Why wouldn't you tell me?"

"Now you know." He looked her up and down. "How does it feel to be betrayed, Gigi?" He spat onto the floor, dismissing her from his life and the chaotic mess he'd gotten himself into.

"Let's go." Ben ushered Andy past Bonnie at the front desk and to a closed door, where he swiped a card before opening it.

Grace watched her brother disappear down the hallway. Unable to process what just happened, she fought the urge to scream at the top of her lungs. What the hell was going on? How was she going to stop everything from spiraling out of control? She eased herself into a chair. Grace winced as each breath was paired with a piercing pain in her back. How far gone was her brother, and how had she not seen it until now? Guilt pressed against her temples to crease her forehead and cause a headache to form. Nothing prepared her for the sorrow as it crawled up her throat to purge from her lips in a heart-wrenching sob. Grace hunched forward and bawled.

CHAPTER FIFTEEN

"Cocaine?" Vera Penner whispered, as she backed herself onto a stool at the kitchen island. Ben had not met Grace's mom until now. The petite woman was an older replica of Grace, beautiful with the same kind eyes. After they got Andy stowed away in a cell, and Ben had left strict instructions with Bonnie that he remain there until he said otherwise, Ben had demanded he go with Grace to tell her parents. He was sure by the way Dave glared at him that the man was not happy to see him standing in his kitchen, with his daughter no less, but Ben didn't give a damn.

"Grace, why is he here?" Dave asked, leaning against the counter with his arms crossed. His tone was even and light, but the commanding nature of his stance and eyes said otherwise.

"If it hadn't been for Ben, Andy would be shuffled off to the county jail," Grace said.

"I will decide what is best for my son, not you two."

"Are you thinking rehab, Dave?" Vera asked, but instead of giving her an answer his lip curled in response.

Dave turned to Ben. "Thanks for your time and help, Detective, but we will take it from here."

Ben nodded, his eyes never leaving the dark stare Dave penetrated him with.

"Daddy, I think it's best Andy stays in the jail. He will not get into trouble then."

"Penners don't go to jail, Grace." Dave picked up his phone and dialed.

Ben watched him from the other side of the kitchen. It'd become apparent Dave Penner was the man in charge of his entire family, and the first duty was to uphold the family name. In a small way, Ben understood the man's responsibility, more than likely passed on by Charles Penner. He had a reason to keep the name untarnished, and if that meant bailing your drug-addicted kid out of jail, so be it. He wondered what other lengths the man would go to in order to keep the family name clean and free of gossip. Murder perhaps? A man like Dave did not relinquish control, and Ben wondered what secrets he held.

"Rhoads. It's Dave..." Grace's father left the room as he continued to speak with the sheriff.

Ben let out a breath. He wasn't the least bit surprised Dave called Rhoads. The prominent people of Oakville had a direct line to the sheriff, and Ben was sure the perks for allowing things to go their way were bountiful. Sheriff Rhoads kept his position, along with the ability to shit the bed when it came to his job, and no one cared so long as their wants and needs were met.

The damn department was run like a bloody circus with a handful of cops who wanted to do a decent job. Enders was one of them, but Ben suspected the others followed suit in accepting bribes from the townsfolk. The back door swung open and wide shoulders filled the doorway.

"Detective." Jules nodded, as he entered the kitchen.

"Jules." Grace hugged him.

"Gracie-girl, how're you doing?" He kissed her forehead and jealousy pinched the back of Ben's neck.

"Ugh. It's been a hell of a night." She leaned her head onto his shoulder and explained what had happened with Andy.

The calm approach the two had with one another reminded Ben of a brother and sister, even though Jules was her uncle, and he relaxed a bit.

"Was Andy staying out at the farm with you?" Dave came back into the kitchen and placed his cell phone on the counter.

"Yeah, why?"

"And you knew he was doing drugs."

"I didn't know what he was doing, Dave, but I knew he wasn't the same kid."

"And you still allowed him to live there."

"What the hell was I supposed to do? Put him out on the street?"

"You were supposed to send him home."

"He would've never come back here, and you damn well know it."

"Well, I sure as hell don't need him running around town either."

"Then you shouldn't have kicked him out."

"You need to keep out of my business, little brother," Dave sneered.

Ben pulled Grace away from them and to the other side of the kitchen island.

"Oh, you mean the business you'd rather ignore. Is that the business you're talking about?" Jules slapped his hand onto the counter. "Damn it, Dave, your son needs help, and you continue to look the other way."

"He wants attention, and it's pathetic how he's getting it."

"Is it any wonder? The only time you pay the kid any kind of attention is with the back of your hand, or a cruel remark."

"Watch yourself, Jules."

"Or what?" Grace's uncle took a step. "You don't intimidate me, Dave."

"Get the hell out of my house."

"You better get a grip, big brother," Jules said. "Andy's in deeper than you think he is, and it could kill him."

Vera gasped, and tears dripped from her lashes. Grace went to her mother and Ben sensed the chill from her absence.

Dave's nostrils flared.

"You can't ignore this. None of us can." Jules' voice softened.

"I'll send him away."

"What?" Vera sobbed. "David, we need to discuss this."

Dave ignored his wife.

Ben wondered what reason Dave had for sending his son away and whether his actions were genuine or being done to keep the gossip from tainting their name.

"Rehab isn't a bad idea," Jules agreed.

"Military school will straighten him out."

"The kid has a problem, Dave. He needs counseling."

"He needs a firm hand and strict rules."

"Listen to yourself." Jules raised his voice. Anger slanted his eyes and drew the corners of his mouth inward. "This is your son, and you want to throw him away."

"And what is it you would do?" Dave yelled. "Coddle him? Tell him it's all okay? Shit, you of all people should talk."

"What the hell does that mean?"

"Look at you. An inmate yourself when you were seventeen. Hell, I bet you still cross to the other side from time to time."

Jules looked at Grace, and Ben saw remorse in the man's eyes.

"Everyone makes mistakes, Dave."

"Yeah, and I'm sure you're still making them."

"Aren't you?" Jules's voice held a warning.

"You sure the shop isn't a front for something else? Hell, Andy is probably getting his drugs from you."

"You're a real piece of work and a piece of shit." Jules's lip curled. "Your son is sick and all you can do is point fingers at everyone else, when in fact you should look in the fucking mirror."

"I won't put forth excuses for the disgrace Andy's become, just like I didn't when you fucked up."

"David!" Vera placed her hand on his shoulder, but he brushed it away.

"Go to hell." Jules left the room, slamming the back door on his way out.

Ben couldn't believe what he was hearing. Dave Penner had spoken of his son as if he were no more than a stranger and of his own brother like he was a derelict.

"Andy can live with me," Grace said. "I will help him."

"Stay out of it, Grace," Dave yelled.

The girl shrunk into herself, and Ben stepped forward.

"You're not needed here," Dave said to him. "Rhoads is bringing Andy home as we speak."

All eyes turned to Ben. He'd seen enough to know where he had to search for answers. He gave a quick nod and left through the front door. The cool night air caressed his cheeks, and he shivered. He hadn't slept more than a few hours a night in weeks, and he guessed it was because of all the turmoil in his life. He still hadn't heard from Chicago, and he was beginning to wonder if he ever would. He unlocked his car and opened the door when Rhoads's cruiser pulled up.

That was quick. Ben wondered if the sheriff even bothered with the paperwork.

Jules's truck was still parked across the road, and Ben figured the man wanted to see the shape his nephew was in. They locked eyes for a mere second before Ben turned away from his car and down the sidewalk toward Rhoads. The kid was behind him, and Ben didn't have to look at his face to know he didn't want to be here.

"What are you doing here?" Rhoads asked.

"The exact opposite of you." Ben drove his shoulder into Rhoads as he passed him. He came face to face with Andy, but before Ben could say a word to the kid, he bolted.

"Ah, shit," Rhoads yelled, but made no move to go after him.

The man didn't have a chance. Ben would bet his paycheck Rhoads hadn't given chase to a fugitive in a long while. He heard Jules's truck start and squeal down the road.

The front door opened, and Dave Penner's wide frame filled the entrance.

"Where's Andy?" he asked, coming down the steps toward them.

"He ran off," Ben said, as he continued toward his car.

Dave turned piercing blue eyes on him. "I thought I told you to leave."

"Was on my way." He smiled.

"Where the hell is my kid, Rhoads?"

Ben got in his car. He flipped on the radio before backing out of the driveway when someone pounded on the driver's side window.

Grace. He was surprised at the way his chest expanded. He lowered the window.

"I'm coming with you," she said in between breaths.

"Gracie," Dave yelled. "Grace."

Her eyes remained locked on Ben's. "Please, I want to find my brother."

"Get in."

She wasted no time running around the vehicle and jumping in the passenger side.

"Where do you think he's gone?" he asked, putting the car into drive and accelerating away.

"He usually heads to Jules's house."

"Do you think he's on his way there now?"

"I don't know."

"What about friends or co-workers?"

She was quiet, and he turned to look at her. One tear slipped from her lashes to fall down her cheek and settle on the ridge of her top lip.

Ben inhaled. The strong desire to kiss her crashed onto him, and he gripped the steering wheel tighter. Not one to take advantage of a situation, especially a girl as vulnerable as Grace was right now, he took another breath. Her fear was clear by the way she sat, bent forward, her arms wrapped around her middle protecting herself from more bad news. Ben wanted to take it all away.

"We'll find him." It was all he could trust himself to say, and even then, he was sure the words sounded short and forced. Damn it. Why wasn't he better at this? He'd had enough time on the job to know how to talk to someone in crisis. But Grace was different... very different. He'd watched the way she collapsed at everyone's demands, including her own father's. Seeing the shock of what Andy had done crushed her, and the horrible accusations he threw at her, including the one about her cousin, had deflated any resolve the girl might've had. Ben wanted to keep it all from her, shield her from the trouble he knew was coming, and steal her away to a quiet place where she could just breathe.

Life wasn't going to give the girl any breaks, and the realities she'd have to face were going to be tough on her.

"Grace?" He placed his hand on her knee. It was shaking, and he clenched his jaw. "Things will work out."

She faced him and nodded.

"We are going out to the farm, right?" he asked, to make sure she wasn't implying Andy would go to Jules's home in town.

"Yes, that's right."

The next twenty minutes were spent in silence. Ben knew she needed time to digest all that had transpired. He pulled the car into the long driveway and heard her sigh.

"He's not here." Her voice was no more than a whisper.

"Let's go have a look, just in case." Ben parked the car in front of the garage and shut off the engine. He didn't think the kid would make it here before them, being on foot, but he had been wrong before.

Headlights came up behind them, and without waiting for Grace, he got out of the car.

Jules pulled the old truck to a stop beside them and jumped out.

"Looks like we had the same idea," he said with a side grin.

"I thought for sure Andy would be here." Grace closed her door.

"Me too." Jules scanned the yard. "No lights on in the house, but that doesn't mean he isn't here." The wide-shouldered man ran up the steps and into the home. Grace followed, and Ben remained outside and have a look around. The sun had gone down an hour before, and the land was covered in murky shadows. He reached inside the car for his flashlight. There were a million places to hide out here. Ben doubted they'd find the kid tonight.

He strolled toward the barn and stepped inside. The scent of hay and the distant smell of cows filled his nostrils. The stalls were empty other than for the field mice, and he kept walking until he stood on the other side of the barn. He stared at the dark field. Charlie Penner had done well for himself. When Ben looked at the map, he'd been astonished to see how much land the man owned.

What he didn't understand was why Charlie paid Carl ten thousand dollars over and above the price of the land he bought back. He'd need to dive into the man's bank statements.

The front door to the whitewashed house opened. Grace leaned against the railing. Ben knew she'd find it difficult to believe the things he suspected of her family, and it was best he kept it to himself until he was sure. There were still too many loose ends he'd need to figure out before he could arrest Dave, but he was sure the man was responsible for the death of Claire White. Ben thought of Carl and wondered how he was faring in the hospital. The doctor had said the next seventy-two hours would tell them if the elderly man would pull through or not. Carl had spent half of his life drinking. It surprised Ben he hadn't succumbed to the effects before now.

He shone the flashlight out over the field, allowing the light to cascade above the cut wheat. Nothing unusual caught his eye, and so he made his way toward the house.

***

Grace closed her eyes and took a deep breath. The cool night air filled her lungs and renewed her tired bones. What was happening to her family? All her life she'd known the Penners to be close, sharing a sturdy foundation built on love and respect. But lately, she'd not seen anything of the sort. Her uncles were at odds, her aunt despised her, and if what Andy said was true, her best friend and cousin had betrayed her. Grace sniffled and wiped her sleeve across the damp lashes.

She straightened. Feeling sorry for herself would not find her brother, but she couldn't shake the past events from her bones.

The day had been horrifying and Grace still couldn't believe what she'd seen and heard from her brother. Disheveled and an emotional mess, Andy had thrown out judgments of her behavior and Ally's betrayal. She'd watched helplessly as he bounced around, twitching and chewing on his bottom lip as if it were a piece of steak.

Grace squeezed the railing. Andy was not the same person she'd known all these years. The little boy she'd cuddled and watched Saturday morning cartoons with was gone, replaced by a stranger with hollow eyes and ashy skin.

What had happened to make him go astray? Could it be Dad and the way he treated him? She'd always turned a blind eye when things got physical between them, often comforting Andy afterward. It was just the way Dad was with him, but did it make his behavior right? She wasn't so sure now. Dad had always been tough and somewhat rigid, but she'd always chalked it up to the responsibilities he'd had growing up, yet now she wasn't so sure. The things he'd said to Jules tonight had been horrible, too. Grace shook her head. Dad looked down on his younger brother because of his past. People made mistakes—it was all a part of growing up—and Jules had been a teenager. She still didn't know what had transpired to make him go to jail back then, and it really was none of her business, but whatever it was had straightened Jules out. He was one of the best people she knew.

Grace sucked in another breath. As much as she didn't want to admit it, Dad was wrong, and it broke her heart to think about it.

"I take it he isn't here," Ben said, coming toward her.

She hadn't seen him in the dark and wondered why he turned the flashlight off.

"Nope," Jules said, opening the screen door to stand beside Grace.

"When Andy was staying here, did you notice anything other than the obvious?" Ben asked.

"I tried to talk to the kid, make him see reason." Jules ran a hand through his dark hair. "But he just kept telling me he had it all under control."

"It's not your fault, Jules." Grace placed her hand within his.

"He's had a hard time of things," Jules said.

Grace led her uncle to the chairs on the porch, and they sat.

"What do you mean?" Ben asked, standing off to the side.

Grace wasn't sure she wanted him to know anything about Dad and Andy's relationship, and she gave Jules a look.

"Andy has got some problems, and I'm not talking drugs."

"What?" Grace knew her brother had issues, but what was Jules talking about?

"I'm sorry, Gracie. Someone should've told you…"

"Told me what? Jules, what the hell are you talking about?" Grace's heart rate kicked up a notch, and she leaned forward.

"Andy suffers from severe depression and anxiety. He has since… well, since he got lost in the forest for those few days."

Andy was eight when he hadn't come home for dinner, and Mom had begun to worry. He'd been missing in the forest outside of Grandpa's land for three days.

The family had been frantic, sending out search parties for the boy when finally, Dad had found him.

"I know the trauma from being lost took its toll on him, but he seemed all right," she said.

Jules shook his head.

Grace thought back to when she and Andy were young. They were close, and yet she didn't even know her own brother suffered from depression. It explained her mom's reluctance to push him in any direction other than the one he wanted to go. Grace didn't think Steph knew about Andy's issues either, or her sister would've shown compassion instead of riding their brother's ass every time she saw him.

"How do you know this?" Ben asked.

"I was taking him to a counselor once a month until about six months ago." She straightened. "For how long?"

"On and off for the last eight years." Jules leaned back in the chair.

Grace's stomach dropped, and the urge to vomit washed over her. Had she even lived in the same house?

"How did I not know?" she whispered, her eyes misting.

"I'm sorry, Gracie."

She let the tears fall from her lashes, not bothering to wipe them away.

"What had the kid so depressed?" Ben pulled out a chair and sat.

Jules shrugged.

Grace didn't think he'd say, but she wanted to know, too. "It's okay, Jules."

"I don't think that's a good idea."

"I don't give a damn what you think." She flattened her lips together, shocked at her words. "I'm sorry."

"Don't apologize, Grace. He's your brother. You have a right to know." Ben placed his hand on her shoulder, and she drew her courage from him.

Jules exhaled. "Dave's gonna have my ass for this."

"Are you afraid of him?" Ben asked.

Her uncle scoffed. "No, although he'd love it if I were."

Grace fidgeted in the seat.

"Andy started becoming a recluse shortly after the incident in the woods. The once fun and free boy refused to go outside or play with friends, and remained in his room. Your mother took him to the doctor... but," Jules groaned, "Dave convinced her he was just doing it to get attention."

She waited for him to continue.

"It was left for a few years until Andy got worse and Vera found drawings in his room."

"What kind of drawings?" Ben asked, and Grace was glad because she didn't trust herself to speak.

"Let's just say disturbing images of someone in the family."

She wiped the wetness from her cheek.

"When Dave found the drawings, he got angry, and things got progressively worse for Andy."

"I know Dad and Andy have a tumultuous relationship, but I never thought it was that bad."

"Yeah, well, the more Dave yelled, the more Andy retreated into himself. The kid wasn't sleeping, he wasn't eating, and your mom asked me to help her. I'd gotten out of jail the year before and thought it was the least I could do."

"You were only nineteen."

"Almost twenty, and I took Andy under my wing. We kind of helped each other, if you know what I mean?"

She did. Jules had found trouble when he was a teen, and being sent away to prison must've been horrible.

"It was very kind of you to help Mom and Andy."

"Well, that was just it. No one was to know. Just us three… until now."

"Dad still doesn't know?"

"Oh, he knows, but he refuses to see a problem. You heard him tonight."

"If Andy wasn't well, why wouldn't Dave want to help his kid?" Ben leaned back into the chair.

"Because Dave is all about appearances. My father and mother held onto the Penner name like it was gold, and when I ruined it back then I was sent away, but when I returned it was never talked about. In fact, no one in town ever said a word to me about it, and if they knew, they never let on."

"Why is that?" Ben asked.

"Not sure." Jules smiled.

Grace thought back to when Jules returned and he was right, it had been as if he were on a vacation. Grandpa and Grandma threw him a homecoming party, and everyone acted like he'd been away doing something amazing instead of sitting in a jail cell for a year.

"What did you go to prison for?"

"You don't have to answer that, Jules." Grace glared at Ben.

"It's okay. I'm not ashamed of my past, Gracie." Her uncle stared at Ben. "I was in with a bad crowd, doing drugs, stealing, and I assaulted a police officer."

"What?" Grace hadn't heard that part.

"Rhoads," Ben said.

"How'd you know?" Jules asked.

Grace turned toward him.

"Just a hunch."

Her family wasn't what they appeared to be, and it made Grace's head spin.

"Now what?" Jules opened the cooler sitting beside his chair and pulled out three beers. He handed one to Grace before he offered one to Ben.

"I've got a murder to solve, but I'll help you any way I can to find Andy."

She knew he would. Ben had proved himself to her, and she had no reason to doubt him.

"Any leads on who might've killed Carl's daughter?" Jules asked.

"Not really."

"Must be tough since it happened so long ago."

"It has been challenging, but thank goodness we have forensics. With technology we can use DNA to help solve murders now."

"Talk around town is you hail from Chicago." Jules took a sip of his beer.

Grace's ears perked. She knew nothing about Ben other than what he'd told her.

"Yeah, that's true," Ben said, but Grace sensed the tension in his voice.

"Why did you come here?"

"I punched my captain."

Grace almost choked on the beer in her mouth.

Ben smiled, and she almost swallowed her tongue. He was handsome, and she ignored the way he made her feel.

Jules whistled. "He must've had it comin'."

"Why do you say that?" Ben leaned forward.

"Well, the man must've done something for you to put your job on the line."

"Actually, he did nothing."

Grace saw the guilt and shame in Ben's eyes and knew he was speaking the truth.

"Why'd you do it then?" she asked, keeping her voice soft.

"I don't know." He blinked. "I was going through a tough time personally." Ben took a breath and Grace placed her hand over his.

"I'm sorry," she said.

"You have no reason to be sorry. I made the decision and I will have to pay for it." Ben stood. "Thanks for the beer. If I hear anything about Andy, I will let you both know."

Grace watched him walk to his car. He'd practically thrown her hand from his, and without even looking at her, he'd left. She took a slow sip of her beer to hide the disappointment Jules would see on her face.

"Don't take it personally, Gracie. The man has a tough job."

She nodded, but the ache in her chest made it difficult to accept.

"Can you give me a ride home?"

"Sure thing."

She followed Jules to the rusted old truck. Her mind raced with all she'd learned about Andy and Ben. Grace wanted to make everything right for them both, but she knew if she didn't find her brother soon things could get far worse.

"Jules?"

"Yeah."

"Do you think Dad loves Andy?" After listening to what Jules had said, she wasn't so sure, and needed to know—to hear it from someone she trusted.

The sound of the engine echoed in the cab of the truck as she waited for him to answer.

"In his own way."

Grace stared out the window into the black fields. An ache she'd never experienced before penetrated her chest and worked its way to her throat. The family was falling apart and the only way she knew how to save them was to make sure the bell was put back together.

CHAPTER SIXTEEN

Ben stared at the papers on his desk. Charlie Penner's bank statements sat in one pile and Olga White's file from the Meadows Care Facility in Riley in the other. He'd sent Enders there to grab it and any other details the staff could remember about the older woman. The deputy came back with nothing to report—the staff at the retirement home hadn't known the woman—but judging by the thick file, Ben figured he'd find out all he needed to know about Mrs. White inside. He flipped open the folder, yellowed from years of being handled and later stored in a box. He scanned the sheets of paper, looking for anything that might stand out. The old woman had been a bit of a hell raiser according to several reports. She was abusive toward the staff, committed arson, and repetitively flushed her meds down the toilet.

Ben rubbed his forehead. Olga White hadn't been easy to deal with, and a part of him felt sorry for the nurses who had to handle her episodes. Where had Olga lived before she'd gone into the care facility? A woman with that many problems couldn't live on her own.

He rummaged through paper after paper until he found the admittance form, and his eyes almost shot from his head.

Charles Penner paid for Olga to be there.

"What the hell?" He read through the document until he found her last known address. "Riley County Mental Hospital?"

Ben blew out a long breath. The Penners seemed to have ties with the Whites that ran long after Claire had died. The question was why? If Charles had nothing to do with the girl's death, why would he pay for Olga to go into the retirement home? He jumped out of his chair and headed straight for Rhoads's office.

"Explain this." He slapped Olga's registration to The Meadows Care Facility down on the man's desk.

The sheriff had just taken a bite of his sandwich and before he picked up the paper; he wiped his hands on the front of his shirt.

Ben frowned.

"It's Olga White's registration for the old folk's home."

"Look who paid for it." He pointed to Charlie Penner's signature on the bottom of the contract.

Rhoads grunted and took another bite of his sandwich.

Ben clenched his hands into tight fists at his side.

"Care to explain?"

"What makes you think I know anything about this?"

"Seems old Charlie paid for many people in this town, you included." Ben would not mention what he'd found until he'd dug further, but the man's dismissive attitude had pissed him off.

"You better watch what you're saying."

"Or what? You'll fire me?" For the first time since coming to the forsaken town, Ben wanted to stay, and it surprised the hell out of him.

"Damn right." Rhoads tossed his half-eaten ham sandwich on the table. "Stop pokin' where you have no business bein'."

"You were on Charlie's payroll. My guess is you're still on it by the way you jumped when Dave Penner phoned you the other night."

Rhoads's mouth worked, and saliva built in between the creases of his lips.

"How does it go? You do what the Penners ask, look the other way, and collect a bit of cash? No harm, no foul?"

"You don't know what you're talking about." He stood and one of the buttons on his dress shirt popped open. The man needed to buy bigger shirts.

"Explain it to me."

"I don't owe you a damn thing."

Ben advanced.

"You gonna hit me like your captain back in Chicago?"

He wasn't surprised Rhoads knew about the incident, nor was he shocked when the bastard used it to bait him. If he didn't play his hand right, Rhoads would toss him out, and he'd be back on probation from another precinct. Ben ground his back teeth. He'd deal with Rhoads later. Right now, he needed to find out why Charlie Penner paid for the old woman.

"Tell me what you know about Olga White's stay at The Meadows Care Facility," he paused, "please." The last word left a bitter taste in his mouth, and before he replaced it with another not-so-nice word, Ben reminded himself of the importance of the matter.

Rhoads sat back down and picked up his sandwich.

Ben took a seat in the chair across from him and waited.

"What I say is off the record."

He nodded and held the glare the other man shot his way.

"I mean it, James. If I so much as hear you spoutin' what I tell you." He pointed a finger at him. "I'll have your ass thrown out of here so fast your head will spin."

Ben held his tongue, and the obscenities he wanted to let fly. The bastard was threatening him. It took everything within him not to dive across the desk and wrap his hands around the arrogant lawman's throat.

"Your word?"

"You've got it," Ben spat.

"Olga lost her marbles after Charlie broke it off with her, and you know of the trouble she caused here in town."

He nodded.

"Well, the boys—"

"What boys?"

"The Penner boys put a stop to it, and—"

"Harassed the hell out of her, telling the town's people she was crazy," Ben finished.

Rhoads raised his brow.

"Dave Penner told me already."

"Did he tell you how far it really went?"

"No."

"Olga had a fear of mice. You know the kind of terror that you see on TV where the people lose all sense and go crazy?"

"Yeah, a phobia. I know what you mean."

Rhoads swallowed, and for a moment Ben thought he saw remorse in the sheriff's beady eyes.

"She kept showin' up at the farm. Wouldn't leave. So Dave locked her in the outhouse." He took a breath. "And, well—"

"Dave let a mouse loose in there?" Ben guessed.

"Far worse than that." Rhoads shifted in the chair.

Ben waited.

"It wasn't just one mouse, but a bunch of them. Two days. He left her there for two whole days with those mice crawling all over her." Rhoads shivered.

Ben's stomach turned.

"When Dave finally let her out, she attacked him. Bit his neck and arms. Damn near ripped him to shreds, and the bastard deserved it." The man shook his head. "The poor woman had lost her mind, literally, and was admitted into a mental hospital shortly afterward."

"Carl didn't know any of this?"

"He knew, and his hate for the Penners intensified along with his drinking."

"He didn't try to do anything?"

"Carl may be a drunk, but he isn't stupid."

"Where was Claire during all of this? She was friends with Dave."

"Pfft. They'd been more than friends."

"She was okay with them treating her mother like this?"

The sheriff wiped the napkin over his brow. "You know kids. They don't pay attention to stuff like that."

There was more to the story, but the man wasn't saying.

"I've asked around, and everyone says Olga left Carl."

"In a way she did, and Claire, too."

"Come on."

Rhoads shrugged. "People choose to believe what they've been told."

"By the Penners?"

The silence spoke more than Rhoads could ever have said.

"Why didn't you do anything?" Ben asked.

He stared at the floor. "I tried, but I'd already…"

"Taken their money," Ben finished for him.

"If I went against them, I'd have lost my job."

Ben pitied the man for what he'd become. He allowed the very people he'd sworn to protect to blackmail him, and yet he failed at that, too.

"And when Jules had gone to jail?" He knew it was off topic, but his conversation with the youngest Penner boy had bothered him.

Rhoads glanced up from his sandwich.

"I know you were assaulted."

"If you want to call it that."

"What was it? A shove? A punch?"

"I was in a hospital bed for over a week."

Ben couldn't keep the surprise from his face.

"I didn't think Jules was like that."

The man grunted.

The youngest Penner brother hadn't seemed the type, and Ben flexed his jaw at how he'd been duped.

"Jules wasn't even there."

"What do you mean?"

"Dave did it while Randy and Rick watched."

What the hell kind of family was this? The more he found out about the Penners, the more Ben could see how they'd gotten away with almost anything they did.

"Why?"

Rhoads picked up the pen sitting on his desk and flipped it in between his fingers. His lips flattened and nostrils flared.

"I think we're done for today."

Ben leaned forward, placing his elbow on the desk. The white lights reflected the sweat glistening on Rhoads's forehead, and Ben knew he'd get no more information from him.

"Are you afraid of them?" he asked, keeping his voice low.

Black eyes stared back at him, and he wasn't surprised to see the answer to his question reflected within the dark depths. Shit. The Penners had bullied the sheriff, and the man was afraid of them. Pity settled in his stomach for the other man.

"Can you please answer one more question?" he asked. The man didn't respond, so he continued. "Why did Jules take the fall and not Dave?"

Rhoads let out a long sigh. "He was a minor."

"But if he wasn't even there, why would he agree to it?"

"Jules had been arrested three days prior for possession of drugs, along with a few of his friends. He'd been so drunk and out of it he couldn't remember what had happened."

"So, you let him believe he'd assaulted you?"

Rhoads nodded, a pitiful shake of the head.

"You charged an innocent man with assault?"

The sheriff stared at his desk but didn't answer.

"I can understand your fear, but he was just a kid."

"It wasn't as simple as you think."

"Seems to me you made it more difficult by being a coward." Ben couldn't keep the anger from his voice.

"Go to hell."

"There's more to it. You just won't say." He steadied his voice and his rage. "And that makes you worse than all of them." He stood, leaving the office and a solemn Rhoads behind him.

Ben's mind recounted what he'd just heard. He'd need to speak with Jules and the other brothers. Maybe one of them would come clean and tell him what happened back then.

He sighed. They were Penners, and Ben doubted he'd get any further with them than he had with Dave, but he'd have to try.

***

"Honestly, Grace, I don't know what to tell you," Steph said on the other end of the phone.

She called her sister looking for sympathy—advice—and all she got was Steph's crass attitude.

"Ally is our cousin, and my best friend."

"I'm not sure you should believe anything Andy says. He is using drugs."

She knew that, but why would he lie to her?

"If he's telling the truth, what're you going to do?" Steph asked.

"I don't know."

"You have to say something."

"What good will that do?" Grace heard Finn squawking in the background and smiled.

"Well, for starters, you won't get walked on anymore."

"I don't get walked on." She lied.

"Everyone walks on you, Gracie."

She was silent. Hearing the truth from her sister didn't make it any easier to digest. Steph was right. She was a doormat. All her life she'd worried about everyone else, putting her feelings aside.

"Ally is family."

"What does that have to do with anything?"

Did Steph not remember how they were raised? Family was everything. If you didn't have each other, you had nothing.

"We are Penners."

"Oh, you sound like Dad."

Had her sister adapted to Tom's way of thinking? Her brother-in-law wasn't much for the whole Sunday family dinner thing, and he didn't come often. Half his family was spread across the country and rarely saw one another.

"What does that mean?"

"Dad's way of thinking is so old school. People mess up, Grace. It's a fact of life, but to cover it up and pretend it didn't happen is wrong."

"Who's covering it up?"

"Then say something to her."

"I'll think on it."

"Yeah, sure you will."

"I'm not like you, Steph. I can't go off on someone without thinking it through first."

"You don't need to go off on Ally, but you need to talk to her. Don't be like Dad and brush it under the rug."

"Dad doesn't do that."

"He sure as hell does, or he solves the problem for you."

"Only if you ask."

"Is that what you think?"

Grace didn't know anymore. She was doubting all the morals and values she'd been raised with.

"Dad was brought up in a different time."

"You're making excuses."

"Since when are you so anti-Dad?" She couldn't keep the frustration from her voice.

"I'm not anti-Dad. I see what no one else does or is too afraid to see."

"Enlighten me."

"Say what you will. Moving to Chicago was the best thing I ever did."

"Why?"

"When I lived at home, I was so wrapped up in all the bullshit we were fed every day. Smile, nod, be polite, any problem can be solved with the right bit of advice."

"What's wrong with all of that?"

"It's not real, Gracie," Steph shouted into the phone. "It's all fake, a facade put on to make people think the Penners are these upstanding citizens, when we are not."

"How can you say that? We had a good upbringing."

"We did because of Mom." Steph sighed. "I'm sorry, Grace, but Dad isn't a model parent. You know that."

She did, and it hurt to think the words.

"Didn't you feel it in school? People were dying to be our friends, or they avoided us, all because of our name."

"I think you're making things up."

"Ugh… you really didn't see it?"

"Not really. I got bullied in grade three because of my glasses."

"I'm not talking about those kinds of things, Grace. I'm talking about the way people look at us, the way they act around us. Not to mention how Dad controls every aspect of our lives."

"No, he doesn't."

"Come on, Grace. We do everything he says."

Steph was right, but Grace didn't want to admit it. She loved her dad, and she didn't want to think poorly of him. He'd provided for them and gave them a good life. Sure, he wasn't always the kindest, and he had rules, but what parent didn't?

"Nonsense." She changed the subject. "Will you come to town and help me search for Andy?"

"No."

"Why not? He's our brother."

"I know you don't think this, but I love Andy and that is why I'm staying here."

"That makes no sense."

"It does. And once you take your rose-colored glasses off, Gracie, you will understand."

Steph hung up the phone.

Grace stared at the screen on her cell phone. A sense of foreboding crept its way up her spine and for the first time in her life, Grace was unsure of everything and everyone.

CHAPTER SEVENTEEN

Holding a wrapped piece of apple pie, Grace stood outside Carl's house. She'd gone to the hospital to visit him, but the charge nurse told her Carl had left yesterday without the doctor's approval.

She'd rushed over to make sure he was okay, stopping first at the diner for a piece of his favorite pie. The front porch hadn't been cleaned since they called the ambulance three days before. She placed the slice of pie on the railing, grabbed the bag sitting near the door and began picking up the papers strewn about.

"Hello." Ben stood at the bottom of the steps, two coffees in his hands. "Thought I might find you here." He smiled.

"I brought Carl apple pie." What a dumb thing to say. Why not, hello? How are you?

"Always thinking of everyone else." He walked up the steps and handed her one of the coffees he was holding. "That's why I like you."

"You didn't have to bring me this," she said, feeling her cheeks heat.

"It was nothing."

Grace couldn't keep the smile from her lips.

"Have you gone inside yet?"

"No, I thought I'd clean up out here first."

"It's a shame no one helps him. You'd think there was some kind of aid for the elderly living on their own."

"I'm sure there is, but Carl is a drunk and most people don't want to be around that."

"You're probably right, but it doesn't sit well with me just the same."

"Me either." She picked up an empty bottle and tossed it in the bag.

"Any word on Andy?"

She shook her head. It'd been three days since he'd run off, and no one had heard from him. Fear pressed against her temples and she squeezed her eyes shut.

"He'll turn up."

"I'm not so sure."

"Why do you say that?"

"I... well..."

He placed an arm around her shoulders, offering the security she needed from the outside world, and she was thankful for it. She'd gone out the last two nights after her shift and walked the streets looking for Andy, and each night she came home even more defeated than she had before she started. Her head was spinning, and until she could comprehend all that had transpired, she'd stayed away from both of her parents and anyone else who knew about Andy.

She stepped away from Ben and picked up more garbage. Her left forefinger stuck to the label from a soup can. She waved her hand to try to get it off. Coffee in one hand and the paper stuck to the other one, she flailed her arm out again.

"Here, let me help you." Ben gently pulled the soup label from her finger, and the corners of his mouth lifted.

"Crazy glue." Grace had fastened the second last piece onto the bell last night, and in the process had gotten some on her finger.

"One more piece left?"

She nodded.

"What will you do when the bell is put back together?"

It was an honest question, but one she wasn't sure she wanted to share the answer to.

"How long has it been in the family?" he asked.

"As long as I can remember."

"What's the significance of it, other than it came from your grandfather?"

"Nothing, really," she lied.

"I'm pretty good at my job and can tell when someone is fibbing." He smirked.

"You'll think it's dumb, like everyone else does."

"Try me." He nudged her with his shoulder.

Grace leaned against the wooden post and opened the lid of the coffee she held. "When I was a little girl, Grandpa used to let me ring the bell. When I did, every single time, they'd come to the farm."

"Who would come?"

"My family. All of them."

"You think the bell had something to do with that?"

He wasn't making fun of her; he was interested in what she was saying, and Grace opened up to him.

"Well, maybe a little." She smiled. "I just know that the bell brought everyone together, and now it's broke and so is my family. It's the last piece of Grandpa I have left and the one thing I can think of that will put everything back together again. Stupid, right?"

"Not at all. I think it's good to believe in something."

"Yeah, well, not everyone thinks so."

"One person going astray does not mean your family is torn apart, Grace."

She met his stare.

"It's not just one person." She sighed. "Have you ever felt like all you've known—all you've been taught—was a lie?"

"I was never taught much from my father, but I kind of know what you're speaking of."

"But you had Malcolm," she said, remembering their conversation a week before about Ben's mentor.

"Yeah, I do, and the old bugger has taught me to always be honest."

"It's nice to have someone who believes in you."

"Your family seems close. I'm sure they believe in you."

She grunted.

"No?"

"From the outside, yes, but I'm finding out things aren't what they seem."

"You mean all that stuff Jules said about Andy and your dad?"

"I've always known my dad didn't treat my brother like me and Steph, but I didn't think it was that bad." She tipped her head to hide the remorse in her eyes. "I made excuses for my father. I didn't want to see the truth."

"We all do it. Seeing the truth is one thing, but to admit it takes a lot of courage."

"I am not a very courageous person." She'd failed as a sister to Andy, and now she didn't know how to make it right.

"I think you are."

She looked at him and the feelings she'd fought surfaced. "How do you know all the right things to say?"

"I don't." He took a drink of his coffee. "I tell the truth. You're a very special woman, Grace Penner."

She sat down on the step.

He joined her.

"Tell me why you hit your captain?"

He blew out a long breath and she could see the memory was painful.

"I was engaged up until last year."

She kept the shock from her face and nodded for him to go on.

"Lana and I had been together for three years. I bought a house in that time." His hand tightened around the paper cup. "I was going to remodel it for her. Kent, my father, was coming around a bit and I was slowly letting him back into my life."

"That must've been difficult."

"It was, but Malcolm and June encouraged me to give him another chance." He stopped, and she placed her hand over his. "I should've seen it. Lana talking endlessly about him. Kent popping over unexpected. But I didn't. I guess I let the fantasy of having a family shadow my intuition that something was wrong."

"You don't have to continue, Ben. I see where this is going," she whispered.

"No. I haven't spoken about this to anyone, not even Malcolm."

"Okay, as long as you're sure."

"It was a Sunday. I came home to both of them sitting at my kitchen table. They were holding hands." He cleared his throat. "Lana told me how they'd fallen in love."

Grace put her coffee down and rubbed the tear from her cheek.

"Kent didn't have the decency to even apologize, instead he smiled—a big cocky grin like he'd just won a million dollars all at my expense."

Grace thought of Ally.

"I buried myself in my work, solving cases," he chuckled, a sad distant sound. "I even cut Malcolm and June out for a while."

"It's understandable. You were hurt."

"Not by them. Those two were the only ones who stuck by my side through everything, and I threw them away like a stale piece of bread."

"I'm sure they understood."

He squeezed her hand.

"Is that why you hit your captain?"

"I'd been working the Reeder case, a serial rapist. I was close to getting him when my captain, thinking I had too much on my plate, put me on desk duty. He was right. I did. But at the time I was angry, and I saw him as a threat—as someone who wanted to take me down, and so I went against his command and worked the case anyway without approval." He stopped, and she watched as his face twisted.

"You saw him as your father."

He nodded.

"You don't have to—"

"I'd gotten a tip about where Reeder was, and I went looking for him. Caught him luring a young girl into his van. I lost it. I beat him so badly he ended up in the hospital."

Grace didn't know what to say. Ben had saved the young girl's life, and her admiration for him grew.

"Cap was pissed, and we got into it. I'd gone too far, and I didn't care. I had so much pent-up anger toward Kent that when Cap started lecturing me, I snapped." He rubbed his face with his hands. "I don't even remember what happened until I was being pulled off of him."

"What you did for that girl should outweigh any of the circumstances afterward."

"Internal Affairs doesn't see it like you do. I crossed several lines that day."

"You were going through a rough time personally."

His eyes glistened.

"When I was asked for a statement, I refused to accept what I'd done was wrong. I held onto my pride, not giving a damn how it affected those around me."

"I'm sure if you apologize—"

He faced her, eyes filled with unshed tears.

"I still believe I was right in doing what I did."

"And you will not apologize for it?"

He nodded.

"What about your captain? Doesn't he deserve your remorse?" She scrutinized him, desperate to see the man she hoped he was.

"I don't know," he whispered.

Grace could see the turmoil he experienced in the averted eyes and hung head. She felt terrible for him.

"I believe your shame is outweighing your conscience and will not allow you to apologize." She brought his hand onto her lap. "From what I can see, you're a good man, Bennet James. The problem is that you won't allow yourself to believe it."

They sat in silence and Grace let him process what she said. The guilt of what he'd done was eating at him.

"How long are you on probation for?" she asked.

"Could be permanently. I was asked if I wanted to stay home or come here. I couldn't sit on my ass every day and stare at the walls, so I took this job."

"Do you regret coming here?"

He was quiet, and she knew he was pondering her question.

"Yes, and no."

"Why both?" She placed the coffee on the step beside her.

"Yes, because the man who punched his captain is not me, but somehow I've lost that. I don't know how to get it back."

"I hardly know you and can tell you're not that kind of man. You just need time to find yourself again."

He smiled.

"Tell me what the 'no' reason is." She bumped him with her shoulder.

"No, because I wouldn't have met you."

Grace didn't know what to say. Over the last month she'd harbored a tenderness toward him she was unfamiliar with. He was in his thirties, and a lot older than she was, but something about him drew her, a force she didn't recognize, and she was tired of fighting it.

"Do you trust me, Grace?" His voice was sincere.

She watched his eyes for any flicker of deceit. Seeing none, she answered, "I do."

He touched his forehead to hers and before Grace knew what was happening, his lips were pressed against hers. She fell into him, allowing his tongue to catch her as he toyed with her bottom lip in a soul drenching kiss. Grace's heart pounded in her ears. She gasped as he tossed his coffee and dug his fingers into her hair, bringing her closer to him. She threw all caution out of her mind and met his lips with the same intensity until she was lying on top of him on Carl's porch. Ben's hand never left the back of her head, holding her to his mouth. She thought he was going to take her right there in broad daylight—and she would've let him— until he tugged gently on her hair to pull her lips from his.

She locked eyes with him, dark depths penetrated right through to her soul. The corners of his kiss-swollen lips lifted, and she damn near fell back into his arms. What was she doing? He'd just poured his heart out to her, and she wanted to jump him.

Grace scrambled off of him. "I'm sorry," she mumbled, patting her hair back into place.

"What are you apologizing for?"

"I... well." She didn't know. It was what she did.

"I kissed you."

His admission didn't make her feel better, and she stepped away from him when his hand grabbed hers.

"This is not an accident, Grace. I meant that kiss."

She couldn't look at him. Her cheeks were hot. Damn it, her face must be beet red. Ben didn't want her like she wanted him. He just got out of a serious relationship, one that broke his heart.

"Let's just forget about it," she said, prying his hand from hers.

He didn't respond, picked up the garbage bag and placed it next to the door.

***

Ben thought Grace's suggestion was easier said than done. The kiss they'd shared had been nothing like he expected coming from someone so young. She set his insides on fire, and he had to keep from devouring every inch of her.

He glanced at her as she picked up another one of Carl's empty bottles. Ben had made a complete mess of things. Grace would never understand his feelings for her were honest and separate from the investigation. He held the breath he wanted to release. She had no idea he thought her father was involved with Claire's murder, a fact she would soon find out. Ben's stomach turned. She'd be devastated, and he'd be to blame for it.

Shit.

It was better for him to keep her at a distance and screw the feelings she stirred inside of him. It was Grace he was concerned about.

"I can check on Carl. You don't need to," he said, keeping his voice neutral.

"No, I want to see him." She picked up her coffee.

He nodded and knocked on the door.

The shuffling inside told him Carl was there, and probably drunk. Ben masked his disappointment and opened the door.

"Carl. It's Ben." He walked inside. The stale odor in the room told him the old man had gotten into the bottle the minute he got home from the hospital. Sympathy nudged at Ben's insides.

He heard Grace behind him as he walked into the living room. Carl sat slumped over on the sofa. He was wearing gray slacks and a dress shirt that was buttoned in the middle, leaving his chest exposed.

"Hi, Carl," he said, and sat down next to him.

Grace picked up the garbage littered on the table and floor.

"What do you want?" Carl slurred.

"We just came by to see how you were doing."

The old man ignored them and stared at the television.

"How are you feeling?" Ben kept his eyes from watching Grace and concentrated on the man beside him.

"Still here."

He didn't know what to say. Carl was still alive, even though the doctor figured he'd not live through the year. It was the way he said the words that caused Ben's chest to constrict with emotion. The man didn't look healthy, and he sure as hell didn't live the way he should, but those weren't the reasons he no longer wanted to live. He was lonely, and Ben didn't doubt his presence and the questions he'd been asking had led to Carl remembering the wife and daughter he'd lost months apart.

Carl coughed, and Ben reached inside his suit coat for a tissue. He handed it to the man, but he swatted it away.

Another cough led to a relay of hacking fits until blood trickled from the old man's lips.

Ben placed his hand on Carl's back. "Here, let me help you."

"Go away."

He glanced at Grace, unsure of what to do next.

She sat down on the other side of Carl and with the same caring nature he'd seen her do with Andy; she offered the old man her coffee. Carl took it, sipping until he no longer coughed. Ben watched the scene and his respect for the girl grew. Most people wouldn't want anything to do with the old man, yet Grace didn't look at anyone that way. She saw all people as equal. A good quality to have, but one that could hurt you, too.

"I brought you a slice of apple pie from the diner." Grace placed the plastic wrapped slice on the coffee table in front of Carl.

The old man's eyes widened, and he reached for it, tearing into the cellophane. He dropped the wrapping onto the floor and shoved the pie into his mouth. Crumbs and cinnamon glazed apple fell onto his chin and chest.

Carl lacked manners, and Ben had to keep from saying something when he saw the shocked look on Grace's face.

"You should've stayed in the hospital," she said.

Wrinkled lids narrowed before they sagged, and he shook his head.

"Why didn't you stay?" she asked.

"What's the point?" Sorrow was evident in his eyes.

"You'd be more comfortable."

Carl stared at his hands.

Aside from the wish to die, there was another reason Carl didn't want to stay at the hospital, and Ben had a feeling it was due to reminders of being all alone.

"I'd have come and visited you." Grace placed her hand over his.

"You remind me of her." It was the first time Carl had brought up Claire without being prompted.

"How so?" Grace asked.

Carl clasped his hands together on his lap. "She was pretty like you."

"What were a few of the things she liked to do?"

"Dance." His bottom lip trembled. "She'd dance in the kitchen while helping her mother make dinner."

Ben glanced away, not wanting either of them to see how Carl's admission affected him.

"Her laugh." Carl inhaled. "I loved her laugh." He placed his head in his hands and whimpered. "Oh, Claire. My sweet, sweet girl."

Grace placed an arm around Carl's back and hugged him to her. "I'm so sorry."

Ben's eyes locked with Grace's, and he saw the empathy she held for the old man. His shoulders sagged, weighted down with the pressure of whether to tell her the truth about her family or not. He'd kept things hidden on purpose and now knew his reasons were selfish. He was an ass. Ben wasn't ready to have those beautiful blue eyes look at him with resentment and anger.

Carl's back shook as he sobbed for the daughter he missed so much. "Claire, Claire, Claire."

Grace wiped a tear from her own cheek, and Ben felt another stab of guilt in his chest.

"I'm going to make us some coffee, okay?" Grace eased away from him and stood.

Too overcome with memories, Carl laid his head on the arm of the sofa.

Ben moved from his seat, and soon the old man's legs were sprawled across the cushions. He pulled the blanket laying across the back of the sofa and laid it over Carl before sitting down on the chair to keep vigil over the poor man. Blue lips wheezed in and out as Carl dozed off.

Ben wanted more than anything to give Carl answers about what happened to his daughter, but he didn't have any solid evidence yet. The things Dave had done to Olga disgusted Ben, and he wanted the man to pay for it, but it happened years ago. There was nothing to go on other than the word of a dirty sheriff, and Ben knew Rhoads wouldn't talk. The Penners got what they wanted one way or the other, and it didn't matter the cost, or at whose expense either.

Dave appeared to be the worst out of all of them. Ben hadn't met Rick or Randy, but he also hadn't heard of them doing anything other than standing by and watching Dave beat on Rhoads years before. He wished the lawman had told him what transpired to lead to such a disastrous event, but Rhoads was afraid of Dave. Ben guessed it was because the oldest Penner was blackmailing him. It was the one thing that made sense.

Ben let out a long breath while running his hand down the length of his face. He had a lot of digging to do.

Grace entered the room holding a coffee cup.

"He's asleep," Ben said.

She smiled and placed the mug on the coffee table. "I'll finish cleaning up in here." She disappeared back into the kitchen before returning with a new garbage bag.

Unable to sit while she cleaned around him, Ben got up and walked around the room when he spotted a turned over box in the hallway. The paramedics must've knocked it over when they wheeled Carl out. He knelt beside it and began shoving the papers back inside when he spotted a brown envelope with Charlie Penner's address on the top corner. He placed it to the side, then rummaged back through the papers for anything else with Charlie's name on it, but found nothing. Ben made sure to put everything back inside the box, except the brown envelope.

"What's that?" Grace asked.

"I'm not sure." He didn't want her to see the name on it and turned the envelope, so the writing was pressed against his leg. "I'll be in the kitchen."

She nodded, but the look in her eyes told him she'd question him later.

Ben sat down and pulled out the stapled papers from the envelope. It appeared to be a contract. He kept reading, and what he saw shocked him beyond anything he'd been prepared for. He scanned the other papers to be sure of what he'd read before putting them back inside the envelope.

"Is everything all right?" Grace stood in the doorway holding Carl's coffee cup.

"Yeah."

"What was in the envelope?"

Ben prided himself on being an honest person, but he didn't know how to tell Grace this and so he hedged. "Nothing."

"Nothing?" She reached for it, and he tugged it toward him and off the table to hug to his chest.

"It's evidence."

"You don't think I can handle it. The same reason you won't tell me what you know about Grandpa."

She wouldn't let that go. Ben eyed her. "If I tell you what I know about Charlie, will you drop this?" He held up the envelope.

She smiled. "Yup."

He clenched his jaw. "Charlie had an affair with Olga White."

Grace's blue eyes grew big.

"I'm sorry." He meant it.

"How long ago?"

"About six months before Claire disappeared."

"Do you think,"—she swallowed—"I mean, could my grandpa—"

"I don't know, Grace." It was half of the truth. He suspected Charlie had something to do with Claire's murder too.

She blew out a breath, moving the hair that had fallen around her face. "Does Carl know?"

Ben nodded.

"The poor man."

Ben was surprised at her reaction. He was sure Grace would've defended her grandpa, but she was more concerned for Carl. His attraction toward her intensified. His mind replayed their kiss earlier, and he shifted in the chair.

"Do you have any suspects?"

"Your father." Shit. He'd been so distracted by her beauty, he'd answered without thinking.

"What? You're kidding, right?"

He shook his head, keeping his mouth shut so he didn't blurt out Charlie Penner's name too.

"Because of Andy? I agree my dad hasn't treated my brother that great, but it doesn't make him a murderer."

Ben remained silent. He'd said too much already.

"What do you have to back this?"

"I can't tell you." It was the truth. He could not compromise a case by telling her about any of the evidence.

"I don't believe you."

"I would never lie to you, Grace."

"But you'll use me to get closer to my father?"

"No. Never."

"Bullshit." She raced out the door.

Ben placed his head in his hands. The more information he found out about the Penners, the more he believed them to be guilty of Claire's murder. The contract was just another piece he needed. In other cases Ben would've been elated to have cracked things open, but with this one all he experienced was sadness. The Penner foundation was about to falter, giving way to a devastation far beyond any of them could imagine, and all Ben cared about was protecting Grace from all of it.

CHAPTER EIGHTEEN

Ben knocked on the wide oak door of a small home with a beautifully manicured yard. The colorful flower beds and globe-shaped shrubs planted below the front windows were inviting.

"Can I help you?" A tall man holding a pair of pruning shears in his hand walked around from the side of the house.

"Detective James. I'm looking for Richard Penner."

"I was wondering when I'd see you, and it's Rick." The man smiled and Ben relaxed.

"Do you have a moment to answer a few questions?"

"Come around back." He leaned the cutting tool against the house and walked away.

With no other choice, Ben followed.

The back yard was smaller than the front yard, but it was decorated just as nicely with pots of daisies and lilacs scattered about. A table with four chairs and an umbrella sat on a cement pad, and a small garden flourished in the corner by the wooden fence.

"Have a seat," Rick said. "Can I get you a drink?"

"No, I'm good, thanks." Ben pulled out a lawn chair and sat down.

Rick slid a yellow cooler out from behind a tall shrub, flipped up the lip, and pulled out a beer.

"Well, what is it you need to ask?" He cracked the cap off and took a long drink.

"I'm sure you're aware of Claire White's body being found out at the mill."

"Yeah. I always thought she'd run off."

"That's what I'm hearing from most folks." Ben pressed his back into the chair. "What can you tell me about that time?"

"Why don't you tell me what you already know, and I'll try to fill in the missing pieces."

Ben couldn't figure out if the man was smart and trying to keep from saying something he shouldn't, or if he was sincere and didn't want to waste Ben's time.

"Well, I know Dave and Claire were together. Charlie had an affair with Olga, who lost her marbles, thanks to your brother, after which your father paid for the woman's care. I also know about the money given to Carl White from Charlie, the payouts to Rhoads, and that Dave continues to do the same."

Rick smiled.

"Surprised?"

"Not at all, more like impressed."

Ben frowned.

"You've got all of it right except the last one. My brother no longer pays the sheriff."

"Why does Rhoads jump when Dave calls?" Ben had only seen it once with Andy, but he was positive it had happened more than once.

"Because of the past."

"Explain." Ben promised Rhoads he wouldn't say anything about their conversation, but something told him Rick was referring to when Dave had beat the sheriff and put him in the hospital.

"You're smart, Detective. I'm sure you know."

"Call me Ben, and I'd like to hear it from you."

"I don't live like my brother." Rick took another drink of his beer, and Ben could tell by the way he gripped the bottle whatever he had to say was difficult.

"What do you mean?"

"I'm an easygoing kind of guy. I never wanted the pressure of having to uphold the family name. It's one of the reasons I refused to be a farmer."

He sensed the man wasn't finished and waited.

"My father was a good man, with good intentions, even if to some it didn't look that way. He made mistakes—we all do—but there was an underlying burden to carry when you're a Penner passed down from generations."

"Keep the name clean?"

"Yeah, something like that."

"But your dad compromised that when he had an affair with his best friend's wife."

"That he did, but he tried to do right by it all afterward."

"I'm guessing it was too late by then."

"Yes, and no. Carl would've forgiven him, but Olga couldn't let it go."

"She was in love with him."

"Ever since high school, or so my mom always said."

Ben nodded. It made sense. Olga had been infatuated with Charlie for a long time, and when he showed her a little attention, she took it too far.

"Whose idea was it to lock the woman in the outhouse?"

Rick ran a hand through his hair and sighed.

"Dave's."

"Were you there?"

"Randy and I both were, and we tried to tell him to leave her be, but Dave refused."

"And why was that?"

"Dave inherited a part of my dad no one liked. The need to control everything." Rick took another drink of his beer. "From a young age Dave was groomed to take on the farm, to be the leader. Never do wrong, and if he did, Dad would bail him out."

"Charlie didn't do that with you and Randy?"

"Of course, but not in the same way as with Dave. If we got into trouble we'd pay, maybe not with the law or by someone else, but Charlie made it so."

"And Dave never had consequences?"

Rick shook his head.

"Not once?"

"Not that I can remember."

"Why was he treated different?"

"He was blood."

Ben leaned forward. "I beg your pardon?"

"Randy and I aren't Charlie Penner's biological sons."

Ben's mouth gaped.

"My mother was already pregnant with us."

He didn't know what to say. Ben had not foreseen this.

"So, Dave is not your mother's actual son?"

"Here's where things get sticky." Rick smiled, but the sentiment didn't reach his dark eyes, and Ben's heart softened toward him. "My mother left my father when Dave was one. She moved back home to Wyoming. I haven't been able to dig it all up, but she got pregnant."

"And it wasn't Charlie's?"

"Nope."

"Are you sure?"

"I have the DNA report in my safe if you don't believe me."

"Do you know who your biological father is?"

Rick shook his head, reached for the cooler, pulled out another beer, flicked the cap off and took a long drink.

"Why would Charlie take your mother back if he was all about appearances?"

"Because of that exact reason. He claimed us as his own and no one was the wiser."

"But how?"

"They told people Mom had just gone home to visit for a while, and no one questioned it." The man blew out a breath. "But Mom made sacrifices, too. In order to give us a better life, she allowed Dad to do as he pleased."

"Have his affairs."

"Yes."

"Are you the only one who knows this?"

"Randy knows, but he refuses to speak of it."

"Too much for him?"

Rick laughed.

"No, it's more of an egocentric kind of thing with Randy."

"I see. What about Dave? Does he know?"

"I think so, but we have never spoken of it, and he'd want it that way."

"The name?"

"The control."

Everything Rick said was just another brick added to the wall of suspicion Ben built against Charlie and Dave, but it still didn't prove either of them had killed Claire.

"Do you think Dave killed Claire?"

Rick fidgeted and the woven lawn chair creaked under his weight.

"No. And I don't think my father did either."

"Are you saying that because they're family?"

"I'm saying it because it's the truth."

"Dave dated Claire right until she went missing."

"That is not true. Dave slept with Claire, but he never dated her."

Ben raised a brow.

"Two different things, Detective. Even you know that."

He thought about the contract he'd found at Carl's house.

"Tell me why Jules was sent to jail."

"You already know why."

The middle Penner was smart, and Ben had to redirect his questions if he was going to get any more information.

"Okay, tell me something I don't know."

Rick laughed.

"You're looking in the wrong direction if you want to find out what happened to Claire."

"How do you know that?" Ben couldn't figure out if the man was toying with him to protect his brother, or if he knew something else that could lead Ben to the killer.

"I won't deny my family is full of secrets and some of them dark, but they'd never kill anyone."

"Do you think what Dave did to Olga was just punishment for a bit of harassment?" He was getting annoyed and tried to keep the edge from his voice.

"If you're asking me if I think it was right, the answer is no."

"She went insane because of what he did."

Rick's eyes watered, and Ben could see he'd hit a nerve.

"Olga White did not deserve what Dave did to her, and if a man can be that callous—that inhumane—then what is stopping him from murdering someone?"

"I won't deny what you're saying, but I will not give you what you want."

"And what is that?"

Rick smiled, but there was nothing jovial about his features. Ben figured it was because after all these years, the man still believed in the family and the name, even though he didn't want to.

"What can you tell me about this?" Ben pulled the contract he'd taken from Carl's house and placed it on the table.

Rick glanced at the papers before he met Ben's stare. "If you've read it, you know what it is."

"Does Jules know?"

"No, and it's best if you keep it that way."

"You don't think he has a right to read this?"

The other man inhaled, and his nostrils flared. Ben had touched a nerve, but he didn't care.

"Dave and Jules don't have the best relationship." Rick pointed to the papers. "This will end any hope of them ever having one."

"How long will you keep covering things up?"

"Until they no longer need to be."

Ben stood, grabbed the folder from the table, and without another word to the man, he left. His mind reeled from all he'd been told. The damn Penner matriarch was an enormous bunch of lies, and the papers he held proved it.

He stopped mid-step.

The contract. The dates. He ran to his car. Once inside, he scanned the papers again. Ben flipped through the pages to where Carl had signed the document. Next to the man's scribbled signature was November 1991, the year before Claire had gone missing. Ben did the math in his head. Claire disappeared in August 1992. Which meant Jules had been born right before Claire had died. The money Charles Penner gave to Carl was in November 1991, too.

Ben jammed the papers into his briefcase. There was one person who could answer the questions he had.

***

Grace held the tray propped on her forearm and winced. She'd had a headache all morning, no doubt due to the few hours of sleep she'd had last night. She couldn't stop her mind from going over all the possibilities of how Ben could think her dad had anything to do with Claire's murder. No longer willing to deny the way Dad treated Andy all these years, Grace also needed to consider the information Jules had told her. But with everything she knew, it still did not make her father a murderer.

Steph hinted at deceit, and so did the ominous envelopes. Grace needed to talk to Jules again. He never lied to her, and she knew if she asked, he'd tell her the truth.

The two coffee cups, cream, and sugar rattled as she walked toward the table by the window. The last place she wanted to be was at the diner, but Grace was not one to fall short on her commitments, and if it meant serving patrons all day when she was dead tired, so be it.

The diner was unusually busy for a Thursday morning, and Mel had been called in because Ally hadn't shown until two hours into her shift. With all the tables full, Mel stayed to help with the rush. Grace avoided her cousin and wasn't sure she even wanted to talk to her after everything Andy had said.

"Here you go." She emptied her tray on the table for the two women sitting there. "Have you decided on breakfast?"

"Bacon and eggs," the woman said, "for both of us."

As Grace wrote down their order, and the instructions about crisp bacon and runny eggs, she glanced at Ally standing behind the beverage counter. A tray full of drinks sat on the ledge beside her. The girl hadn't taken them to her table yet, too busy texting on her phone. Ally had four tables to take care of and Grace had only seen her go to one of them.

"That'll be right up," she said, before making her way to Jose in the kitchen.

"I'm going to kill your cousin." Mel came up behind her with a tray full of dishes.

"Get in line," Grace growled. She clipped her order on the reel and spun it around toward Jose in the kitchen. "Two orders of bacon and eggs, runny and crisp please."

"Sure thing, Miss Grace," Jose called.

She smiled, turned from the counter, grabbed a clean tray, and walked toward her cousin still on her phone.

"Are you going to deliver those drinks?" she asked in a clipped tone.

"I'll get to it in a minute." Ally turned, hiding the phone while she texted.

The last couple of days had been some of the most difficult ones Grace had to endure, and she was in no mood to deal with her over-privileged cousin. Her brother was still missing, she hadn't talked to her mom and dad since that night, and all she wanted to do was fall onto her bed and sob.

"Your table is waiting." She tried again to get Ally moving.

"Would you be a dear and take their drinks for me?"

Grace ground her back teeth and picked up the tray. Steph would've dumped the five pops onto Ally and told her where to shove it, but Grace didn't have it in her. It was better to keep things civil, on smooth ground. No turbulence meant an easy ride for everyone, even if that meant Grace's heart got broken in the midst of it all.

She dropped the drinks off at the table and took their order. Grace scribbled the notes onto her pad and whipped around colliding with Mel and a steaming pot of hot coffee. The decanter dropped from the other woman's hand, hit Grace's leg and spilled the scorching contents all down her calf.

She held in a scream. The heat from the coffee felt like someone had branded her with a metal iron. Grace limped to the back before she let out a whimper and pulled up her soaked pant leg. The skin was bright red, and two blisters formed.

"Oh my gosh, Grace. I am so sorry." Mel knelt in front of her with a cold cloth in her hand.

"Please, don't touch it," she begged, holding shaky hands out toward her.

"That doesn't look good. You need to go to the hospital."

Grace knew the other woman was right, as the pain radiated up her leg.

"What happened?" Ally walked toward them, her phone out.

"You'll need to take my tables. I have to go to the hospital." She held back another sob, but she couldn't contain the tears as they dripped from her lashes.

"Oh, it's just a burn, Gracie. I'm sure you'll be fine."

Ally had to be out of her mind to think this was just a minor burn. Grace thought her leg was going to explode the pain was so intense.

"It's not, and you'll need to take Grace's tables," Mel said.

Ally ignored the other woman and placed a hand on Grace's shoulder. "In a few minutes she'll be back to normal."

"I'm hurt, Ally. Look at my leg."

"You're fine."

Grace couldn't breathe. All the years of being stepped on by her cousin gripped like a vise around her lungs. She forced herself not to cry any more than she already had, and damn it, not to apologize.

"I'm going to the hospital," she said.

"No, you're not." Ally laughed.

Mel growled before walking away.

"I'm hurt."

"Ugh. Stop being a baby. The diner is full, and you can't leave."

"You're unbelievable," she whispered.

"Grace?"

"You're so selfish. You don't care that Mel and I have busted our asses this morning because you showed up late, or that my leg feels like it's on fire. You didn't care I needed your help with Andy the other night, either. Instead, you hung up on me."

"Your brother's problems are not mine."

"He's family, Ally. We help each other. That is what we do."

"C'mon, Grace. You know that's not true."

"It is true."

"Maybe to you, but the rest of us are normal."

"What does that mean?"

"You live in a fantasy world where everything is all rainbows and sunshine. Just like the damn bell. None of that is true. It's time you grow up, Grace."

Had she been living life like a child, believing everything was perfect and there were no problems? It was clear just in the past week the family had their share of issues, but wasn't she raised to stand by them no matter what? Steph didn't think so, and now neither did Ally. She flexed her toes, regretting it a second later when pain shot down her leg. If none of what she'd been told all these years were true, then what was, and who the hell was Grace Penner?

"I don't have time for this," Ally said.

"That is typical," she muttered.

"Oh, I'm sorry. I didn't know I had to answer to you, Grace." Ally turned to walk away.

"I never saw it before." Her eyes misted. Desperate to hold on to any composure she had left, Grace bit the inside of her cheek.

"What?"

"It's always about you."

Ally rolled her pretty green eyes. "Whatever, Grace."

"It's the truth, and," she held up her leg, "it's evident right here."

"You're fine. Feeling sorry for yourself will not get any sympathy from me."

She squeezed her hands together until her nails bit into the flesh.

"Get up, Grace, and walk it off."

"No," she hissed.

"You're behaving like your lazy brother."

She straightened, every muscle in her body flexed. Grace wanted to lunge at Ally for thinking of her brother the way she did. Andy's words echoed in her mind. *You're so stupid, Gigi. Ally's been seeing Josh behind your back this whole time.*

"What have you been doing the last few months when I've been covering for you?"

Ally shrugged, and her eyes shifted from Grace to the floor.

"Oh, right. Ally, the honest friend and cousin." The last word left a bitter taste in her mouth.

"I have no idea what you're talking about."

"Yes, you do. But you're too much of a coward to admit it."

"Fuck off, Grace."

The tears were close. She blinked them away. The betrayal stabbed into her, and she ignored the pain when she inhaled. She opened her mouth to say something when it hit her. The cool layers of Ally's eyes took on a whole new meaning now. The girl didn't give a damn about anything she said. Grace searched her cousin's face. Ally held no guilt, no remorse over what she'd done, and the recognition slapped Grace across the face. How did she not see this? All this time she'd considered Ally to be like a sister, and now when she looked at the woman, Grace saw a stranger.

A tear fell from her lashes, and before she could wipe it, another one followed. Damn it. She wanted to be stronger.

"Please, just tell me the truth," she whispered.

"What are you talking about?"

"I know."

"You're delusional, Grace. I think the burn on your leg is making you hysterical."

"Say it," Grace screamed. "Tell me what you've been doing with Josh."

Ally crossed her arms.

"You're sleeping with him."

She shrugged.

Another blow to her already beaten spirit. She tipped her chin.

"At least admit it."

"Poor, Grace." Ally cooed and placed a hand on her shoulder. "You weren't enough for him."

She bit the inside of her cheek.

"Josh needed someone with confidence."

Chest tight from the sob she refused to let go, Grace gripped the chair beneath her.

"Besides, he wanted me all along."

She closed her eyes.

"You're too basic, Grace, and everybody knows, boring and *fragile*. You should be happy for me, not jealous."

Ally's last words were like a knife to her heart. Grace hung her head as her body shook. The need to escape the girl and her onslaught of judgments overwhelmed Grace, and she stood. "I'm leaving."

"To go to the hospital, I suppose."

"I quit."

"What? You're being dramatic, Grace."

"No. I'm not." She didn't know where her strength came from, and when she met her cousin's eyes, she did not turn away. "I quit this job and I quit you."

Ally's full lips opened. "Grace, you cannot be serious. Over a boy who didn't love you?"

There was nothing left to say. Grace limped to the cupboard, pulled out her purse, and left the diner.

*****

Despair sunk into Grace's chest, and she moaned. Her ribs hurt and her back ached. The pant leg she'd hiked past her knee slipped down to rub against the burn as she hobbled toward her car. Biting her lower lip, she willed the tears to stop, but they dripped from her eyes like a spring rain.

She was pathetic. She'd made it so easy for Ally to go behind her back with Josh. Just like everyone else in her life. The soft-spoken one, Grace went out of her way to help, even if it meant she was going to pay for it. Where had it gotten her? She clenched her jaw. The kindness she'd shown had been reciprocated with betrayal.

She pulled out her phone and stared at her reflection in the black screen. She bit her lip, refusing to fall apart, and took another step. The throbbing in her leg intensified. She inhaled a sharp breath. Grace wanted to go home to her bed and her dog—to hide away and never come out.

She wasn't calling her sister after Steph's refusal to help look for Andy. She didn't need the 'I told you so' either. Grace couldn't understand why Steph wanted nothing to do with their brother. Steph was just worried how Tom would perceive her feelings on the issue. It seemed everyone was in it for themselves. Everyone except Grace.

She thought of Ben and her anger toward him softened. She was baffled at her own emotions toward the lawman, especially after he'd divulged that her dad was a suspect. How could she feel anything for someone willing to put that allegation on her loved one? She paused and gripped the phone tighter. Ben hadn't lied to her like everyone else, she'd give him that, but he was against her, and it was enough to make her resent him.

She tossed the phone into her purse and dug into the bag until she found her keys.

"Grace?"

Ben stood behind her. She'd recognize his voice anywhere. She ran her forearm across her eyes.

"Leave me alone." She sounded pitiful and wished again to be more like Steph.

"Are you okay?"

"I'm fine." Her hands shook from the pain in her leg, and damn it, she couldn't get the key in the lock.

"I saw you limping. Are you injured?" He was beside her.

"Well, you are a detective." She winced at her crass remark.

"Did something happen to your leg?"

"A pot of coffee dumped on it." Why was she telling him?

"Which one?" He crouched down beside her.

"The left." She squeezed her eyes closed. Grace Penner was pathetic.

He lifted the pant leg, and the air stung the swollen skin. Once he finished with his inspection, he carefully replaced the cotton back to cover the wound.

"Are you going home?" He was beside her now, but she refused to look at him. She shook her head. One tear. Damn it.

He wiped it with the pad of his thumb. "It hurts. I know."

He had no idea how much.

Ben scooped her up into his arms and carried her to his car.

Grace said nothing, too afraid if she opened her mouth, the life she'd so carefully been trying to hold on to, would crack and the depth of everything she thought was real would bury her. She stared over Ben's shoulder at the diner when a hooded man caught her attention. Dark jeans and a faded black sweatshirt. Grace was sure she glimpsed blond hair. Andy?

"Stop."

"You need to go to the hospital." Ben kept walking.

"No. It's Andy. He's here." Grace's heart raced inside of her chest, and she stretched her back to get a better look.

Ben stopped, and she wiggled out of his arms.

"Andy." She waved, but the boy disappeared behind the diner into the alley. "Wait. Andy." Grace limped as fast as she could. Ben was behind her. Pain radiated up and down her leg, but she ignored it and forged on. Andy was more important. He was here.

When she finally got to where she'd seen him there was no sign of the boy and her heart sunk. Grace took another step, but the pulsing in her leg stopped her, and she lifted the limb balancing on her other foot.

"You need to go after him." She turned to Ben.

"He's gone, Grace."

"No. He isn't." She looked back into the alley. Out of breath, she placed her hand to her chest. "He was just here. He can't be far."

"You have to go to the hospital."

Anger curled around her spine and she stood taller. "No. I need to find my brother."

"Not right now." His voice was soft and warm.

She rejected the way his nearness made her feel and took off down the alley.

"Grace."

She ignored him and limped past the garbage cans and back doors of the other stores until she came to a dead end. She bit her lip to stifle the cry that wanted to break loose from her lips.

"Come on, sweetheart." Ben tugged on her hand.

She yanked free of his hold.

"I need to find my brother." She had nothing left to hold on to, and the weight she'd carried this past week came crashing down around her. Unprepared for the desperation wrapping around her neck, she gasped. Grace wanted to scream, to pull out her hair, to claw and scratch—to inflict pain—the same pain she felt. The outcome was not what she'd expected. She should be embracing her brother right now, but the only thing she embraced was desperation and fear. A raw, gut-wrenching fear. The need to escape rushed through her body like waves colliding against the rocks, the force so strong it weakened her knees and tore away any sense of sanity she had left. She had to escape, leave this damn town, and everyone in it.

"We will find him."

"No, we won't."

"Grace, I promise you."

"Don't do that." She sucked in a breath. "Don't make a promise we both know you cannot keep."

"I don't plan on breaking it." He smiled, and it was the last thing she wanted to see. His smile—the only thing that made sense amidst the mess around her.

"You don't get it, do you?"

He was silent.

"No one is who they say they are. The people you've trusted your entire life, they betray you." She held her eyes shut, remembering the conversations with Ally, Steph, and Andy. "They fucking betray you," she rasped.

"You're better than they are, Grace."

"How?" She wiped at her eyes. "They use me. Every one of them. And why wouldn't they? I let them. I never say no. Grace the fucking doormat. Come on, stomp on her, she won't do a damn thing." She slapped a hand over her mouth to stop the sob wanting to escape her lips.

"There is nothing wrong with being a kind person, Grace."

"Where has that gotten me?" She stepped away from him.

"Grace…"

"No one is who they say they are." Her hands shook. "Nothing is the same, and I don't know how to fix it." She combed her fingers through her hair and pulled.

He was silent.

"How do I make things right? How do I fix my family?"

"I don't know."

"I feel like I'm drowning, and I can't breathe. I can't fucking breathe." She said the words—the truth. Exposed herself, like slitting her wrists to bleed in front of him, and damn it, her entire body ached from the confession. How had she been so foolish? So bloody naïve?

He took a step.

"No, please." Her voice trembled. Fresh tears doused her cheeks to cover her in despair. Grace could no longer stop them or the pain as it spread across her chest. She wrapped her arms around her waist, hunched forward, and wept.

He pulled her toward him.

With nothing left in her to fight, she allowed his strong embrace to shield her from the outside world and all she'd been forced to deal with. It was wrong to lean on him, the person who wanted to place her father in jail, but for now none of it mattered. He was all she had.

Chapter Nineteen

Ben sat on the edge of Grace's bed. He'd insisted on driving her to the hospital and home afterward, leaving his car parked at the diner. She hadn't disagreed with him as she was too tired from the events of the last few weeks, but he'd used it to his advantage. He rubbed his eyes. He was an asshole—he knew it—but if being a jerk meant he could spend more time with Grace, he'd gladly be called anything.

It saddened him to see her eyes, once bright blue and full of enthusiasm, now downcast and dull. She'd been forced to face some awful things, and he hadn't told her all of what he knew yet. He'd battled with what was right and wrong in this situation and came out still not knowing the best way to go about telling her everything. Maybe he was selfish. He was an asshole, so why not be a greedy bastard, too?

He grunted.

He enjoyed spending time with her. She'd captured a part of him he thought died when Lana left. Did he want a relationship with Grace? He didn't know. He couldn't give himself to another person again, and yet, he wanted to spill his whole life story to her. The situation perplexed him, made him second guess the case he was working on and fight off the desire to kiss Grace Penner every time he saw her.

Reluctant to leave her alone this afternoon, he'd tucked her into bed and kept vigil as she dozed. It was the first time he'd been inside Grace's home, and he was surprised at how tidy she kept it. Every trinket had its place and pictures of the farm and her family covered the walls. It was a testimony to how much she cared for them all.

The emotional toll from everything was wearing her down. Ben could relate to the same trauma of having your world torn right out from underneath you.

He placed his head into his hands and sighed. How could he keep secrets from the woman who trusted him? Grace never wavered in her dependability or willingness to help him. So why should he deceive her? From what Ben could tell, Grace and Jules seemed to be the only two worth saving out of the whole Penner bunch. He didn't know much about Andy, other than his addiction, but something told him the kid had a lot buried deep down. Ben witnessed Dave's lack of affection for his only son, and as far as Ben could see, there had never been any. He couldn't understand why, but then again, he'd lived the same thing with his own father. Kent was the biggest bastard Ben knew, and it tore him up knowing they shared the same blood. Andy must've thought the same way. If Dave is as cruel as everyone says he is to the boy, then the kid probably hates his old man, and Ben couldn't blame him.

He'd come to know the Penner family, but what bothered him was how much he cared for a few of them. If he were in Chicago, he'd have done what the law stated; go with the evidence, and to hell with anyone's feelings. There'd be no worry of Grace, Jules, or Andy. He had a job to do and all emotional connections would be kept at a distance. It was how he stayed sane.

When he first started out as a detective, he prided himself on getting to know the families of the victims, often eating dinner with them, watching a sibling play baseball or going to the funeral after the remains were found. The sentiments were formed out of his empathy for them, but what he didn't count on was the emptiness that followed whenever a case was closed. He no longer visited, watched games, or stopped in to check on them, and in the end it was Ben who was left alone.

His captain took him aside and taught him how to do his job without becoming too emotionally involved. At first Ben worried he couldn't be a detective without really getting to know the family, but he soon realized he could have understanding and compassion without becoming attached. It wasn't until later that he admitted to himself the connection he desired was from not having his own family. Ben fought hard to make sure he kept a distance, all while showing he cared.

He glanced over his shoulder at Grace, her chocolate lab, Zeke, cuddled in beside her, a plaid quilt pulled tight over her shoulder and tucked under her chin. For the first time since meeting Grace, he allowed himself to study her. She was small-boned with dainty features. Chestnut brown hair fell across the white pillow she snuggled into, and her petite nose turned upward a fraction, but you really had to look to see it. A few freckles sprinkled across its bridge to cascade onto her flushed cheeks.

Ben stretched his fingers. He fought the urge to run his thumb across her pink lips, slip his arm under her sleeping frame and pull her to him.

A loud knock, followed by three more stronger ones, rattled the front door. Zeke popped his dark head up from beside Grace and barked. Ben moved to the bedroom door when Grace sat up. Her blue eyes wide and startled.

His chest expanded, and the need to protect her at all cost took hold of his heart.

"Grace," a loud voice called from outside.

"It's my dad." She combed her fingers through her hair before turning toward him. "Stay here."

"Grace—"

"No, Ben. My dad will flip if he sees you here."

He didn't want to upset her more than she already was, so he nodded.

"Promise me you will not come out." The desperation in her eyes made him feel on edge. Was she afraid of Dave, or was it because she didn't want to explain things to him? Whatever it was, he'd stay hidden, but he wouldn't promise more than that if things got physical between Grace and her dad.

"You have my word." He meant it.

She wiggled out of the bed to stand, the pain from her leg evident when she bit her lip.

He took a step toward her, but before he could offer his help she limped past the door, shutting it behind her. Ben positioned himself against the wall to listen.

***

Grace rushed to the front door of her small condo before her dad banged on it again. She swung it open.

"Hi, Daddy."

He pushed his way into the kitchen.

"Where is he?"

"Who?" Did he know Ben was here? She refrained from glancing back at her bedroom door.

"Andy! Where is your weasel of a brother?"

"Daddy, Andy is not a weasel."

He faced her, his eyes narrowed to thin slits and his forehead folded into a deep frown. She'd seen him mad before, almost always at Andy, but this time was different. She inspected him. His white dress shirt was buttoned halfway, his blond hair messy, but that wasn't unusual. When he was working construction, she'd often see him change shirts before heading out to run errands. On the outside her dad looked normal, so why were the hairs on her arms standing? Grace had never been afraid of her father, but today he seemed off—restless and annoyed.

"Gracie?" He stood a few feet from her, concern now in his brown eyes, and she relaxed.

"Andy isn't here, Dad," she said.

"I know you two are close. Maybe give him a call. He will answer if he sees it's you."

She sat down at the table, her leg hot and aching. "I've tried calling him. He doesn't pick up. I'm worried about him."

"Well, don't be."

"How can you say that, Daddy? He's in a lot of trouble."

"He is now."

"What do you mean?" Had Andy done something against the law again? Grace's stomach tightened.

"He broke into my office." Her dad's face reddened. "And into my safe."

"How? He doesn't know the code."

"He probably found it in my desk."

"You keep the code to your safe in the office?" Why would her father do such a stupid thing?

"Have you heard from him? Be honest with me, Grace."

"No. I haven't." She sat back in the chair. "How do you know it was Andy who broke into the safe and not one of your workers?"

"You sound just like your mother."

"It's an honest question, Dad. Why are you assuming it was him?"

"Because I know damn well it was your brother, and when I get my hands on him—"

"You'll what?" Grace stood, surprised at her own actions. Heart pounding and feeling as if she were going to faint, she grasped the edge of the table.

"Don't test me, Grace." There was an even tone to his voice, but she didn't miss the threat.

"Why do you treat him differently than me and Steph?" She couldn't believe the words had left her own mouth, and she gripped the table harder to stop herself from slapping a hand across her lips.

"I'm not getting into this with you."

"Why can't you answer me?"

"Because I don't need to." Dad was a big man, well over six feet with wide shoulders and an aura that would frighten a lion, but Grace wasn't backing down. She had to know.

"All these years you've been horrible to Andy and I've stood by and watched it. I never had the guts to ask why."

"Horrible?" He laughed. "You're ridiculous."

"Answer my question, Dad."

"Who bought this condo, Grace?" He raised his voice.

She planted her feet on the floor, refusing to move as he advanced around the table toward her.

"Who made sure you never had to worry about anything? You always had extra money, a running car, food in your fridge."

"You," her voice squeaked.

"And you disrespect me this way?"

"Daddy, I—"

"I'm disappointed in you, Grace. I always thought we had a special relationship, you and I." He wiped at his eyes, but she saw no tears there. "How could my own daughter think I didn't care for my son."

"I'm sorry, I just thought…"

"You've been hanging around that new detective in town, and he's filling your head with nonsense."

How had he known that she'd been spending time with Ben? Was Dad following her?

"From what I hear, he is the one you should be leery of, Gracie. Rhoads said he was sent here because of a major incident involving a case back in Chicago. He killed someone."

That couldn't be. Ben told her he'd hurt the bad guy, not killed him, and she wouldn't care if he did. The bastard deserved it for hurting all those girls. She assessed her father before choosing the words she said.

"I haven't seen him since the day at your office."

"I don't like it. And in fact, Grace, I forbid you to spend a minute with the man. He's dangerous."

"I'm not a child. You can't forbid me from seeing anyone, Dad." It was a big mistake to say those words, and Grace regretted them immediately when Dad's jaw flexed and his face slanted.

"Is Andy here?" he growled.

"I already told you he wasn't."

He slammed his hand on the table, rattling the pot of flowers she'd placed there last week.

Grace jumped.

Large fists pumped at his sides, and his chest moved in and out as if he'd just ran a marathon. Dad wasn't going to talk to Andy. He was going to hurt him.

She watched as he walked the length of the small kitchen and went from room to room. When he came to her bedroom door, Grace froze remembering Ben was in there. She opened her mouth, but nothing came out. Panic set in and she bolted to her bedroom to stop him when Dad swung the door open.

She held her breath, squeezed her eyes shut, and waited for the curses to fly.

Silence buzzed in her ears and she peeked through her lashes to see Dad pacing in front of her. Where had Ben gone? Perhaps out the window? She was thankful they had taken her car and left his at the diner. Dad would've seen the cruiser and known she was lying.

"How much money is missing?" She needed to distract him, just in case Ben was still hiding in the bedroom.

"I don't know."

He didn't know much money was missing? That was odd, especially since he was the one who did all the ledgers. Grace knew this from when she worked for him.

"When I find him, he'd better have those…" He stopped.

Why hadn't he finished? Those what? He'd let Grace think it was money Andy had stolen.

"How much did you say was missing?" she asked again.

"I don't know, Grace. Damn it. I need to find your brother."

"Did he take all of it?" Something wasn't right. She kept pressing.

"What?" He looked confused.

"Did he take all the money inside the safe?"

"Has he called you?"

Her dad was avoiding her questions, and it made Grace uneasy.

"No. I haven't spoken to him since the night he was arrested."

"I don't believe you."

Dad had never questioned her before. She straightened. "What else is missing?"

"Phone him." He picked up Grace's cell phone from the table and handed it to her. She kept the surprised look from her face when she recognized Ben's phone instead.

"What did Andy take, Dad?" she asked again, refusing to dial her brother's number.

"Leave it alone, Grace." His words were short but laced with a warning, and Grace heard it loud and clear. She'd already pushed him today and wasn't sure she wanted to walk that line again. This time Dad might not be so easy on her. But he was hiding what Andy had taken, and she wanted to know what it was. Tired of backing down like she always did, Grace stepped toward her father and pointed a finger at him.

"I know all about Andy and his issues."

"Good for you. It's all an act. A ploy to pull your mother and I apart."

"Is that what you think? Andy wouldn't do that."

"Then you don't know your brother."

"Lately I don't know anyone in this family."

"Phone Andy. Now." His whole demeanour changed. Shoulders back, he lifted his chin. Calm and composed, Dad was in control and when his dark eyes bore into her own, Grace stepped back.

She pressed shaking fingers into the buttons on the cell and dialed her brother. Andy wouldn't pick up—he hadn't all the other times she phoned—and he most certainly wouldn't when he saw it was Ben's number.

The first ring startled her. She pressed her cheek into the phone. Another ring.

"Hello."

Grace hung up the phone. It killed her to think she could've spoken to her brother, asked if he was okay, but with Dad standing a few feet from her, it was the only option.

"You didn't let it ring long enough. Call back."

"It went to voicemail," she lied.

Dad stared at her, the same way he had when she was small and did something wrong, or when she was older and raised her voice to argue.

"I see a change in you, Gracie, and I don't like it."

What was he doing? Why was he turning this around on her?

"You've become distant. Blaming the family for the broken bell."

How could he say that when Janice was the one who broke it? He saw the letters with the missing pieces attached. Where did he think they came from?

"I'm not blaming anyone, Dad."

"You need to take a good hard look at yourself, Grace, and remember who you are. Where you come from."

What did that have to do with anything? She just wanted the bell not to be broken, the family to stop fighting, and to have everything back the way it was. "I know where I come from, and I want the bell to be put back together."

"Your incessant nagging and prodding have placed the family at odds. Because of your obsessive behaviour you've also blamed some of them and I will not have it."

Grace blinked. Dad was talking about Janice. Why was he sticking up for her? She swallowed. Why didn't he see how much the bell meant to her, and why wasn't he on her side? Grace couldn't form a word and knew if she tried, her voice would break. Dad thought she was wrong. He'd gone against her, and she withdrew from him, understanding for the first time in her life how Andy must've felt all these years.

"We are family and we stand together. No matter what. So, whatever it is you think happened to the *bell*, I don't want to hear another word about it."

Grace stood still as he strode to the door.

"If you hear from or see your brother, you *will* call me, Grace." He walked out the door, leaving it open behind him.

She rushed over and closed it, pressing her face against the smooth surface. Her conversation with Steph replayed in her mind, and Grace now knew everything her sister said was true.

"Grace?"

Not wanting to turn around and let Ben see how much her conversation with her dad had affected her, she remained with her face pressed against the door.

"Are you okay?"

It was a simple question, one she was sure on any other day she'd be able to answer with a cheerful smile, but not right now. In fact, Grace wasn't sure if she'd ever be okay.

"I heard everything."

She didn't doubt he had. Ben was a detective, a job that required him to listen when he wasn't supposed to. She should be angry at him for eavesdropping, but she was glad he'd heard. There was no way she'd be able to tell him without showing the uncertainty she had about her father.

"I need to talk to you about a few things." His voice sounded weak, slightly withdrawn.

She turned to face him.

"But I need to tell Jules first."

Grace raised a brow.

"You can come with me," he hesitated, "if you want."

She nodded, knowing what he was going to tell her uncle was serious and again would change her outlook on how she perceived the family, but she needed to know.

CHAPTER TWENTY

Ben sat on the wicker chair on the veranda of Charlie Penner's home. Grace perched on the edge of her chair beside him, while Jules stared at the papers Ben gave to him. While Grace's uncle gripped the contract written years before between Charlie Penner and Carl White, Ben was sure he'd seen the man's eyes mist a time or two.

He couldn't help feeling responsible for what Jules was going through. Had he not found the contract at Carl's house, no one would've known. Grace inched closer and Ben knew she was itching to find out what the papers said, but it was up to Jules to tell her.

"What does it say?" she asked, impatience getting the best of her.

Ben was shocked she'd even come with him. The car ride over had been silent, and he figured Grace had been thinking of the conversation she'd had with Dave. It had taken all the strength he had not to show himself when Dave swung open Grace's bedroom door. The promise he'd made to her is what stopped him. If he couldn't shield the girl from who her family was, then he'd make damn sure she could believe in him.

While in the bedroom, he also concluded that Grace had a right to know about everything he did. The decision was made after he'd heard the way Dave had treated his daughter. The man played on Grace's emotions and guilt about Andy. Ben was sickened by the way Dave was able to maneuver the conversation from whatever Andy had taken from his safe to how much of a disappointment Grace had been.

Dave was hiding something. Grace had picked up on it, too. He didn't know what it was, but his gut told him Andy was in danger. While Grace drove them to see Jules, he had texted Enders to look for Andrew Penner, and he hoped to hell the deputy found the kid before his father did.

"Jules? What do the papers say?" Grace asked again.

"I'm still a Penner," the man said solemnly. Jules placed the contract onto the wooden table they sat around, his chiseled features motionless. "And Claire White is my mother."

Grace gasped.

"I'm sorry you had to find out this way," Ben said, and he meant it. He considered Jules a friend and didn't want to hurt him.

"Where did you find this?" Jules asked.

"At Carl's."

"I'm sorry," Grace said. "But you need to explain to me how Claire is your mother and Grandpa is your father."

Jules laughed.

"Gracie, Grandpa isn't my father."

"Well then, who is?"

Jules glanced at Ben before he said, "Dave."

"Dad is your father, not your brother?" Grace sat back in the chair, her eyes wide and cheeks pale.

Ben placed a hand on her knee.

Jules raised a brow.

He ignored the other man and left his hand there.

"I need a drink." Before anyone could reply, Jules reached under the table and slid out a cooler, he placed three beers on the table. They each took one.

"So, my dad is your dad, and he slept with Claire White?"

"Way to break it down, Gracie." Jules inhaled the beer, almost emptying the bottle in one swig.

"So that makes you my brother," she said, astonished.

"Yup, guess so."

Ben could see the tension on Jules's face, the reality of it all sinking in for the other man.

"If you don't mind, I can explain it to Grace, so you don't have to," he said to Jules.

"That'd be great." He cracked another beer, downing it the same way he had the first one.

Ben turned toward Grace expecting to see disappointment flash in her eyes, but instead he saw trust, a yearning to know the truth shadowed by a sliver of fear. He understood all the emotions she was feeling and decided to take his time. He wanted to tell it once, for Jules's sake.

He took a long breath. "The papers on the table are a contract dated November 1991, between Charlie Penner and Carl White."

Grace nodded.

"In the contract it states that Claire White's child, who she carried at the time, would be signed over to Charlie and Anna Penner to raise as their own."

"But why?" she asked, and when he glanced at Jules, he knew the other man wanted to know too.

"I don't know. All I can tell you is what the papers say." He held them up.

"Go on."

"For the rights to the child, Carl White is paid thirty-five thousand dollars, and Claire's medical bills are paid along with a five-month stay at Rolling Acres Ranch until the baby was born."

"Did no one wonder where Claire was for five months?" Grace asked.

"My guess is if Carl and Charlie had come to an agreement, then they also hatched up a story as to where she was all that time."

"More lies," Jules muttered.

"I just don't understand why Dad and Claire couldn't raise Jules as their own?"

"Claire was seventeen, Dave eighteen," Ben said. "Times were different thirty years ago."

"Had nothing to do with the times," Jules said. "A pregnant teen would tarnish the family name. A baby out of wedlock didn't happen to the Penners."

Ben thought so, too, but he didn't want to be the one to say it. The Penners were a force to be reckoned with, and he didn't doubt there was some bullying going on to push Claire to agree.

"I'm sorry, Jules," Grace said. "Everything I've ever known or been told seems to be a sack of crap."

"I know. Me too." His broad shoulders slumped forward. "I don't care that they never told me. I'd rather be raised by Charlie than Dave." He winked at Grace. "No offence."

She smiled.

"What bothers me is that I was raised to stay away from Carl, and I was never told about his daughter."

"Why do you think you were told to steer clear of Carl?" Ben wanted to know.

Jules shrugged. "Not really sure other than the obvious. He's a drunk."

"Maybe they thought Carl would say something," Ben suggested.

"Could be right." Jules ran his hand through his hair. "Son of a bitch. I wondered for years why I wasn't close to any of my brothers. I always thought it was the age difference."

Ben had experienced something similar between himself and his own father. He had accepted long ago that Kent James would never love him like a father should love his son. The admission hurt like hell, but he faced it, taking years to fully come to grips with the reality of what family he'd been born into.

"What do you mean?" Grace asked.

"I can't explain it. Randy and Rick ignored me mostly. I was never close to them and Dave. Hell, he'd just as soon forget we were even related, but because of our *upbringing* he pretends to want to be around me. They all do. It's what Penners do. They fucking pretend."

Grace stared at her lap. She saw it now, too.

"There is no love there. Shit, looking back I don't think there ever was. Rick wanting to be left alone, Randy's need to have the best of everything, and Dave's desire to control us all." Jules grabbed another beer.

"Grandma and Grandpa loved us," Grace squeaked. "Right, Jules?"

"Yeah, kid. They did."

Grace nodded while wiping the tears on her cheeks.

Ben wasn't so sure Jules believed the words he'd said, but he remained quiet, allowing the man to vent his emotions.

"Are you going to talk to Dad?" Grace asked, and Ben didn't miss the fear in her voice.

"Damn right I am. I have questions that I need answers to."

"He won't admit to any of it. That is how he is."

Jules clenched his jaw, the bone protruded from his face. "I don't give a damn whether or not he denies it. He will know that I found out his secret."

There were more of those, Ben thought, but again kept that part to himself.

"I can't believe after all these years of walking past Crazy Carl, the man was my grandfather," Jules said.

"He knows you're his grandson," Ben added. "He signed the paper."

"I wonder if that's why he hates us so much?"

"What do you mean?"

"Carl despises us Penners. Has all my life anyway."

"Do you know why?" Ben asked.

Jules shrugged.

"Probably because Grandpa slept with Carl's wife," Grace said.

"Where did you hear that?" Jules asked.

"From me," Ben said, and he took another deep breath because what he was about to say would shock them both. "Charlie and Olga had an affair. I'm not sure how long it lasted, but from what I've been able to drag up, he ended things shortly after it began, and she wasn't too happy. A few months before Claire died, and I'm assuming was still at Rolling Acres waiting to deliver Jules, Olga began harassing Charlie. She was in love with him, or so I've been told."

"Despite being married to Carl?" Grace asked.

"Yes, and according to the files, she carried on this way for a few months until Dave put a stop to it."

"Oh, I'm sure he did," Jules added.

"What do you mean?" Grace's voice was light and unsure.

He couldn't turn back now. "I'm sorry, Grace. Dave locked Olga in the outhouse on the ranch and left her there for days." He cringed before adding the last part. "He knew Olga had a fear of mice, and he deepened this fear by dumping a bucket of mice on her."

"No," she whispered.

"What a rotten son of a bitch." Jules's anger intensified, and he grabbed another beer without asking either of them if they wanted one.

"Olga went clinically insane because of it." Ben finished.

"Shit," Jules whispered.

"My ... my dad did that to another person?" Grace blinked as she digested what Ben had told her.

He knew she was trying to understand Dave's motives, but there was no way to look at it other than the man was wretched.

"Why? Why would he do that?"

"The name," Jules said, before Ben could answer her.

Grace turned toward her brother. "What do you mean?"

"Ah kid, you know how it's been all your life. The Penner name is like gold around here. When I went to jail, I tarnished it. No one was pleased, and Dave never let me forget what I did, either. He used it against me whenever we would argue."

Ben fidgeted in the chair. Every part of him wanted to tell Jules about what Rhoads had said, but he gave his word to the sheriff, and now he regretted doing so.

"I've heard him." Grace inhaled. "Steph thinks the same way."

"Probably why she moved."

Grace nodded.

"We all have ghosts," Ben said, trying to ease their minds.

"Do your ghosts murder people?" Jules growled.

"Jules." Grace sat upright. "How can you say that?"

"I never thought I would, but the more things I find out about our *glorious* family, the more doubtful I am that some of them are innocent."

"But to say one of them murdered Claire? You're going based on your feelings, not on—"

"How I was raised?" Jules leaned into Grace and Ben stiffened.

"I wasn't going to say that," Grace whispered.

"I was raised the same way you were, Gracie, to not go against the family. Ever."

"You make it sound like we are some kind of royalty."

He scoffed. "More like the bloody mafia, harming anyone who stood in our way."

"You aren't like that, and neither are Uncle Rick or Randy."

"I assaulted a police officer, and as for your uncles, who knows what they did, but I can assure you their slates aren't clean."

Ben swallowed down the confession he wanted to let fly.

"I didn't have a terrible upbringing, Jules, and neither did you."

"No, but Andy did."

Grace blinked back the tears forming in her eyes at the mention of her brother.

"I never went against Charlie, and you didn't go against Dave, but imagine what would've happened if we did?"

"You think Grandpa and Dad would've harmed us?"

"All I know is if a man can bully a young girl to give up her son, and another can do something as inhumane as what Dave did to Olga, then yeah, I think so."

"Maybe Claire wanted you to have a better life," Grace said.

"You think she was okay with selling me?"

"She didn't get that money. Carl did." Ben reminded them. "You won't know the truth of how, or why it happened until you talk to Dave."

"I won't get the truth from him either," Jules growled.

Ben's cell phone beeped. When he glanced down at the message from Enders he leaped out of his chair.

"Carl's house is on fire."

Jules was on his feet and down the steps before Ben.

"We'll take my truck."

"I'll drive," Ben said. "You've been drinking."

Grace ran along beside him.

Jules tossed him the keys to his truck. With Grace squished between them, Ben started the old Chevy and sped out of the driveway.

Chapter Twenty-One

Grace said a silent prayer for Carl. The sky glowed orange as they got closer. She refused to think Carl's house would be gone when they arrived, or the man she'd come to care about had perished within the flames.

"Go faster," Jules yelled, holding onto the dust-covered dashboard.

"I can't risk someone darting out in front of us," Ben said, as he steered the truck around a corner and came to a screeching halt at the alley where Carl's house was.

Two firetrucks blocked the entry and firemen lined the east side of the house dousing it with water. Another row of firemen sprayed the businesses surrounding Carl's home.

Grace pressed on Jules's shoulder to get him out of the truck and took off into the crowd.

"Carl," she screamed, pushing her way through the people standing around.

"Grace!"

She didn't know if it was Jules or Ben yelling her name, and she didn't care. All she thought about was the poor old man suffocating from the smoke.

"You can't go past here, ma'am." A tall fireman grabbed her arm.

Soot and ash covered the man's face. Grace needed to get to Carl, or to know if he was all right. She shoved him, but he was too strong, and his grip tightened on her arm.

"Where's the man that lives here?" she yelled, her voice hoarse from the smoke filling the air. She pressed a palm to her breast to calm the restless beating in her chest, but the worry she felt for Carl couldn't be ignored. She looked frantically around the chaos for her friend.

"Grace. What the hell are you doing?" Ben was beside her, his breathing labored.

"Shit, Gracie, you scared us," Jules said.

"Where's Carl?" she asked.

"I'll find him." Ben turned to Jules. "Don't let her out of your sight."

"No problem." Jules put a heavy arm around her shoulders, cementing her in place.

She watched as Ben disappeared among the men and women who were fighting the fire.

"What if he dies?" she said, more to herself. But she wasn't surprised when Jules pulled her closer to him.

"Let's wait and see what Ben finds out."

The minutes ticked by slowly as she observed the commotion around them. Instructions were shouted from one firefighter to another as they held long white hoses near the burning home. Blue and red lights flashed at both entries to the alleyway as the police blocked off the road.

Grace stood on her tiptoes to get a better view of where Ben might be, but she saw nothing through the thick fog of smoke.

"I'm going to need you to move over there." A young police officer ushered them another twenty feet back and away from the flames.

"Have you seen Detective James?" she asked him.

"No." The man stretched his arms out sideways, creating a barrier against the crowd.

Flames shot into the air, eating at the wooden structure and everything Carl had left in this life. The home was engulfed in fire and unsalvageable. The boards heaved and cracked, spitting sparks into the air. A loud bang caused Grace to jump, and she watched horrified as the roof caved in.

"Oh, no."

Jules hugged her to him. The comfort did little to ease the profound sadness she felt for the old man and all he'd lost. Carl had been through so much already, and now he'd be homeless.

"Carl is safe," Ben said, running toward them.

Grace wormed her way out of Jules's embrace and wiped at her face.

"Can we see him?" she asked.

"We will have to go this way, but…" He stopped. When his eyes locked with hers, the severity of the situation reflected within the dark depths shadowed by a deep, penetrating sadness.

She inhaled, taking in the importance of what had happened. Carl wasn't okay, and Ben didn't know how to tell her.

"I want to go."

He nodded, took her hand and pulled her along. Jules followed behind.

They walked around the trucks to the other end of the alley where an ambulance was parked. Carl sat on the ground, a green blanket was strewn about his bony shoulders. He had a white bandage wrapped around his head, and a bottle cradled in his lap.

"How did the fire start?" Jules asked.

"The old man," Ben said.

Grace knelt in front of Carl, who had ash in his silver hair and black smudges on his hollow cheeks.

"Hi, Carl," she said, and reached for his hand.

He lifted his head. Pale blue eyes looked up at her, and Grace held onto the small reserve she had left so she didn't fall apart in front of him.

"Are you okay?"

"Gracie, my house," he whimpered. The strong scent of alcohol cascaded from his lips.

"I know, and I'm so sorry." She moved to sit on the ground beside him. "What happened?"

Carl shook his head. "I don't know."

It seemed to be the story as of late. The drinking evaporated the memory like raindrops on a warm summer day.

"You're lucky to be alive," Ben said.

"I should've died years ago," the old man slurred.

Grace glanced up at Jules. His features drooped with regret. He was looking at Carl for the first time as his grandfather, and it must hurt like hell.

"It's okay. We will help you." Ben placed his hand on the old man's shoulder.

"I want to die." He wept. "Why can't I just die?"

"Is that why you started the fire?" Ben asked.

Carl raised a hand in the air, his bottom lip jutted outward, and an angry growl rumbled in his throat.

Grace sent Ben a pleading look to not upset the poor man any more than he'd already been.

"I want to go home," Carl moaned.

She couldn't contain the anguish from constricting her throat, and tears washed her smoke-ridden cheeks.

"Mr. White, I'm Jules." He sat down in front of Carl. "Your grandson."

Grace wasn't sure now was the time to tell Carl what he already knew, and she nudged Jules with her hand.

"I don't have a grandson," Carl stated, as he reached for the bottle in his lap.

"You're coming home with me," Jules said matter-of-factly.

Grace was astonished at how the man she'd thought of as her uncle all these years, and now her brother, was dealing with everything he'd found out tonight. Her heart swelled with pride at how Jules handled his newfound grandfather.

"I ain't going anywhere but back to my house." Carl's wrinkled hands held tight to the bottle while he brought it to his lips and swallowed half of it in one guzzle.

"Your home is gone." Ben patted his shoulder.

"Bah." Carl shoved the palm away. "I want to go home."

"I'm sorry, but you can't."

The old man's lip quivered, his eyes crowded with tears, and a low sorrowful moan blew past his lips.

Grace looked away, unable to watch Carl fall apart.

"Let's help him up," Jules said. "We can take him out to the farm."

Ben nodded.

She stood watching while they hoisted Carl to his feet, each man holding on to an arm so the old man didn't fall over.

"I know you," Carl slurred.

"Yeah?" Jules smiled.

"You're that rotten Penner."

"Carl," Ben warned.

"Where's Claire?" he asked, and before anyone could answer, Carl dropped his bottle and dove for Jules's throat. "Where's my daughter?"

Jules was quick and a lot stronger than Carl. He dodged his attempt at choking him, while Ben grabbed Carl from behind.

"You killed her," Carl shrieked, the sound so unnerving the hair on Grace's arms stood. "It was him. That man. He killed my daughter." Carl's arms thrashed wildly toward Jules.

"No. He didn't. You have the wrong guy," Ben said in an even tone, trying to calm him down.

"Bah." Carl spat. "I hate the lot of you Penners."

Grace's entire body shook with anxiety. She didn't know what to do. Carl was out of his mind, and there was no way to help him. She glanced at Jules, the rough and rugged features of his face, now soft and sagging as the old man spewed his contempt toward him.

The two paramedics who attended to Carl earlier ran over to help.

"He needs to be taken to the hospital," Ben said, straining to hold the old man up and away from Jules.

Grace stepped beside her brother and placed a hand within his shaking one. She watched helpless as the two men assisted Ben and strapped a screaming Carl to the gurney before they wheeled him to the waiting ambulance.

"I'm sorry, Jules," Grace said.

"I definitely did not expect him to accuse me of murder when I told him I was his grandson." Jules let go of Grace's hand and massaged his face.

"I think the years of drinking have finally caught up to Carl." Ben was back beside them.

"The way he looked at me..." Jules shivered. "It was as if he were certain I'd killed his daughter."

"It's impossible," Grace said, trying to take the worry from Jules's face. "You were just an infant."

"Yeah, but Dave wasn't," Ben said. "Maybe he got you two mixed up."

"Stop it," Grace shouted. "My dad would never—" Her voice trailed off when Jules turned to look at her and shook his head. He thought it, too. Grace's mind replayed all she'd learned about her family since Ben told her of Claire White's death. The lies. The abuse. The control. The threats. She inhaled a quivering breath. Her father was the only one with reason. He had given up his son, he'd caused an old woman to go crazy, and he was going to hurt Andy when he found him. Grace could no longer deny what was right in front of her.

Ben balanced the disposable tray of coffees as he walked across the parking lot of the diner toward Jules and Grace. Not ready to leave either of them for the night, he'd suggested a cup of coffee before they departed. Grace refused to go inside the diner, and he volunteered to grab the brew and meet them back outside.

He wished more than anything he could change the situation for his friend, and especially for Grace. The anguish clouding her features tore at his soul. He had no hard evidence against Dave, other than his horrendous behaviour, and there was no way the district attorney would see fit to charge him. He'd been in the job long enough to know the rules, and until he had a confession or DNA—and that was unlikely—Dave Penner would walk.

He thought about Carl. The man had been through hell with his wife going crazy, not knowing where his daughter was all this time, and now he was homeless. He doubted the man would come back from today.

"Thank you," Grace said, as she took her coffee from the cardboard tray.

"It'd be better if there was whiskey in here," Jules smirked before he took a sip.

Ben didn't disagree with him. He could use a stiff drink himself. He'd come to this town to avoid his own problems, and instead he'd taken on the problems of Grace Penner, the woman who had charmed him with her infectious smile. He'd reminded himself time and time again it was just another case, like all the others he'd worked on, but somehow it had become so much more. He wanted victory for the girl with the long brown hair who stood before him sipping on her coffee. He wanted the bell she cherished so much to be put back together, and the smile she'd worn on the first day he met her to never leave her angelic face again.

He sighed.

There would never be anything between them. She'd forever see him as the man who thought her father was a murderer. It was probably for the best. Ben didn't know whether he'd have a job to go back to, and at this very moment he wasn't sure he even wanted it.

The truth sunk into him like a snake biting into his flesh. Ben didn't deserve to have his job back. He'd gone against his captain, something he should've never done. Looking back now, he regretted all of it. His behaviour that night and the days leading up to the incident were filled with anger along with the desire to belong and the yearning to have someone believe in him. He'd felt inadequate—weak for so long. A strong desire to prove himself to Lana and Kent burned inside him, fueling the rage he'd held onto the past year. The problem was, they didn't care, and innocent people paid the price.

Ben watched Grace. If it wasn't for her, and the example she put forth, he would've never seen a brighter side to the sad story he'd been living. His shoulders lifted. It had been his fault. He was to blame for all of what had happened that day. Ben owed his captain an apology. A big one. He needed to make amends, even if he never got his job back.

"James. James." Enders ran toward him from across the street where the firefighters were still hosing down Carl's house.

The frantic look on the young deputy's face had Ben sprinting toward him.

"There was a call into the precinct. Andrew Penner is at Dave's house, and he's got a gun," Enders panted. "Rhoads is on his way now."

Ben swung around and ran toward the car.

"What's going on?" Grace asked.

"It's Andy."

"Is he okay?"

"I'll explain on the way over." He needed to save the kid from killing his father and spending the rest of his life in prison.

Chapter Twenty-Two

"Andy?" Ben called through the door. "It's Detective James. Can I come in?"

Rhoads's cruiser sat across the street. He sauntered over just as Ben knocked on the door. He'd given strict instructions to both Jules and Grace not to burst inside in case Andy got spooked and fired his weapon. They were behind him on the step. Grace's whole body shook, and he felt the step vibrate underneath him.

"Kid's got a gun." Rhoads stood on the grass.

Ben frowned. The bastard should be talking to the boy already, instead he'd hid in his car until they arrived.

"Andy?" Grace yelled.

"Gigi, is that you?"

"Yeah. Can we come in?"

"The cop has to leave his gun outside." Andy's voice cracked, and Ben knew the kid was scared.

"Okay." Grace answered.

"Andy, it's Detective James. Me and Rhoads will leave our guns on the step."

"I swear, Gigi, if I see one gun." He huffed. "One gun. I'll shoot."

"I promise, Andy," Grace said. "They're putting them on the step now."

Ben gave her a nod of reassurance, then removed his gun from the holster and placed it on the corner of the step. Rhoads did the same.

"The guns are gone," Ben called. "Can we come in?"

Silence.

"Andy?" Grace knocked on the door.

"Come in."

Ben motioned for everyone to get behind him before he turned the knob and slid the door open slowly. When he stepped into the living room he was shocked to see the whole Penner family huddled in the small room.

Grace rushed in, and Ben grabbed her arm.

Wide blue eyes swimming with tears stared at him.

He smiled. The only way he thought to relax her.

"Hey, Gigi." Andy said, from the other end of the room, a gun in his hand.

"Take a breath and be calm," Ben whispered loud enough so she could hear.

Grace inhaled before she addressed her brother. "Hey, bro."

"Get over there with the rest of them," Andy said and waved the gun.

Whimpers from the family caught Ben's attention, and he scanned their faces while he walked to stand next to them. Vera sat on the couch, a girl who looked an awful lot like Grace, probably her sister, held the sobbing woman's hand. His chest tightened. A mother shouldn't have to see her son fall apart like this.

He recognized Rick crouched in the corner with his arms around two more girls and his wife. Another man, who must be Randy, sat on a chair with a dark-haired woman on his lap, and another woman who Ben remembered seeing at the diner, stood behind them. He zeroed in on Dave Penner, a few feet from the rest of the family on his own chair. His arms were crossed, and he had a glare fit to scare the devil himself planted on his face.

"Andy, why don't you put down the gun so we can talk," Ben said.

"I've tried that," Rick said from the floor. "He doesn't want to listen."

"He doesn't want to listen because he's a drug addict," Randy's wife stated, and Ben decided he didn't like the woman.

"Hey, kid," Jules said. "You don't look so well."

The man was right. Ben inspected the boy and saw the red-rimmed eyes, disheveled hair, and wormy jaw. Andy bounced from one foot to another as he kept the gun trained on them. He was high on something other than marijuana, and it frightened the hell out of Ben. The kid could go off at any moment, and it would be because of whatever drugs he'd ingested. He'd need to tread lightly.

"Gigi, remember the bell?" Andy asked.

Grace nodded.

"Do you think it will fix this?" he laughed.

She hung her head, and Ben wished he could comfort her.

"Put the damn gun down. Now." Dave Penner stood.

Andy fired a shot into the ceiling and white paint chips fell onto his hair. "Sit down."

Dave did as he was told, but Ben saw the man was seething.

"Can't control me now, Dad." Andy hopped to the other foot. "All my life." He pulled on his hair with his free hand. "All my fucking life you've said when, where, how much, and if I didn't, a good beating would fix it, isn't that right?"

Ben's chest ached for the kid. It was obvious Andy went through some sort of trauma other than the obvious bullying he'd received from his father.

"Did you know he locked me up?" Andy went on.

"Andy." Dave made a move to stand, but the kid was quicker and pointed the gun directly at his father.

"Do it," Andy ordered. "Do it. Stand up so I can blow your fucking head off." His eyes welled up and his bottom lip shook.

Ben needed to get the situation under control, and fast.

"What are you talking about, kid?" Jules asked.

Andy's glossy eyes focused on them.

"I'm listening." Jules smiled. "I've got your back."

"You always did, Jules."

"I still do."

"Remember when I went missing?" Andy stammered.

"When you were nine? Yeah, I remember." Jules was doing an outstanding job with the kid, and Ben let him continue while he surveyed the room for a way to get around the back and tackle the boy.

"Ol' Dave here locked me up on the farm. In the outhouse." Andy's body shook.

"No way," Randy said. "You're lying."

"Of course, he's lying," Dave yelled. "That's all he ever does."

"David?" Vera stared at her husband.

"Why'd he lock you up?" Jules asked.

"Why are you asking him?" Dave pointed at Andy. "He's a bloody liar."

"You can tell me, kid. Why were you locked up?" Jules repeated, ignoring the other man.

"Tell them, Dad." Andy waved the gun at Dave. "Tell them."

"Look at him," Dave growled. "He's out of his mind on drugs. I have no idea what he's talking about."

"Does this have to do with what you took from Dad's safe?" Grace asked, interjecting herself into the conversation.

Ben knew Dave's visit earlier today had bothered her. She wanted answers.

Andy stared at her, and Ben could see the kid's features soften. He loved his sister. Whatever he'd gone through at the hands of his father had ripped Andy in two.

"You bet it does, Gigi."

"Dad, what did Andy take?" she asked.

"Shut up, Grace," Dave yelled.

"No," Andy screamed and pointed the gun at his dad. "Do not talk to her like that."

"This is ridiculous. I'm leaving." Randy's wife stood.

"Sit the hell down, Jan," Jules barked.

"Watch who you're talking to," Randy said.

"You can all go once everything is out." Andy laughed, a high-pitched sound that had the hairs on Ben's neck standing.

"Why did Dave lock you up, Andy?" Jules asked again, trying to grab the kid's attention. Grace's new-found brother would make a great cop. He was doing a fantastic job at keeping the kid calm.

"Ask him," Andy pointed to Rhoads, cowering in the back by the wall.

Damn it. Ben knew the bastard hadn't told him everything about the Penners.

"I don't know what the kid's talking about," Rhoads whined.

Ben caught Dave staring down the sheriff. A warning, no doubt to shut his mouth.

"If you know something, now is the time to tell it," Ben said to the lawman.

Rhoads's pinhole eyes darted about the room and his forehead perspired.

The room was silent as all eyes stared at Rhoads, waiting to hear what he had to say.

"Tell them," Andy screamed and pulled at his hair.

Grace jumped, and Ben wished more than anything he could take her away from all of this.

"Aww, hell. The kid's tellin' the truth," Rhoads mumbled.

"You son of a bitch," Jules said to Dave.

"Well, let's hear it." Randy whined, as if it was all too much for him.

"The whole town was out lookin' for Andy. I'm sure you all remember. I'd come upon him at the outhouse just after Dave did." Rhoads glanced at Vera. "I'm sorry." His voice shook. "Dave was threatening the kid that if he ever spoke of being locked up to anyone, he'd take him where no one would find him."

"Why would he lock Andy up in the first place?" Rick asked.

Rhoads swayed, sweat trickled down his temples. "Because the kid knew some things."

"What exactly are those *things*?" Rick asked.

"The affairs." Rhoads wiped his mouth.

Vera gasped, and Grace's sister placed a protective arm around her mother.

"That's not all," Andy sang.

The sheriff gave the kid a pleading look.

"Tell the rest."

"Come on, kid," Rhoads begged.

"Say the rest of it," Andy screamed.

"And the two kids," Rhoads whispered.

"What kids?" Rick asked, as he got to his feet. "Dave, what kids?"

"The ones he's been hiding for ten years," Andy shouted, pulling out the papers from the inside of his shirt. "The twin boys he refuses to acknowledge. The ones I was forced to keep a secret about for the last ten years." The kid wiped at his eyes. The burden his father made him carry had taken its toll on Andy.

"Daddy?" Grace said.

Dave Penner sat in the chair, a smug look upon his face.

"Tell me, Dave," Jules said. "Is this how it happened when my mother, Claire White, got pregnant?"

"Ah shit," Rick muttered.

Vera placed her head into her palms and sobbed.

"Claire was trash," Randy said. "You should be thankful Mom and Dad raised you as their own."

"You better watch your mouth." Jules stepped toward the other man.

"Or what?" Randy stood.

"Sit down," Ben yelled.

"There's more," Andy screeched, halting any more words between Ben and Randy.

Dave dove for the kid. The entire room moved at once to protect Andy from his father's rage. The gun went off, this time above Dave's head, the bullet stuck into the wall and the family picture hanging there. Andy pushed the gun into Dave's forehead.

Everyone froze.

"I fucking hate you." Andy's face was flushed, and sweat trickled down his cheeks.

Ben watched Dave for any signs he would lunge at the boy again.

"Sit down." Andy pointed the gun at them. "Everyone, sit the hell down."

Dave was the last one to take his seat. His dark eyes bore into his son, telling of the things he'd do to him once this was over.

The threat didn't faze the kid. He smiled a lopsided grin.

"Okay, kid. What else?" Jules asked, drawing Andy's attention away from Dave.

"Ask him why you went to jail." Andy pointed the gun again in Rhoads's direction.

Shit. Andy knew why Jules had gone to jail. Now was not the time for Jules to find out. Ben stepped closer to the man.

"You told him," Rhoads accused Ben.

"I didn't say a damn word." The kid knew a lot of things, and Ben wondered if he also knew if his dad murdered Claire.

"Told him what?" Jules asked.

Rhoads looked at the youngest Penner and shook his head.

"I know all about it," Andy shouted.

"How?" Rick whispered.

"I overheard Dad talking to Grandpa about it just after Jules came home from prison." Andy looked at Dave. "Didn't know that, did you, Dad?"

"Ah, hell," Rick sighed, his face pale and eyes downcast.

"He doesn't know what he's talking about," Dad yelled. "He's a liar."

Andy laughed and pulled at his hair. "Tell Jules the truth." The gun aimed at Rhoads.

The sheriff shook his head.

"Say it," Andy screeched.

A droplet of sweat fell from Rhoads's chin as he shook his head again.

"Fucking tell him or I will." Andy's bottom lip shook. His neck twitched to the side.

Ben's shoulders tensed as he watched the kid closely. Andy's eyes held no color, his whole body began to shake. The kid was close to losing it.

"I … I'm sorry, Jules. I truly am."

"Sorry about what?" Jules asked.

"You didn't lay a hand on me back then." Rhoads's wiped at his forehead.

"Of course, I did. I saw what you looked like. Shit, I put you in the hospital." Rhoads shook his head, and the jowls hanging from his cheeks quivered.

"I will have your job," Dave said, from the other end of the room.

"No. You won't," Ben barked at the man.

"You're on thin ice as it is, Detective. So, you'd better watch what you say to me."

Ben knew the man was talking about Chicago and all that happened there.

Dave smirked. The man thought he was above the law.

"Say it." Andy held the gun outward, facing them. The kid was getting impatient.

Ben zeroed in on the gun and the sweaty hand holding it. A slip of the finger could mean a life. He had to get the weapon from the kid.

"It was Dave who beat me," Rhoads said in one long breath.

Jules's mouth gaped.

"I was going to arrest him for what he did to Andy." The sheriff's shoulders sagged.

"You bastard." Jules charged for Dave.

"It wasn't just Dad. Was it?" Andy said, stopping Jules, who was halfway across the room.

"Tell me the rest of it," Jules shouted. Anger pushed the veins from his forehead.

"Rick and Randy were there, too," the kid crowed, before Rhoads said any more.

"You all knew?" Jules flexed his hands. "You let me go to jail for something I didn't do—let me carry this guilt around for the past ten years?"

The room was silent except for the quiet whimpers coming from Vera Penner.

"You're right. We were wrong, and I'm sorry," Rick said, the truth reflected in his eyes.

"It's too late for that." Jules clenched his jaw.

Ben saw through Jules's tough exterior and knew the lies and deceit had cut deep. He'd never be the same.

Rick wrung his hands together. "I wanted to tell you so many times, but—"

"Oh, would you shut up already," Randy said. "It had to happen, Jules. You were a minor. Dave wasn't."

"You should thank me." Dave leaned forward in the chair. "Your sentence straightened you out some."

"You piece of shit." Jules walked toward the man.

Dave stood.

Ben knew things were about to explode, and before he could step in between the two Jules punched Dave, connecting his fist with the man's jaw. Dave fought back. Rick jumped in to pull them apart, but he was no match for either of them. Ben locked his arms into Jules swinging ones and wrestled him away from Dave while Rick pushed his eldest brother back, breaking the two of them apart.

"Andy," Grace yelled.

Ben released Jules and spun around when he caught sight of Andy. He ran toward the kid to try and catch him before he fell. The boy's eyes rolled to the back of his head, the muscles in his neck and back spasmed, and he let go of the gun before he collapsed onto the floor.

Ben dived to the ground to help the boy.

Jules scooped up the gun.

Andy was in full seizure. He rolled the boy to his left side.

"Call an ambulance."

"Andy." Grace knelt beside her brother. Worry creased her forehead and eyes.

White foam bubbled from the boy's mouth, and his body convulsed.

"Andy." Vera moved from the couch to be with her son, placing her hand in his stiff one. "Mom's here. Everything will be all right."

Ben wasn't sure, but damn it, he hoped so. The kid didn't deserve to lose his life to a drug, and all because of an abusive father.

"How much time before they get here?" he asked.

"They're a minute out," Jules answered, still on the phone with the emergency operator.

Ben held the boy on his side while his bony body vibrated.

The sirens and red lights filled the room as the ambulance pulled into the driveway, and seconds later two paramedics rushed into the room.

"He's taken drugs," Ben said to the man closest to him while the other injected Andy with an anti-seizure medicine.

"Do you know which ones?" They asked in unison while they worked quickly to stabilize the kid.

"Cocaine, and possibly something else," he told them.

"Okay, we will take it from here."

That was his cue to move away and let the men do their jobs of saving Andrew Penner's life, but Ben couldn't make himself leave. He needed to be there for the boy. Andy was a reflection of himself. Broken, abused, and begging someone to love him, and he'd be damned if he'd desert the kid now.

"Sir?" the paramedic said.

"I'm staying right here."

The man nodded while taking Andy's blood pressure.

Another injection was placed in the kid's arm, and Ben blew out the breath he'd been holding when Andy's body went limp.

"We have to get him to the hospital before the medication wears off, and he slips into another seizure."

Within minutes, Andrew Penner was loaded onto a gurney with tubes in his arms, and an oxygen mask over his mouth. Then they wheeled him out the door and into the waiting ambulance.

***

Grace watched in disbelief from the window as the ambulance raced away. Andy could die. The thought stole the breath from her lungs. She bent forward and gasped for air. She would not cry. Not here. Not now. She pressed her fingers into the tops of her thighs until they ached from the pressure.

Ben placed a hand on her shoulder. The sudden comfort pulled at every nerve in her body and she wanted nothing more than to fling herself into his arms. She blinked. The whole evening seemed like a bad dream. A bloody nightmare that she wanted so desperately to wake from. Her vision blurred.

"What are you doing?"

She peeked around Ben to see her father questioning her mother.

"I want a divorce," Mom said, taking off her wedding band.

"Come on, Vera. You're being ridiculous."

Grace knew by the way Dad stood with his chest puffed out and the look of defiance on his face he would not let that happen.

"You hurt our son." Mom pointed a finger at him. "All this time you knew what was wrong with him, and you told me he was doing it for attention."

"He was. Look at what he's become," Dad yelled.

"That's because of you." Mom pounded her small hands into his chest. "You bastard. This is all because of you."

211

"Vera, it's okay, sweetheart." Jules pulled her away.

Grace stood beside her Mom, Jules, and Steph.

"Why, Dad?" she asked.

"Stay out of it, Grace," he growled.

"No." She stood taller. "I don't even know who you are." She looked at the rest of the family still in the room. "I don't know who any of you are."

"This is not our problem," Randy said.

"How do you figure that?" Jules asked. "You were there when Dave beat Rhoads, and you were there when I got sent to jail."

"That was a long time ago," Randy scoffed.

"You lived your life while I was sitting in a cell, and it never bothered you?"

Grace's uncle shrugged.

"Not one of you cared," Jules continued.

"What's more important is Dave's affairs and the fact he has two sons," Jan sneered.

"He has four sons," Steph said, and placed her arm around Jules.

"I've heard enough," Dad shouted. "I need to speak with my wife. Everyone, get out."

"No, David, you can get out." Mom pointed to the door.

"Not yet." Jules walked right up to her dad and for a moment she thought her brother was going to punch him again, but instead he asked, "Did you kill my mother?"

"This is absurd." Dad grabbed his keys from the fireplace mantel.

"Answer the question," Jules said.

"I'm leaving. Vera, I will be back tomorrow to talk to you."

"Are you going to see Andy?" Rick asked.

The only answer was the door slamming on his way out.

"I need to see my son," Mom whispered, a lost look in her eyes.

"Okay, Mom. Let's get your purse and Ben will drive us to the hospital." Grace ushered her mother to a chair.

"Gracie, I'll go grab her things and a sweater. She looks cold," Steph said.

She nodded to her sister before facing the family. Jan, Ally, and Randy were gone.

"They left a few minutes ago," Ben said.

Grace was surprised she didn't feel upset. She blew out a long breath and straightened. Her relationship with Ally was finished, and she wanted nothing to do with her uncle or aunt.

"Are you okay?" Ben whispered into her ear.

"Once I know how Andy is doing, I'll be fine." She was thankful he was here, and she'd tell him so later.

Elle and Zoey, silent all this time, ran toward Grace, smothering her with a warm hug.

"We love you, Gracie," Elle said.

"We are coming with you to the hospital." Rick placed a hand on Mom's shoulder. Fran walked to the other side of the chair and sat on the armrest before she leaned in to hug Mom.

Grace's heart ached for her mother. Vera Penner looked distraught, confused, and the sorrow Grace saw in the woman's eyes almost killed her. She wished there was more she could do to help ease the hurt Mom was feeling right now.

The evening was a monstrosity of accusations and truths, only some of which Grace had known. She stole a peek at Jules, standing off to the side and dealing with his own emotions from all he'd been told. Nothing would change between them. Grace adored Jules. Her protector all her life, and now her big brother. She'd always be in his life. She'd make sure of it. As for Rick or Randy, that was up to Jules.

CHAPTER TWENTY-THREE

Grace had been home from the hospital to shower and change before going back to see Andy and so far, all she'd done was sit and stare at the damn bell.

Andy was in a coma. He'd suffered an overdose from the drugs he'd taken, and the doctors weren't sure what kind of state he'd be in once he woke.

She pulled the chair closer to the table and reached for the bell, gripping the heirloom she'd been trying to put back together for weeks. If she'd found the other piece would any of this have happened? She turned the porcelain chime in her palms until the side with the hole faced her. There was no magic. No spell or aura that pulled the family together. She'd been a fool to ever think there was. It was just a dumb bell, like everyone said.

The family was dismembered, falling apart at the seams, and she didn't foresee the Penners coming back together anytime soon. If at all.

Grace shuddered when she thought of her father. He hadn't shown up at the hospital to see Andy. Disgust tainted her tongue. How was she ever going to look at him again after what he'd done? The man who raised her, taught her how to fish, drive a car, and BBQ a steak, was living a double life. He showed one side of himself to his son and anyone who might cross him, and the other to his wife and daughters. He'd managed to keep them all in the dark when it was he who lived a life in the shadows.

Andy figured it all out, and he paid for it. Her father was a cheat, a liar, and worst of all, a sociopath, stomping on anyone who stood in his way. Grace was sure he had something to do with Claire White's death. Her stomach turned. There was nothing left to defend him with, no recourse to excuse his actions. The proof was in the things her father had done.

He'd sold Jules to his parents, beat and bullied Andy, and ignored the twin boys he'd sired ten years before. Grace didn't know whether to cry or slam her hands onto the table. Rage mixed with sorrow, tightened the muscles in her back as she fought against the despair wanting to tear her apart. Her kidneys ached from the trauma of the false life she'd lived. The room spun as she squeezed her eyes shut, refusing to allow the pain to win.

She would not cry. But her eyes welled with tears, mocking the little strength she had left. She bit her bottom lip to stop the scream wanting to expel from her and pressed her fingers into the bell.

"Grace?" Ben opened the door. She'd left the hospital while he'd gone to check on Carl, and she didn't expect to see him again until tomorrow.

She didn't have it in her to greet him, much less look up from the bell she held. The gift from her grandfather was nothing more than a farce. She should smash the bloody thing on the floor.

She squeezed the chime harder.

"Don't break it," Ben said, placing his hand over hers.

"Why not?" She sniffled. "It means nothing to me now."

"Sure, it does."

She scoffed.

"No. It doesn't."

He stared at her, and she looked away from the remorse she saw there.

"Everything I thought it stood for is gone." She let go of the bell to wipe her nose. "My family does not exist anymore." The truth hit her like a tidal wave washing onto the shore and her chest constricted.

"I know you're hurting, Grace, and I'm so sorry for that."

"All my life I thought they cared for one another. I thought the family dinners, the nights out at the farm, the laughter were all real."

Ben wiped her cheek.

"This means nothing now." She held up the bell. "Grandpa let me believe in the lie. The fairy tale of a little girl who loved her family more than anything, but I was too blind to see how much they hated each other." She sniffled.

"Aww, Grace, that's not true."

"My aunt Janice and uncle Randy didn't even stay to see if Mom was all right tonight. Ally betrayed me, and Uncle Rick knew all this time Jules had gone to jail for something he did not do. What kind of family does that? My father is a monster and, worse yet, my grandfather either looked the other way or supported him."

He nodded.

"Do you know how it feels to find out your family is corrupt? To know they'd step on you if it meant they'd eat first. I never thought they were like that. I put them on a pedestal. I spoke so highly of them and for what? For what?" Her soul crushed, the weight of all the family transgressions on top of her. She slammed her hand on the table, shaking the wooden structure and rattling the bell. "My poor mother. I can't even imagine the pain she must be going through. And Andy." Grace wept. "How he must've felt being locked up, so small, and by the man who was supposed to protect him."

Ben didn't move, but his silent support filled the room. Grace gave in to the sorrow, the despair, the grief, and as she bared her deepest fears, Ben remained fixed in the chair beside her.

"How did I not see any of the signs? How was I so blind to not know my brother was in such turmoil? And now," she whispered, "he could die." The anguish infected her insides to poison the past and make the memories rancid within her mind. The misery lay heavy upon her chest, clawing its way through to her heart, crippling any resolve she hoped would come.

"I know you feel like everything around you is broken, sweetheart, much like this bell." Ben picked up the memory bell. "But it's not."

"How can you say that?" she whimpered.

He cupped her cheek within his palm. "Because it's the truth."

She shook her head.

"You told me the bell was a symbol of your family, right?"

She nodded.

"And now it's broken, much like your family. But the bell can be put back together, and so can your family."

"I don't think so." She pointed. "There is still a piece missing."

Ben sighed. "Even if you don't put the last piece in, it doesn't mean the bell won't work."

She examined the heirloom.

He smiled.

"Even with the bell cracked"—he pinched the top stem with his fingers, swinging the bell until it chimed—"the bell still rings."

"But it doesn't sound the same."

"You're right, but it rings just the same."

"No, it's broken."

"To you the bell is broken, but you're not looking close enough."

Grace squinted, but the heirloom still looked the same.

"Your family is this bell, Grace, cracks and all. The missing piece signifies the ones you have lost." He reached for her hand. "I know it doesn't seem like it now, but everything will be okay. You will all heal and be closer than ever. Much like the crazy glue you used to put the bell back together. Now the bell is stronger, and you will all be, too."

"And it should ring differently because we will never be the same?"

"Exactly, but in a good way. The family you have left knows all the secrets and still chooses to stay together." He smiled. "They choose to work it out, no matter what happened in the past, and sweetheart, that's what's important."

Grace understood what he was saying, but she let doubt shadow any sense from her mind. She couldn't see past what happened, and she didn't think the family would either.

"I have to get back to the hospital," she said, wanting to end the conversation but more importantly, wanting to be with Andy.

"I can drive you." He stood and pulled her along with him.

"Ben, thank you."

"You don't have to. It's my job."

His words halted any more she wanted to say. He wasn't here because he cared for her, or the family. He was here because it was what the job required, and he was looking for a murderer. It was another knock to her already beaten spirit, and Grace nodded, too afraid to speak. She'd taken his comfort for more than what it was and allowed herself to believe he'd wanted more from her. In turn, she'd been a fool again.

Grace grabbed her purse from the counter and followed him out the door. She'd not showered or changed, like she planned, and she didn't care. Desolation sunk into her heart, and Grace embraced the despair masking any feelings she had for him.

***

"How's the old man doing?" Jules asked, catching Ben as he exited the hospital room where Carl still lay hooked up to oxygen.

"Pissed off."

"He's a bit of a handful."

"He inhaled a lot of smoke, and the doctor suspects that the lack of oxygen mixed with his abuse of alcohol caused him to become confused." Ben tossed the coffee he'd been drinking into the trash.

"Makes sense. Do they think he'll pull through?"

Ben shrugged.

"I hope so. He deserves to find out who murdered his daughter." Ben didn't miss the flicker of regret in Jules's eyes, and he knew the man wanted to know what happened to his mother, too.

"Were you able to find out any more about why Charlie and Anna raised you?"

"Yeah. Rick and I spoke for a few hours last night and he told me."

Ben waited, not wanting to push his friend, but needing to know for the case.

"Dave wanted Claire to have an abortion. Carl was going to pay for it, but she refused."

"Carl didn't want you either?" Ben regretted the words immediately when he saw the sadness in Jules's eyes. "I'm sorry, I didn't mean—"

"It's okay. There's no other way to say it."

"So, Charlie initiated the contract?"

"Wrong again."

Ben raised his eyebrows.

"Carl wanted the contract after he attempted to get Claire to the clinic to abort me and she ran off. According to Rick, he didn't want anything to do with the Penners. Hated us all because of the affair and what Dave did to Olga."

"Understandable."

"Carl assumed when he signed the contract it was for rights of Claire because she was a minor. The deal was that she would still abort. Claire was to be sent away to Rolling Acres to have an abortion, but instead she finished out the pregnancy."

"Charlie and Anna deceived Carl?"

"Yup."

"And that's how they got custody of you then?"

"Claire didn't have a say either, thanks to the old man."

"Carl didn't know Claire had you?"

Jules shook his head.

"Not until she came home and began sneaking out to go see me. Rick said she never wanted to give me up. She was forced by Dave, Charlie, and Anna. They used the contract to solidify the adoption, if you want to call it that. To sum it up, I was stolen from her."

"Shit. Jules, I am so sorry."

"Claire kept showing up at the ranch unexpected, and Dave didn't like it. He and Vera had just started dating. Carl followed her one night and realized I was never aborted. He dragged her home." Jules sighed.

"Do you think Dave did something to Claire so Vera wouldn't find out the truth?"

"I don't know, but it's the only logical reason. Rick said she showed up a few more times after the day Carl dragged her home begging to see me. Charlie refused to allow her past the gate, but Claire wouldn't give up and snuck around through the field. Dave got so mad he hit her, and she ran off. It was the last time anyone saw her."

Ben didn't know what else to say. There was no evidence other than hearsay to arrest Dave Penner for the murder of Claire White. He hadn't heard from Dawson in a few weeks and made a mental note to phone the coroner when he got to the office.

"Is Grace still here?" Ben asked. He needed to apologize. This morning she'd thanked him, and all he could do was tell her it was his job. She was more to him than the work, and he didn't know why he just didn't say so. He witnessed the look of disappointment in her eyes and knew he'd hurt her.

"She's still sitting with Andy."

He nodded.

"You better not hurt her." Jules stopped to face him. His wide shoulders stretched out, and Ben knew by the man's stance he wasn't messing around.

"I have no intention of doing that."

"What exactly is your intention?"

He smiled.

"That is between me and Grace." Ben's cell phone rang, and he glanced down to check the call display. It was the Internal Affairs office. His finger hovered over the button to answer, but not ready to hear his fate, he let it go to voicemail.

"That's where you're wrong. I'm her big brother. It's my job to protect her." Jules placed a hand on Ben's shoulder. "Answer the question."

He admired Jules and hoped their friendship lasted well past the case and his possible return to Chicago.

"It's up to Grace." He spoke the truth. Ben spoiled things between them for now, but once the last few days sat easier in everyone's minds, he'd tell her how much she meant to him.

"You're correct there. She's been through a lot. I don't want to see her get hurt."

"I'd never do that."

Jules smiled.

"I'm going to head to the office. If you need anything, call me." He walked away. The cell phone heavy in his palm, Ben knew the answer to his future with the Chicago PD was in the message left by IA. The sun greeted him as he walked outside. Not willing to wait another minute, he checked the message. Neck tense, he clenched his jaw while he listened. The misconduct charge held, he'd be relocated, probation continued for another year and worse, he'd be behind a desk. No fieldwork.

Ben leaned against his car door. The punishment wasn't what he'd been hoping for, but it was what he deserved. His actions placed him in the predicament, and he'd have to face them for the rest of his career. Ben looked around the parking lot. He'd come to like the small town an hour east of the big city, even hoped he might stay, but that wasn't going to happen now. Malcolm always said things worked out for the best. He thought of Grace, and for the first time in his life, Ben didn't believe him.

CHAPTER TWENTY-FOUR

Grace sat beside Carl's bed while the old man slept. Three days passed since the ordeal with the family, and her brother still hadn't woken from the coma. Needing to escape from the room and the constant questions Mom and Steph were asking the doctors, she'd decided to come here.

Purple bruises splattered down Carl's forearms from his attack on Jules, and Grace was careful not to touch them when she reached for his hand. There wasn't much to the old man. A veil of translucent skin covered fragile bones and sunken eyes gave way to hollow cheeks and thin, veiny lips. She wondered where he'd go if he ever got well enough to leave the hospital.

There was nothing left of his home except a pile of blackened wood. The firefighters tried to salvage some of his belongings, but when the roof caved in, their fight turned to controlling the blaze rather than saving what was inside. She couldn't help feeling sorry for all Carl lost, and most of it at the hands of her family.

Ashamed for the first time in her life to be a Penner, Grace considered changing her last name. She didn't want to be associated with the hurtful things her father and grandfather had done.

Mom still refused to speak to Dad. She'd turned off her cell phone, and instead of going home to shower, she'd gone to Grace's house. She knew their marriage was over, and even though she understood why, a part of her was saddened by the outcome. Steph stepped up and offered mom a place to stay once Andy got well enough to leave the hospital, and Grace was surprised when Mom took her up on the offer. She wanted to get Andy the best kind of treatment and knew she'd find the help in the city, but Grace knew a lot of Mom's decision came from not wanting to be in the small town where gossip and the Penner name held more than just the two syllables.

Grace wanted to flee, but not to Chicago where Ben would be. She hadn't seen him since their talk, and she missed him. Admitting to herself for the first time how much she cared for the detective, Grace needed to accept Ben did not have the same feelings for her. She'd never been in love before, and she now realized her feelings for Josh were only an infatuation. When she looked at Ben, the world around her seemed to halt, and even though they shared one kiss, his touch ignited her soul. She yearned to see him—desperate to be near him, to hear his voice, to taste his lips. He'd invaded her mind, nestled himself into her heart, and Grace knew she loved him.

"Hey, kid, thought I might find you in here." Jules walked into the room, a coffee in his hand. Her brother never left the hospital except to go home and change before coming right back. She was grateful for his presence, and she knew Mom and Steph were, too.

"Thought I'd come see how he's doing." She glanced at Carl, who was still asleep.

"Doc been in yet?"

Grace placed her name down as Carl's next of kin when he'd been rushed to the hospital a few weeks before, so she was the only person the doctors would speak with when it came to the sick old man.

"He just left. He said Carl may be cranky when he woke again."

"Because of the alcohol?"

She nodded.

"It's unlikely he will ever quit." Jules sat down beside her.

"Where will he go when he's discharged?" She worried the man may become homeless.

"I'll take him to the farm."

"Do you think that's a good idea?" she asked, remembering how Carl reacted toward Jules the other day.

"You're probably right. I'll pay for him to be placed in a senior's facility."

"Might have a fight on your hands. I don't think they allow alcohol there."

"The old man can't live on the streets. He doesn't have much of a choice."

Jules was right. Carl had nowhere else to go.

"Whatever happens, he will be taken care of. I'll make sure of it."

"I can't help but consider how similar Andy is to Carl." She'd been thinking about how the two dealt with their lives by turning to addiction.

"You mean the drugs and alcohol?"

"It's so sad neither of them felt they could go to anyone for help."

Jules nodded.

Shame filled her, and she gasped.

"You're not to blame for any of this, Gracie."

"I am." She needed to confide in Jules, to get the words out. "All of these years I watched Dad abuse Andy, and I never said anything to anyone."

"We all did." He sighed, and she knew he suffered from the guilt, too.

"Why didn't we?"

Jules met her tear-filled eyes. "Because we are cowards."

"We all knew it was wrong, and we made excuses."

They sat in silence for a long time, lost in their own remorse for how things turned out for Andy.

"Where do we go from here, Jules?" she whispered.

"We learn from our mistakes." He reached for her hand. "We become better than what we were."

She smiled. He always knew how to make her see the brighter side of things.

"Do you think Andy will be okay?"

"Yeah, kid. He'll pull through, but it will be a tough road ahead for him."

Grace agreed. She'd been reading up on addiction now that she was living it, and she wanted to know how to help someone who fought the disease.

"Rehab?"

"Possibly. No matter which way you spin it, Andy has to be the one who wants to get better. Whatever he chooses, I'll be there every step of the way."

"We can always count on you, Jules."

"And now I'm your big brother, so I'm never leaving."

She smiled.

"Counselling?"

"Definitely. For all of us." He smirked.

Grace laughed and leaned into him.

"Ah, Gracie-girl, I love you."

"I love you, too, bro."

He put his arm around her and squeezed.

"Has Dad come to see Andy yet?" She knew the answer but held onto a glimmer of hope she'd missed his visit while walking the halls of the hospital.

"Nope, and I don't expect him to. He never saw Andy as his son, just like me and the two boys he ignored. I don't see that changing now."

"After things settle down, and we are all feeling the weight lifted from this whole situation, I'd like to meet them."

"Me too."

She smiled, comforted by the little bit of good that came out of such an awful situation.

***

Ben wiped the side of his briefcase with the sleeve of his suit coat and leaned into the chair. His left leg bounced, a nervous habit he'd formed when he was a kid.

Today he'd do the right thing, something he should've done a long time ago. Ben looked around the familiar room. His old office was at the end of the hall. The worn gray door still showed the scuff marks at the bottom from when his hands were full of files and he kicked it open. Now it was occupied by another detective. When two of his old colleagues walked by, he averted his eyes and shifted in the chair. Humiliation coated his throat, and he reached for the bottle of water.

The meeting with Internal Affairs that morning was long, filled with apologies and papers to sign. The permanent position in Charleston meant he'd have to leave Oakville. He'd been reluctant to take the job three hours from the city, but nothing else was offered. The requirements were simple; sign the papers and be there by the end of the week.

The change was for the better, he reasoned. He needed time away from the past reminders of Lana and his father—to start fresh. He'd miss Malcolm and June, but he'd made a pact with himself to phone and visit the elderly couple more often.

He squeezed the bottle of water.

He'd miss Grace, too—more than he wanted to admit. He'd held onto a sliver of hope the board would allow him to remain in Oakville for at least another month. Ben had planned on telling Grace how much he cared for her when he arrived back at the hospital, but not now.

He sighed. Grace was different. A simple caress of her eyes, a subtle stroke from her hand, and Ben was sure he'd come undone. She'd affected him in ways he never thought possible. If he hadn't met her, he wouldn't be sitting here right now.

Pride kept him from doing the right thing and apologizing, even though he'd known he was wrong. Being around Grace pushed him to reflect on his own life, the choices he'd made, and who he wanted to be. She pushed him to be better, and when he was with her, he wanted to be better. He sighed. Now he'd have to leave her behind.

The case of Claire White would be handed over to Enders with the help of a few others in the precinct. The deputy would find justice for Carl. Ben was just sorry he wouldn't be there to do it himself.

Within the week Rhoads would be brought in to answer questions. Ben told the men and women interviewing him today about the White case and how Jim Rhoads had been influenced throughout his career in Oakville. A part of him felt sorry for the other man who would probably lose his job, but the other half knew he deserved what was coming.

The door swung open and a large man with gray hair and a handlebar moustache filled the doorway.

Captain John Powell.

Ben's legs shook as he stood.

"Hey, Cap."

"James." John moved to the side for Ben to walk past him and into the office. Memories of the night he'd attacked the other man invaded Ben's mind. He blinked, trying to focus.

"What do you want?" John didn't mince words, a trait Ben admired.

He refused to hang his head, meeting the captain's stare instead.

"I came by to talk."

"Well, that's a first. Haven't heard a word from you in months."

John wiped at his nose, and Ben's insides turned. The bump on the bridge and lopsided curve were all reminders of how much damage he'd done to his captain.

"I know."

The leather chair whined as John sat down.

Ben inhaled a deep breath, holding it for a few seconds before expelling the air in his lungs along with the fear and nervousness.

"I want to apologize for what happened that night." His chest lighter, he took another breath.

John examined him.

Ben waited.

"Heard you were placed on another year of probation and relocated."

"I deserve it."

"You're a good detective, James."

"Sir?"

"There was more to that night than what happened between you and me."

Ben remained silent. Cap was right, but he wasn't here to be vindicated, he was here to own up to his responsibilities.

"If any of us saw what that bastard had done to those girls, we'd have done the same thing."

"I don't think so—"

"You were on edge—had issues at home—and I provoked you." John shrugged. "I was pissed you went behind my back, and I said some things I shouldn't have."

"I should've never hit you, Cap." Ben's cell phone buzzed. He ignored it.

"Probably not, but life is full of lessons."

Ben raised his brow.

"I'll accept your apology if you'll accept mine."

"Excuse me?"

"I know you've had a difficult go of things the past year."

How had the captain known about Kent and Lana? He hadn't spoken of it to anyone.

"People talk." John smiled. "I've known you for a long time."

Ben nodded.

"You could've come to me, but I understand why you didn't." Captain cleared his throat before continuing. "Now for a few lessons. Know when you are wrong and admit it." He smiled.

"That's why I'm here."

"Exactly. We were both in the wrong." He stood and extended his hand.

Ben grabbed hold of John's hand, shaking it in a firm grasp.

"I hope we can work together again."

"I'd like that." The cell in his front pocket vibrated again.

"Someone needs to talk to you," John said, before he walked toward the door.

Ben followed.

"Thank you. I owe my career to you."

"I'd say half of it." He smirked. "You're a good man, and a damn fine detective. Lesson number two: learn from the past mistakes and be better for it."

He smiled.

"If you ever need anything, you know where I'm at."

"Yes, sir." Ben watched his captain walk down the hallway. The tension in his neck eased, and he flexed his shoulders. He felt lighter, and for the first time in a long while he didn't walk the hallway of the precinct with his head down.

His front pocket buzzed. He pulled out the phone. "Hello."

"Ben?"

"Dawson, it's about time."

"I've got the report back on the piece lodged in Claire White's jawbone."

"Great, what was it?"

"Cellulous. It is a plant material used to make rope."

"What kind of rope?"

"Jute rope comes to mind. Normally this type of rope will decompose into the ground and is commonly used by farmers."

"Why didn't this one decompose?"

"We also found a small trace of pesticides on the fiber."

"Is this why the rope didn't waste away into the soil?" Ben couldn't contain his excitement. Jute rope and pesticides went hand in hand with farming. He tossed the bottle of water into the trash. "You may have just cracked my case, Dawson! Thank you."

"That's not all." The coroner stammered.

Ben pushed through the double doors of the precinct and sprinted toward his car. The bright afternoon sunshine reflected off the windshield and he squinted.

"Hold on, there's more. Ethyl and methyl butyric acid were also found on the fiber."

"What are those?"

"Both are commonly found in alcohol."

"A lot of people use disinfectants. I'll check to see if either Charlie or Dave had any type of injury at that time."

"Not rubbing alcohol. Drinking alcohol. Like rum."

Ben dropped the keys he'd been holding. "What are you saying, Dawson?"

"Those two compounds were more prominent on the rope, and that's why it did not decompose. The alcohol preserved the fiber."

Ben's entire body turned cold. There was one person he knew who consumed rum. His mind raced with the events of the past month. Carl's outbursts. His accusations toward Jules. Ben's hands shook. The rope he'd found in Carl's shed formed into a noose. The empty bottle of rum lying next to it.

"Hello, Ben?"

"Get Enders to the hospital, Dawson. Tell him to make sure no one goes into Carl's room."

"Is everything all right?"

He needed to phone Grace and tell her to stay away from the old man.

Ben hung up the phone without saying goodbye and dialed her number. It went straight to voicemail.

"Shit."

His whole body vibrated as the blood drained from his head.

Carl White murdered his daughter.

Chapter Twenty-Five

"How are you doing, Carl?" Grace stayed most of the day waiting for him to wake.

The old man opened his eyes, and she was glad to be the first person he saw. She didn't want him waking up to an empty room.

Carl moaned.

"Are you in any pain?"

He shook his head. The wrinkles on his face were more prominent than before, and Grace figured it was due to the strain of the past few days.

She grabbed the Styrofoam cup from the table beside the bed and placed it underneath his lips so he could take a sip of water.

"Here, this will help."

"Why can't I just die?" he whimpered, turning his head away from the water she offered.

She set the cup aside, sat down on the edge of the bed, and covered his hand with both of hers.

"You can't die just yet." She smiled.

Carl stared at his feet.

"I'd miss you." She squeezed his hand. "You're not alone anymore."

Gray eyes focused on her. A tear hovered within the few lashes left.

"I know you don't think so, but I am your friend, Carl."

"I don't have any friends."

"You have me."

His shoulders slumped forward.

"I'll never leave you. I promise."

Another tear fell from his lashes and he placed his other hand over hers.

She wanted to make things right for the old man, help him in any way she could, but the sad reality was he'd been left alone because of her family.

"I'm sorry you lost your house, Carl, and…" she paused, "for the horrible things my dad did to your wife back then."

His bottom lip quivered.

"You haven't had it easy. My family treated you poorly, and I am so very sorry." She wanted to let the old man know she wasn't like them, that she was here for him. There was no way to remove all the wrongdoings from the past, but she could learn from them and be better.

Carl's hands tightened around hers.

She gave him a small smile, hoping to reassure him of the truth she spoke.

The pressure on her hands intensified.

Grace tried to jerk them away.

His fingers snaked around her wrist, biting into the flesh. Narrowed eyes, feral and predatory, bore into her. The dark slits mirrored the horror within them.

She shivered.

"Carl?" She strained and tried to pull away again, but he pressed harder into the skin crushing the bones in her hand. "You're hurting me."

"P… P… Penner," he whispered in a slow drawl.

Grace's eyes darted about the room for a nurse or doctor to call out to.

"Just us." Carl's voice was pitchy and low, like a mountain cat calling to his prey.

"I should go." She went to stand, hoping he'd release her, but he drove the pad of his palm into the top of her knuckles.

Grace winced. She'd never seen this side of Carl before, and every nerve in her body screamed to escape.

"Please, let go of my hands," she begged. "If it's alcohol you want, I'll get it for you."

"I hate the lot of you Penners." He sneered.

"I'm not like my father, Carl."

He growled.

She tried another tactic and softened her features. "I'm your friend, remember?"

His eyes glazed before a dark shadow soaked into them.

"Bah! You're one of them." He spat.

Repulsed, Grace could do nothing but let the spittle drip from her cheek.

"I have always been kind to you." Desperate, she tried to make him see she was not like them.

"No one is kind to me!" The veins on his forehead protruded. "You are just like her."

"Like who?"

"Claire! Infatuated with those Penners." His top lip curled, showing yellowed teeth.

"I am not Claire, Carl."

"She wouldn't listen," he yelled.

"You're mistaken. I'm not her."

"You've fallen for them, too!"

None of what he said made sense. The room was hot, and a sheen of sweat beaded on her forehead.

"Claire is dead. I am Grace Penner." She tried again to reason with him.

"I know who you are."

"Please, let go of my hands."

"She wouldn't leave it be. Kept going there to see that baby!" The last word spewed from his lips as if it were poison.

"The baby is Jules, Carl, your grandson."

"He's a bastard and one of them." The once innocent man she'd grown to care for turned right before her eyes. Carl's face drooped downward into jagged points.

The room blurred. Grace blinked.

"He killed her." Spit flew from his thin lips. "He killed her."

"Jules was a baby."

"A Penner baby." Bloodshot eyes, wild and crazed, stared at her. "She didn't listen. I had to stop her."

Grace swallowed.

"What do you mean?"

"I couldn't let them have her, too." He sat up and the muscles in his neck pushed out.

"What did you do, Carl?" Fear snaked up her spine, every muscle in her body tense.

"She didn't listen. Wouldn't stop going there," he gasped. "I followed her one night out to the mill. She crocheted a blue blanket for that baby—she was bringing it to the Penners," Carl screeched. The sound vibrated off the walls.

What was he saying? Did he do something to Claire?

"She was just like her mother. In love with the lot of them." His eyes grew big. "I couldn't let her go." His face twisted. "Oh, how she begged me to let her go, to loosen the rope… telling me she couldn't breathe. I almost did until she told me how much she loved him."

Grace inhaled.

"How much she loved that bastard baby. I needed to protect her from them." He looked at Grace. "And I did."

The hair on Grace's arms stood.

"Please let me go."

"I hate you. I hate you all." Carl's back straightened, a purple hue washed over ruddy cheeks, and his lips pursed. He released her hands to clutch his chest.

Grace jumped away from the bed.

"Carl." Afraid to go closer, she watched as the old man gasped. Desperate to know what happened to the girl, she asked, "What did you do to Claire?"

"I saved her. I saved her from them," he wheezed before he slumped to the side.

The room swayed. Grace reached out a shaky hand to steady herself. Carl killed Claire. She sucked in a breath. He killed his own daughter. Understanding punched her in the chest and she gasped. Her vision blurred, and the room blended together in a kaleidoscope of colors. Grace placed a trembling finger to her lips and moaned. Carl hated the Penners so much he'd taken Claire's life—stolen any chance of happiness from the young girl. Claire never knew her son, and Jules never got to know his mother.

The Penner family destroyed so many. Hate, greed, lust, and revenge infected those she loved like a plague. The result was disastrous, spreading the disease to anyone they thought warranted their wrath.

Grace wrapped an arm around her waist and bent forward. A hoarse cry expelled past her lips, as tears bled from her eyes to drip onto the floor. Despair dug into her ribs. The pain was so intense she panted. How did she come from such horror? The lines of good and evil so parallel, they crossed from one to the other fooling everyone, presenting themselves as angelic citizens when in truth they were horrible.

Grace dropped to her knees and wept.

Strong arms wrapped around her trembling shoulders.

"Grace?"

Ben was here. He was here. She leaned into him taking shelter from the room, from Carl's admission, from Grandpa's sins, her father's horrid behavior, everything she'd found out about the people she loved, burying her head into his chest.

The truth ravaged her soul, eating away any semblance of serenity she'd ever known, casting her into the fires to burn right along with them. The wretched beast pressed on her vocal cords until a cry she did not recognize as her own left her mouth.

Ben's lips pressed into her temple as he hugged her to him, but it did little to ease the anguish wanting to rip her in two.

"It was…" She sobbed. "It was Carl."

"I know, sweetheart."

"All because of my family." She thrust her fists into his chest. "The things they did to him were so cruel."

"Shush."

"How do I come back from this? How do I go on knowing Carl killed his daughter because of them?"

"Grace." He hooked his finger under her chin, forcing her to look at him. "Carl didn't have to kill Claire. He was sick. Your grandpa and dad bullied him, did terrible things to him, but they did not make him kill his daughter."

Grace didn't know if she'd ever be able to comprehend Carl's thoughts, or how he'd suffered after his wife slept with Grandpa and all the events that followed, but she couldn't excuse her family's behaviour.

"They should've left him alone," she cried. "Why didn't they leave them alone?"

"I don't know." He pressed his lips to her forehead. "We may never know the reasons they acted so heartlessly."

He helped her up, keeping his arm on her shoulders. Ben led her outside to a bench where they sat.

Grace crossed her legs and, clasping her hands together, she stared off into the distance.

"Nothing makes sense to me anymore," she whispered, her voice sore from crying.

He placed his hand over hers. "Sometimes life doesn't make sense."

"What's the point then?"

"I thought the same thing when I first arrived here."

"What do you mean?"

"I wondered what my life was all about. Why I'd been dealt such a shitty hand. And why I had to come here."

She nodded.

"I realized while trying to solve Claire's murder that the only person you can count on is yourself. The only person you should want to be proud of is yourself."

Grace knew where this was going, and she didn't want to hear it. He'd made it clear earlier he was here because of the job. She held up her hand to stop him.

"There's no need to continue. I get it. Count on no one but yourself."

Ben smiled.

"I wasn't finished."

She faced him.

"After Lana, I didn't think I'd find that love again, and I haven't."

Why was he telling her this?

"What I found was kindness, gentleness, and an honesty I'd never known before." He sighed. "I wasn't looking, and I sure as hell didn't plan on it, but I can't stop thinking of you, Grace."

"What are you saying?"

"You make sense to me." He smiled.

Grace closed her eyes. "I come from an awful family."

"But that doesn't define you, Grace. You're not like them. You are the complete opposite, just like your mom, Steph, and Jules. Those are the parts of your family you've inherited."

"Oh, Ben. I can't forget what they've done."

"You're not supposed to."

She tipped her head.

He sighed. "Grace, we can't choose our family, but we can choose our own path—our own actions and the way we treat others."

She nodded.

"You're Grace Penner, beautiful inside and out."

She inhaled his words—his scent until the truth of what he'd said sunk in. When she looked at him everything became clear, the past faded from her soul, and all she saw was Ben.

"Thank you," she whispered.

He placed his forehead to hers.

"Grace?" his voice shook. "I have to leave on Friday."

She wasn't surprised. He'd been on probation, and he could be called away at any moment.

"What I said earlier is the truth. I had no intention of falling for you." He closed his eyes. "Shit. Grace, I like you and I don't want this to end."

"I like you, too."

"Do you think we can figure something out?" He smiled. "We can take it slow and see where things go between us?"

For the first time in weeks, hope took root inside Grace's heart and she nodded. Ben touched his nose to hers. She inhaled a shaky breath before he pressed his lips to hers in a soft kiss that whispered of hope, of promises, but most importantly of love.

CHAPTER TWENTY-SIX

Grace fidgeted in the chair beside Mom.

"How much longer?"

"Any minute now," Mom said, before taking a sip of her tea.

When would Andy get here? She tapped her fingers on the table. The aroma of pot roast teased Grace's nose, and her stomach growled. She'd arrived at Steph's ready to face whatever greeted her when Andy walked through the door. After his overdose, her brother was admitted into The Rising Sun Rehabilitation Center for a three-month stay. No contact was allowed with the patients, and she was anxious to see him. How did he look? Was he better than the last time she'd seen him? She glanced at Mom picking at her lip, and knew she experienced the same nervousness.

Andy's recovery would go further than the three months of extensive therapy he'd completed. For his possession charge he was sentenced to a fine and community hours which he'd serve while living with Mom in the city.

Mom glanced at her watch.

"Impatient?" Grace nudged her.

"Yes, a little." Mom looked tired, and Grace suspected the puffy eyes, pale skin and slouched shoulders were the result of lack of sleep and too much stress. Dad wasn't making it easy on her. He'd held firm on not giving her the divorce she wanted.

Mom proved to be a lot stronger than Grace ever realized. She fought to get Andy into the best treatment facility. Grace knew her determination came from the guilt she had over the way Andy was treated by Dad. Life changed for Mom, and Grace knew she struggled to adapt to the new normal. Being married to Dad for twenty-five years suppressed any of her hopes and dreams, always doing what Dad wanted. With Mom's newfound freedom she didn't really know what to do. She moved out of the house and into a small apartment in the city a few blocks from Steph's. They were small steps to becoming independent.

Steph helped out whenever possible, inviting Mom over almost every day for dinner, and Grace spent every other weekend with her. For the first time in her life, Mom was in control. Grace knew this excited and frightened her, but no matter which road Mom chose to walk, Grace wouldn't let her do it alone.

"Gracie, did you bring the bell?" Steph asked, bouncing Finn on her hip.

"Yes, but I still don't know why you wanted me to."

Last week Steph invited Grace to Andy's homecoming party and asked if she'd bring the memory bell along. Reluctant to do so, and curious why her sister wanted her to bring it, she'd placed the small box inside her overnight bag this morning.

"Well, take it out," Steph said.

Grace reached into her bag, pulled out the worn box, and placed it on the table.

"It's too bad you weren't able to get the last piece back." Steph took the bell out of the box. Finn's pudgy hands waved in the air, trying to grab hold of the glass ornament.

"It doesn't really matter." Grace hadn't taken the bell out in months, refusing to look at it.

"I wonder if it still rings?" Mom asked.

She shrugged.

"Let's try it." Steph held it out toward Grace.

"I don't think so." She'd accepted the essence of the bell didn't exist, and when rung no magical element illuminated from the heirloom. It was just a bell.

"Come on, Gracie. Ring the bell," Steph said. "Just once."

Mom took the bell from Steph's hands and placed it into Grace's.

"Just one time," Mom whispered. "For Finn."

Her nephew's big blue eyes watched the bell.

"For Finn," Grace said, and moved the bell from left to right. A tinny clink echoed in the room as the rock hit the inside.

Finn giggled.

Grace rang it again.

"Well hell, the damn thing still rings," Jules entered the room.

"Sounds terrible if you ask me," Andy said.

Grace squealed and jumped out of her chair to smother her brother in a warm embrace.

"Hey, bro. I missed you."

Andy looked great. He was twenty pounds heavier and a rosy glow filled his cheeks.

"Hey, Gigi. I missed you, too." He wrapped thick arms around her waist and swung her around.

"Looking good, little brother." Steph kissed Andy's cheek and handed him Finn.

Andy's eyes bulged.

"What? Can't Finn see his favorite uncle?" Steph smiled.

"Of course, he can." Andy took the baby and placed a light kiss on Finn's chubby cheeks.

"Wait a minute. I thought I was the favorite uncle." Jules winked at Grace.

"No, you're my favorite older brother," Steph said.

"I'll settle for that."

"Hello?" Uncle Rick popped his head around the corner. "Heard there was a party going on."

The room got louder as Aunt Fran, Elle, and Zoey piled into the kitchen.

Steph scrambled to get more chairs and place them around the table. Mom leaped into action, checking on the pot roast while Aunt Fran started to make gravy.

Jules opened a chip bag and dumped the contents into a blue bowl and placed it on the table.

"Sounds like disorder and mayhem."

Grace spun around to see Ben standing behind her. She jumped into his arms.

"What are you doing here?" She was just in Charleston two days before.

"I was invited." He smiled.

Grace's eyes sought out Steph.

"He's one of us now," her sister said from across the room.

"He sure as hell is," Jules added, tossing Ben a soda.

"Gracie, come sit." Uncle Rick pulled out a chair beside him.

She grabbed Ben's hand, weaving her fingers with his, and pulled him along.

"How have you been?" Rick asked.

She hadn't seen her uncle or aunt since they'd been back from their vacation to Bali.

"I'm good."

"I know things have been rough, but I want you all to know Fran and I are here for you always."

Grace smiled.

"Gigi, since you brought the bell?" Andy said through a mouthful of chips.

"Yes," she answered in a cautious tone.

Her brother weaved his way through the family gathered around the table until he was beside her. He reached into his pocket and pulled out a white glass shard.

Grace covered her mouth.

The room grew silent. All eyes were on Grace.

"It was me all along." He took her hand and dropped the last piece into her palm.

Grace blinked.

"Why?"

Andy's blue eyes welled with tears, and his bottom lip quivered. He swallowed before he said, "I couldn't handle the secrets anymore. They were eating me up inside. I thought the messages would get the family talking, and maybe Dad would come clean with everything he'd done." He blew out a breath. "I'm sorry."

Grace rolled the glass in her palm, and her vision blurred.

"What are you waiting for?" Jules said, holding a small tube of crazy glue. "Put the last piece in."

Grace looked at the bell still on the table, and then to her family gathered around. This was what mattered, not some glass ornament. She rang the bell, and they came, but she also knew Steph had orchestrated the whole thing.

"I don't think so," she said.

"What?" Steph asked.

"Why not?" Andy placed his hand on her shoulder.

"Gracie, are you sure?" Mom walked toward her.

"Grandpa told me the bell was magical. A symbol of our family, and when it broke, I didn't see how we'd all come back together, and some of us didn't." She glanced at Ben. "Then someone told me to look closer." She picked up the bell and twirled it within her hands. "See the cracks and the missing piece? This is who we are. Broken. A little rough around the edges and imperfect. We accept each other for our downfalls, our wrongdoings, and our insecurities. The bell is exactly as it should be. Stronger from the glue holding it together and able to withstand any storm that may come its way."

The family huddled around the table, arms interlocked, bonded by their love for each other and… unbreakable.

The End

Dear Reader,

When I started this book it was never intended to be what it became... and isn't that the case with most things? I wanted to create a story we could all relate to—one that pulled at your emotions and made you consider life a little differently.

I hope you enjoyed Grace's story. She is a little bit of each of you—your hopes—your dreams and the love that burns inside of all of us—ready, willing and able to give.

Thank you for sticking with me throughout the years, I adore every one of you.

God Bless,
Kat

Note from the Author

Word-of-mouth is crucial for any author to succeed. If you enjoyed *The Memory Bell*, please leave a review online—anywhere you are able. Even if it's just a sentence or two. It would make all the difference and would be very much appreciated.

Thanks!
Kat Flannery

About the Author

Kat Flannery's love of history shows in her novels. She is an avid reader of historical, suspense, paranormal, and romance. A member of many writing groups, Kat enjoys promoting other authors on her blog. Kat has been published in numerous periodicals throughout her career and continues to write for blogs and online magazines. A bestselling author, Kat's books have been on Canadian, USA and International bestseller lists. *The Branded Trilogy* is Kat's award-winning series.

Thank you so much for reading one of our **Women's Fiction** novels.
If you enjoyed the experience, please check out our
recommendation
for your next great read!

The Apple of My Eye by Mary Ellen Bramwell

"A mature love story with an intense plot.
This book has something important to say."
**–William O. Shakespeare, Professor of English,
Brigham Young University**

View other Black Rose Writing titles at
www.blackrosewriting.com/books and use promo code
PRINT to receive a **20% discount** when purchasing.

www.ingramcontent.com/pod-product-compliance
Lightning Source LLC
Chambersburg PA
CBHW010733100726
47899CB00009B/3028